SAYONARA, *My Sweet*

LEA O'HARRA

Black Rose Writing | Texas

ISBN: 978-1-68513-595-9
PUBLISHED BY BLACK ROSE WRITING
www.blackrosewriting.com

Printed in the United States of America
Suggested Retail Price (SRP) $20.95

Sayonara, My Sweet is printed in Garamond Premier Pro

ACKNOWLEDGEMENTS

Life has been kind. I am grateful for whatever I might call it—fate, destiny, or karma—that has led me on the path I've followed. Or perhaps I should thank serendipity.

Of course, I am indebted to my dear family for the support and love that has sustained me in all my endeavors, including crime fiction writing. My husband, Takehito Nakanishi, is a Japanese orange grower, and we have three sons: Taiki, Kei, and Makio.

My dear friend Suzanne Kamata, a fellow author and long-term ex-pat living in Japan, has inspired and encouraged me to write fiction. I also wish to acknowledge the helpful advice and suggestions many others have given me as I composed this novel.

Finally, I am glad that circumstances led me, in my late twenties, to Japan, where I have lived and worked for forty years. It boasts a unique culture, and the part of the country I have been fortunate enough to inhabit—Shikoku, which is the smallest and most rural of Japan's four main islands—is, I think, particularly representative of traditional Japanese customs and thought. While I worked in Japan for many years as a professor of English at a university, living in Japan proved an education in itself. I learned as well as taught, finding Japanese life challenged assumptions that I had thought universal and teaching me the value of self-discipline and the importance of politeness and kindness in daily interactions.

It seems perverse to write crime fiction set in Japan—perhaps the safest country on earth at present, with a wonderfully efficient police force, almost no gun violence, and a low level of offences recorded, especially compared to other so-called 'developed' nations. It is an eminently civilized place with, for example, minimal anti-social behavior or graffiti or litter. The people are law-abiding and peaceable, and their interactions are harmonious. But crime does occasionally occur there, and I hope I have explained—particularly for readers who have never visited Japan—its context.

PRAISE FOR
SAYONARA, MY SWEET

"Fans of Seicho Matsumoto's *Inspector Imanishi Investigates* have a new hero as Lea O'Harra's Chief Inspector Ito doggedly works to solve the mystery of who killed young Kaori Hirakata. *Sayonara, My Sweet* delivers gritty, Japanese crime noir!"
–Cam Torrens, bestselling author of the *Tyler Zahn* suspense series

"When a young, attractive, strait-laced woman named Kaori dies of poisoning in a peaceful town in rural Japan, the obvious culprit is her ex-*yakuza* boyfriend, Hiroki, who mysteriously disappears. But when Chief Inspector Ito digs into the case, he discovers a surprising web of possibilities and his greatest fear and regret, a crime he failed to solve a decade earlier. As much a deeply emotional family coming-of-age drama as it is simmering Japanese suspense, *Sayonara, My Sweet* by Lea O'Harra concludes in a grand finale that will keep you on your toes, asking, 'Did that just happen?'"
–Michael Summers, author of *Cherry Blossoms in Winter*

"Murota, the fictitious setting of Lea O'Harra's latest Japan-inspired whodunnit, is a town of church-goers and tea sippers, with a renowned ornamental garden. However, something sinister lurks behind the genteel façade; the locals are haunted by a *yakuza* shooting years ago and the more recent bizarre death of a beautiful young woman. Right up until its twisty end, *Sayonara, My Sweet* is infused with late Showa Era vibes and a delicious sense of dread, while the authentic details of daily life are informed by the author's decades-long residence in Japan. But be forewarned: You may never look at a box of chocolates the same way again."
–Suzanne Kamata, author of *Cinnamon Beach* and *River of Dolls and Other Stories*

"*Sayonara, My Sweet*: 'A haunting and poignant mystery of love, hope and redemption set against the vivid backdrop of a small Japanese town where the innocent are delivered from the evils of the past...'"
–Jared Cade, author of *Murder on London Underground*

SAYONARA, *My Sweet*

CHAPTER ONE

Monday 19 September 1988
***The Nippon Daily*, evening edition**

**Mysterious Death in Murota
by Koji Yanagihara**

A young woman died in mysterious circumstances yesterday evening in the town of Murota in northern Kyushu. At approximately half-past eight, alerted by screaming, a resident of the Kitaguchi district rushed to her neighbors' house, where she found the parents with their daughter, a twenty-three-year-old employee at a local business, convulsing and vomiting. She summoned an ambulance, but the young woman died shortly after arriving at the hospital. The authorities are treating the death as suspicious and have not yet released the victim's name. Chief Inspector Ito of the Murota police force has launched an investigation.

Chief Inspector Ito
Monday 19 September 1988

Chief Inspector Ito of the Murota police station wasn't happy. He sat in his office feeling as aggrieved as if he'd suffered a personal affront. He lifted a large, stubby-fingered hand and rubbed it through thick black hair streaked with gray. The swivel chair he was sitting in groaned under his weight as he swayed uneasily back and forth, trying to marshal his thoughts while a fan in the corner emitted a cooling breeze.

He looked around at his office, a room so familiar he barely registered its details from day to day. Glass-fronted cabinets held law books. A few feet from his large desk, two armchairs faced a coffee table with a sofa on the other side. Ito swung around in his chair and looked out the window behind him at a heavily wooded hill in the distance, surrounded by houses, stores, and factories. Despite the earliness of the hour, it was already bright and hot outside, and the familiar scene shimmered and trembled under a cloudless blue sky.

Ito shook his head as he inspected his territory, giving an involuntary shudder. His work as a police officer was uneventful, and he liked it that way. Murota was a peaceful town with a population of less than forty thousand. Violent crime was rare. It wasn't every day a young woman was killed by poisoning.

No, not day, he corrected himself. Night. The hospital officially pronounced the woman dead at ten thirty the previous evening. The chief inspector shuddered again. His only child, Aiko, was just a year younger than the victim identified as Kaori Hirakata, a name that initially had made him start and search his memory until it came to him that he'd met her twelve years earlier when Kaori was eleven years old, and he was investigating an attack on her father.

Of course, Ito couldn't help thinking of his own daughter when summoned to the hospital mortuary at midnight to see Kaori's corpse. He'd felt a surge of anguish when the doctor lifted an upper corner of the white cloth covering the body on the slab to reveal the face of a young woman, her beauty only slightly marred by discoloring in the face and tightness around the jaw showing the agony she had suffered in dying. Her eyes were closed, so the inspector couldn't see if they had the bloodshot appearance common in cases of poisoning.

The chief inspector loved his job. And because he did, he put up with the inevitable component of it he hated but couldn't avoid—being forced to look at victims of violent death shortly after their demise. But Kaori Hirakata marked a departure from the norm. The bodies he'd seen in the past tended to be mangled and bloody, the casualties of traffic accidents. In fact, this was his first murder. That made it even more poignant. While nobody could predict a car collision, it seemed somebody had deliberately killed this young woman. What a waste!

Ito shook himself impatiently. It was no good allowing himself self-indulgent reflections. He needed to concentrate on the case, particularly the victim. What had she been doing the previous day? How had the poison been administered? Who could have wished her harm? And how was her family coping? But he shied away from reflecting much on the last question. It was too painful to imagine their suffering under this sudden, unexpected blow.

Still, despite his good intentions, Ito could not control his thoughts. He pressed his lips together, recalling how emotional he'd felt sitting across from his daughter Aiko at the breakfast table. Naturally, he'd maintained his usual impassive manner and said nothing about the girl nearly her age he'd seen on the mortuary slab only hours earlier. His asking for just toast, as he had little appetite, was the only sign that anything was amiss. His wife had looked at him in surprise and even put a hand on his forehead. Passing him his cup of coffee, she had asked him what called him away the night before, but he dismissed her concern by saying it was an unexplained death. The chief was careful not to discuss his police work at home. He maintained a clear distinction between his professional and personal life. His daughter was busy with her chopsticks, relishing the meal of miso soup, rice and grilled fish her mother had prepared and that he could not face himself. He couldn't help thinking of how Kaori Hirakata would never eat breakfast again. Unwittingly, the chief gazed at his daughter so intently and for so long, he jumped when she suddenly stood and threw down her napkin.

"Stop staring at me!" Aiko said, looking exasperated. "I got home *before* eleven last night like you asked me to. I'm twenty-two, not a child! The sooner I find my own place and move out, the better!" Then she stormed off to her room, leaving her breakfast half-eaten. The chief glanced up to see his wife looking at him reproachfully.

"She's too old to have a curfew," she said. "You should be proud of her. She's got a good job and helps around the house. I'll be heartbroken when she leaves. If Aiko goes because you're over-protective, I'm not sure I can forgive you." Then, picking up some dishes on the table, she disappeared in the direction of the kitchen. Ito put down his cup, puzzling, as he'd often had occasion to do as the sole male in a household of women, at the unfathomable nature of the fair sex.

Kaori Hirakata
Sunday, 18 September

If she'd known she'd be dead in fourteen hours, Kaori Hirakata might have been less concerned about her appearance. But she didn't. Death was the farthest thing from her mind. Life had never been sweeter. She was in love.

Knowing she'd see her lover soon, Kaori spent her last morning making herself beautiful for him. She applied makeup, put on perfume, and filed her nails before giving them a fresh coat of soft pink polish. It was Sunday, so she'd been able to linger in bed instead of springing up at seven to get ready for work, and she was still in her bathrobe as she sat at her dressing table. Finally, she brushed back her thick black hair, twisted it into a ponytail secured by a clip, and gazed at herself in the mirror as intently as if she'd been inspecting a stranger's face.

Which, in a sense, was true, Kaori thought. She *was* a different person. She'd been a loving, obedient daughter all her life. Now she was on the point of running away without her parents' knowledge or consent. And why? Because she knew they'd never agree to the man she'd chosen. Hiroki Sato, a high school dropout living with his mother in a small house in a rundown part of town and working on the assembly line at the local Nissan car factory, wasn't the son-in-law they would have picked for her.

Leaning forward on her stool, Kaori looked at her reflection. She noticed how her soft pale skin glowed as if happiness had lit a light from within, and her lips curled in a smile as she realized how much she resembled one of the girls in the manga drawings Hiroki was always laboring away over in that sketchpad he kept in a back pocket. Like them, she had large brown eyes, a small nose, and a rosebud mouth, and her hair was so thick and lustrous it fell to her shoulders in a dark, gleaming wave.

Kaori used to disdain manga, but Hiroki had changed her mind, and now she was bingeing on whole series of them just like her twin sister Yumi used to do. Maybe it was as well Yumi had gone to England. Otherwise, they'd be fighting over who got to read the newest *Sailor Moon* first.

Hiroki! That strange boy who'd come into her life just three months before. She owed him so much. He'd opened up the world for her while also making her aware of the smallness of her own life. After graduating from college in Tokyo and returning to the family home in Murota two years earlier, Kaori had allowed herself to become a child again, relying on her father for money and on her mother to do the chores. Kaori had a job, but it felt like a hobby, a way to spend time for want of anything better to do. She worked at an expensive boutique four days a week, helping well-dressed women spend the money they had too much of.

Kaori spun on her dressing table stool, looked around her, and frowned. She wished she hadn't chosen the Western style when *Okaasan*— her mother—had offered to redecorate her room and her sister's twelve years earlier. After what happened to their father, they'd known she'd proposed it as a treat and a distraction. Now Kaori thought she'd been lazy in relying on fashion rather than consulting her own preferences. Once, when all her family were away, Kaori had invited Hiroki into her house. Showing him her bedroom, his verdict was, "Middle class. Comfortable. Boring."

Kaori smiled, thinking of how her sister Yumi had chosen Japanese décor for her own room—a futon mattress rather than a Western-style bed, a tatami mat floor, *shoji* screens at the windows, and even insisting on a *tokonoma* where she could hang ceremonial scrolls. That was Yumi all over—strong-minded and independent. It was no surprise that once she'd grown old enough, she'd not only left home to begin a new life but had gone as far away as England to do so. From the day they were born, it seemed the twin girls felt they had to conform to their birth order.

Although Yumi was only a few minutes older, she was the self-reliant, responsible one and Kaori the pampered darling.

Now Kaori jumped up, opened her door, and stood in the hall where she took in the familiar appetizing scent wafting up the stairway from the kitchen that was accompanied by the rattle of pots and pans. Breakfast must be nearly ready. *Okaasan* was a stickler for doing things the old-fashioned way, insisting on serving a traditional Japanese breakfast every morning. A steaming bowl of rice would accompany green tea, miso soup, grilled fish, some boiled vegetables, and a small saucer holding pickled vegetables. Many Japanese had turned to the convenience of toast and coffee for their first meal of the day, but not *Okaasan*. Kaori felt a sharp pang, thinking how much she loved her mother's cooking and how much she'd miss it. It was exasperating she wouldn't even be able to savor it one last time. She had to feign illness to get out of going to church so she could prepare for her elopement that night.

Kaori returned to her room, planning to go down in a few minutes and act out that charade of feeling ill. She sighed because she was hungry, but also because she was worried about her father. He was jumpy and irritable lately, and she hoped he wouldn't be in one of his moods. A few nights ago, when she'd headed for the kitchen for a glass of milk to help her fall asleep, she'd been astonished to hear raised voices from the living room. Her parents never argued. Kaori sometimes teased them for their doting ways, their habit of holding hands as if their romance kept the old heat of the heady days of their courtship. That night, the door to the living room was closed, and she'd paused at the foot of the stairs, trying to listen.

"You can't do it!" her mother exclaimed.

"I can't *not* do it," her father replied.

Shocked and reluctant to make her presence known, Kaori had given up on the milk and retreated back to her bedroom.

Now, walking back to her dressing table to check her appearance in the mirror again before heading downstairs, Kaori stubbed her toe on the edge of a small green suitcase poking out from under her bed. She nudged it further under until it was out of sight. That's when she heard it—a creaking sound followed by a thudding noise. Somebody must have climbed up the huge clematis vine that wound up the house's front wall and jumped off onto her balcony! At first, she wondered if it was her younger brother, Aki, who'd done it a few times and been scolded for it by their mother. She looked at her window and saw the silhouette of a male figure that looked taller than her brother. He stood still, apart from rubbing his hands as if they were painful, then slid the window open.

Hiroki!

His sudden appearance in her room was a big surprise, but the one that followed was much bigger. The next five minutes turned her world upside down. Then Hiroki was gone, his departure as sudden as his unexpected appearance. Kaori sat at her dressing table shaking her head, close to tears.

There was a light tap at her bedroom door.

"Don't come in!" she shouted, thinking it was her mother, come up to summon her to breakfast. "I'm getting dressed."

But the door flew open, and a thin boy with delicate features rushed in. He stopped for a moment, then hurled himself at her, giving her a shove that almost toppled her off the stool.

Seeing Aki, Kaori felt a mixture of exasperation and relief. She needed a distraction. Hiroki's news had come as a stunning blow. Her spoiled younger brother's customary insistence on her full attention meant she couldn't brood over what Hiroki had said.

She felt surprised she could act so normally. Kaori and her brother enjoyed roughhousing, so she stood and gave the boy a playful shove back, then attacked, tickling him and saying she wouldn't stop until he apologized for entering without permission. She expected Aki to retaliate, to tickle her back, and for the two of them to end up rolling on the floor laughing. But this time was different. He broke away with an angry jerk and even lashed out a foot to kick her as he said, "I hate you!"

Kaori rushed to her brother to catch him in an embrace. "Stop! What's wrong?"

But, somehow, she knew. He must have heard.

Chief Inspector Ito
Monday, 19 September

Murder! That's what it looked like, Chief Inspector Ito thought as he sat mournfully in his office at the Murota police station waiting to get the test results promised by the doctor at the hospital. From the start, it was impossible to believe it had been a so-called "natural" death. That's how and why the police had become involved. Her rapid deterioration had dismayed the emergency room doctor who'd treated her at the hospital. He'd rung the station shortly after abandoning the resuscitation measures, saying he felt he must report it as a suspicious death.

The duty sergeant had contacted the chief inspector at home despite the lateness of the hour. Lying in bed next to his wife, he told her to go back to sleep and rang his second-in-command, Lieutenant Miyagi. Then he rose, donned his uniform, and stood outside his house, waiting for Miyagi to pick him up. He interviewed the doctor at the hospital—a thin young man wearing a mask, a weary air, and a blood-stained surgical coat—who said that the suspicious death he wanted to report was that of a local woman named Kaori Hirakata, an apparently healthy, well-nourished individual in her early twenties.

He told the inspector that, according to her parents, Kaori had her evening meal at seven, eating with a normal appetite. She then retired to her bedroom. Her brother had raised the alarm shortly before nine, summoning his parents to her bedroom, where they found her collapsed on the floor, rolling about as she clutched her stomach, vomiting, convulsing, and racked by uncontrollable coughing. A neighbor had shown up when she heard the commotion. Once she saw what was going on, she hurried down to the hall phone and called an ambulance. The emergency room staff had done all they could, but the young woman had died at approximately half past ten.

"I suspect she may have been poisoned," the doctor told Ito. "But I'll need to take blood and urine samples to verify my diagnosis."

"If it was poison, any idea what kind?"

"All the evidence points to thallium."

"That used to be commonly available as rat poison. But haven't they banned it?"

The doctor shrugged and heaved a great sigh. "Where there's a will, as they say."

"In the cases I've heard of, it was administered so gradually the victims suffered symptoms initially dismissed as due to natural causes," Ito said.

"That's not what's happened here. Miss Hirakata must have ingested a huge amount for it to take effect so quickly." The doctor sighed, adding, "And fatally."

The chief inspector sighed, too. "The parents?" he asked, looking around as if expecting to see them sitting quietly in a corner.

"I've sent them home by taxi. They were in such a terrible state I worried I was going to have two more patients on my hands." He paused. "It was odd. The father kept saying it was his fault."

"Did he explain?"

"No," the doctor said, kneading his forehead with one hand as if trying to erase the memory of laboring unsuccessfully over the girl. "No, no, no. Anyway, I'll take those samples and tell you what I find. I've also contacted the forensic pathologist in Ishizaki. He'll perform the autopsy tomorrow morning, and you should have the results in the afternoon."

"I can't get them sooner?"

The doctor, his face drawn and lined, looked up, an angry glint in his eyes. "Not a chance!" he spat out with a surprising burst of energy.

I shouldn't have pressed him, Ito thought. *It was the last straw.* Shrugging his shoulders, he rang the Hirakata residence.

"Muraji here," said a tired, dull voice.

"May I please speak to Mr. or Mrs. Hirakata?"

"No," she said flatly, only condescendingly explaining after a long pause. "They've gone to bed. She's in such a state I thought we'd have to call an ambulance for her, too."

"And you are..."

"I'm her cousin. I live just down the road from their place. Her husband rang, told me the tragic news and asked me to come by to help." She sighed. "Incredible!"

"I need to ask for your help, too, Muraji-*san*," Ito said. "This is Chief Inspector Ito from the Murota police. Please tell Mr. and Mrs. Hirakata I'll come by to interview them tomorrow morning. Also, given the sudden nature of their daughter's death, the house is a potential crime scene. I'll be sending over an officer to spend the night to ensure nothing—no potential clue how she died—is tampered with."

"Bedding," she groaned. "One more thing for me to do."

"That won't be necessary. Lieutenant Miyagi will be happy to spend the night in an armchair. And please don't wash the dishes or do any clearing or cleaning."

Hanging up, Ito instructed Miyagi to drive him home and head to the Hirakata household. Since the Murota police force was too small to have its own dedicated forensics unit, Miyagi also needed to arrange for a forensics team from the larger, neighboring city of Ishizaki to be dispatched early the next morning to inspect the Hirakatas' house.

"Miyagi, I know they're experts and probably won't enjoy being offered advice but instruct them to pay particular attention to any food remaining from the evening meal. I'd like them to inspect and take samples from any unwashed dishes, whether in the sink or the dishwasher, as well as leftovers in the fridge and peelings or scraps in the bins. We'll need to test all these items for any trace of poison."

"Yes, sir."

"Thank you, Miyagi. Let's talk in the morning."

Aki Hirakata
Sunday, 18 September
Aki had been loitering in the hall outside Kaori's room when he heard voices. Pressing his ear against her door, he listened. His sister had a secret visitor! A *man*! But how had he got into her room? Then it came to him. He must have climbed the big clematis vine winding up the front of the

house, just as Aki had done a few times himself. But a man in Kaori's room! It struck him he might be the strange man he'd seen her with at a bus stop a few months earlier.

That indistinct murmur of voices went on and on. Aki hoped his mother wouldn't come to the foot of the stairs, see what he was doing, and yell at him. Finally, his curiosity got the better of him. He had to see his sister's mysterious visitor! Moving as slowly as he could, he turned the knob and opened the door an inch, peering through the crack. As he'd guessed, the weird bus stop man sat beside Kaori on her bed.

They were talking so intently that they didn't notice him. Aki closed the door gently and waited, his ear pressed against the door. Finally, he heard the man say goodbye, followed by the sound of the window opening and the faint creaking of the vine.

Aki felt stunned. What he'd heard had shocked him. It seemed his sister meant to run away with that loser. Could that be possible? He hadn't been able to catch everything they'd said, just the general drift. He decided he had to see Kaori, even though he couldn't ask her directly about that man and their plans. If he did, she'd know he'd been listening. Of course, that's exactly what he'd been doing, but he didn't want to admit it.

Aki felt hurt that Kaori would even consider taking such a step. She was his favorite in the family. He loved his mother, but she was too anxious, and his father was distant and sometimes bad-tempered. His big sister Yumi had left them so long ago that Aki was beginning to forget what she looked like.

Aki burst into the room and came to an abrupt halt, seeing his sister sitting on her dressing table stool. He suddenly felt gripped by fear and anger, thinking he couldn't bear it if Kaori left. He threw himself at her and was glad to see her nearly fall. She looked shocked but, recovering her balance, rose and shoved him back, then grabbed one of his arms and poked him in the ribs where he was the most ticklish. He couldn't bear being touched by her. *Traitor*! After he'd struggled from her grasp, he stared at her in disbelief and fury, then lashed out, kicking one of her legs hard, feeling ashamed even as he did it. It was a childish reaction, as if he was a furious toddler rather than an eleven-year-old boy. He did it because he knew she loved him so much she'd forgive him no matter how badly he behaved. This meant he indulged in immature behavior around her he'd never dare to attempt with anyone else.

"I hate you! I hate you!" he said.

"Stop! What's wrong?" Kaori said.

He gave himself away. "You're going away with that loser. I hate you."

"Come here. We need to talk."

In a few minutes, there was another tap on the door. This time, it was their mother. "Breakfast!" she said, casting a curious look at her children. Kaori and Aki were sitting on her bed, their arms around each other.

When Aki left Kaori's bedroom and went downstairs, he found his father already at the table, his lips pressed together in a thin line, obviously irritated his family wasn't yet gathered around him so he could say grace before the meal. Aki was silent as he took his place. His sister had made him promise to say nothing.

Finally, Kaori appeared, and the tension dissipated. Everyone knew she could wind her father around her little finger.

Aki noticed his father startle at seeing Kaori still in her bathrobe. No wonder. Their parents insisted on formality even at home and were always impeccably dressed; he had never seen them in nightwear. His sister put on an anguished look and clutched her belly.

"Sorry I'm late," she said.

Their mother rose, a worried expression on her face. "Are you alright?"

"I got a tummy ache last night. It woke me up. I still feel a bit sick."

"You should go right to bed," *Otoosan* said, rising to put a hand on her forehead. "You don't have a temperature, but you need to take some aspirin and try to sleep. We'll make your apologies at church."

Aki felt amused. What a chump! Still, it made his father—who could be forbidding and distant—human.

But then Aki regretted what he did when his sister turned to go up the stairs. He hated the thought of having to go to church without her. He relied on her to entertain him during the pastor's interminable sermons. On impulse, he jumped up and rushed over to her. He knew it was idiotic and childish but couldn't help himself. He kicked her again, aiming his foot at one of her ankles as he hissed, "Liar! You're not ill. You just don't want to go!"

He would always remember her expression when she turned to look at him. There was surprise and concern but, above all, love. "I'm sorry, sweetie," she said.

Not so easily appeased, he clawed at one of his trouser pockets and pulled out a good luck amulet she had given him when he was five, which he always carried. His face contorted with anger, he threw it at his sister, saying, "I don't need this. You do!" Then he'd rushed upstairs.

He did not know his sister would be dead before the night was out.

Chief Inspector Ito
Monday, 18 September

Puzzled, Chief Inspector Ito sat in his office the following morning. Murder seemed so improbable. Apart from that unfortunate business concerning the victim's father, the Hirakata family was the model of integrity and respectability. Ito knew a bit about the family from that previous case over a decade earlier, and in small-town Murota, it had been easy to keep tabs on them. Despite the scandal, the father continued to work at Taniguchi real estate company, one of Murota's most prosperous firms, and the mother was a pillar of Murota's sole Christian church. A twin sister had reportedly left the country to live in England while a younger brother named Aki still lived with the parents. Did the young woman's death have anything to do with what had happened to her father over a decade earlier? He looked forward to interviewing them. Had they heard anything, seen anything? He could only hope.

The clock on the wall ticked while Ito drummed his fingers on his desk impatiently. He was restless, longing to spring into action. He had already phoned Miyagi at the Hirakata home and asked him to assemble a list of names with the contact information for the victim's friends, neighbors, workmates, and members of the church she attended should these individuals need to be questioned. Ito had set up an appointment to meet the family at ten, but he wanted to know first if it really was murder. The doctor had promised the results of the blood and urine tests soon. Ito decided to treat the case as murder without the autopsy results if those tests indicated poisoning.

Ito heard a tentative knock.

"Come in!" he barked. It was already a quarter past nine.

Miyagi put his head nervously around the door and then walked in. His thin face looked drawn and even more sallow than usual. He hunched his shoulders slightly, trying to be as inconspicuous as possible.

"I told you to go home after your shift at the Hirakata house," Ito said, regretting the brusqueness of his words as they left his mouth. His lieutenant was reliable and dogged even if the inspector didn't care for his perennially anxious air. Miyagi was middle-aged but moved and acted like a man in his sixties.

"I just wanted to let you know the forensics team from the Ishizaki station arrived at the Hirakata house at 8:30 and is busy at work."

Then Miyagi held out a piece of paper, adding, "And I wanted to give you this in person. It's the contact list you asked me to draw up."

If he had anything more to say, it would have to wait. The phone on the inspector's desk rang. Ito put the paper on his desk and picked up the receiver. Miss Hino, the pretty young receptionist who also acted as the station's switchboard operator, asked if he would take a call from a doctor at Murota Hospital.

At last, Ito thought.

"We've found significant quantities of thallium in Kaori Hirakata's urine and blood samples," the doctor said in a weak, tired voice. "As I'd expected, it appears she consumed a massive amount of it."

The chief inspector was both horrified and relieved. The period of fruitless speculation was over. It was murder. He now knew what he was dealing with and what he had to do.

"And the autopsy results?" he asked.

The doctor sighed. "The autopsy is being performed right now. As I told you last night, we can't get those results to you for hours yet, not until this afternoon." The tiredness in his voice leached through as he disconnected the call.

The inspector glanced up to see Miyagi loitering by the door, looking at him expectantly. On seeing his boss nod, Miyagi approached his desk. "She died of thallium poisoning," Ito said.

"I'm not tired at all," Miyagi replied. "Please don't send me home. I'm fine."

"Very well. Why don't you assemble a team of officers?" Ito looked irritated, but he was actually relieved, knowing he could rely on his lieutenant. "Maybe five or six. And set up an incident room. It will need to include at least one telephone, three typewriters, a photocopier, and one or two whiteboards that we can cover with photographs, timelines, and maps."

"Yes, sir," Miyagi said, adding, his eyes bright. "Our first murder enquiry."

"There's nothing to be excited about," Ito said, feeling compelled to rebuke him for his eagerness. "The poor woman was only twenty-three."

"All the more reason for us to catch her killer, sir," Miyagi said. "And as quickly as possible." Then, looking aghast at his own presumptuousness, he hurried from the office.

Ito glanced at his watch. It was nine-thirty. He'd need to leave in a few minutes if he was to arrive at the Hirakata house at ten. He had brushed off his tunic, readying himself for his visit, when the phone rang again. It was Miss Hino saying that Mr. Hirakata had just called, begging the inspector to delay his visit until four o'clock as his wife had only now fallen asleep, having paced their bedroom all night.

"He said she's desperately tired, sir," Miss Hino said. "She wasn't able to drop off even though the family doctor gave her tranquillizers. He hopes she can get some rest before she's questioned."

"Call him back and tell him that's fine," Ito said.

Consulting Miyagi's list, Ito sent off some officers to take statements while he assigned others the task of transcribing and collating them as they trickled in.

As he was reaching for the phone, Miyagi knocked on his open door.

"Yes, what is it?"

"Sir, we just learned Kaori Hirakata had a boyfriend." Behind his lieutenant was a man from the Ishizaki forensics team who identified himself as Officer Suzuki. He was stout and middle-aged, and his face glistened with perspiration.

Suzuki bowed and held out a small yellow notebook that he laid on the chief's desk.

"The rest of the team is still at the Hirakata household, sir," he said. "But I thought it a matter of urgency to give you this as quickly as possible. We found it in a suitcase in the young woman's room. It appears to be a diary."

Suzuki wiped his face with a handkerchief as he added, "My apologies. After checking the diary for fingerprints—there were only the victim's— we took the liberty of opening it. We looked at some of the latest entries to confirm a theory based on other objects in that suitcase. Besides the diary, we found the victim's passport and birth certificate, an envelope stuffed with South Korean currency, clothes, a pair of shoes, and a bag of cosmetics and medications."

"And your theory is..." said Ito, picking up the book and leafing through it.

"That the victim was on the point of eloping to South Korea with an individual whose name figures largely in the latter third of the diary's entries. Someone named Hiroki Sato." He paused, adding, "It would be helpful if you could get Hiroki Sato's fingerprints for us. There's one set of prints we found in the woman's bedroom that we could not identify. They were on a box of chocolates we found on her bed."

Suzuki paused and looked nervous. "Of course, we can't be sure until we've examined the contents, but it's a strong possibility that the poison that killed the victim was contained in the chocolates, given that nobody else in the household was affected. The box was only half full."

Ito stood, bowed, and thanked him, and Miyagi left with Suzuki. After they'd gone, Ito eagerly flipped through the diary. It seemed wrong, like an impertinence, to read the young woman's intimate descriptions of her feelings for this Hiroki Sato and the hopes she entertained for their future life together. But it had to be done. As Suzuki had reported, the plans outlined in the last pages of her diary made it plain Kaori Hirakata had intended to run away with her young man, and on the very night she met her unfortunate end.

Ito immediately secured Hiroki Sato's address, and then dispatched an officer to bring the young man to the station for questioning.

Officer Fujii was excited but nervous to interview someone connected with a murder, but when he arrived at the address, Hiroki Sato wasn't there. A neighbor, alerted by the loud and persistent knocking, popped her head out her door to tell the officer that Hiroki worked on the local Nissan assembly line.

When the officer arrived at the factory, he was told Hiroki hadn't come in that morning—and it was unusual, as he was one of their best and most reliable workers. But it wasn't a wasted visit. Officer Fujii gained access to Hiroki's locker, where he found a sketchpad, a comb and a mirror. Putting on gloves, he placed them all in a clear plastic bag to take back to the station.

Fujii could also find Hiroki's mother through the personnel department. They not only had Hiroki's photo and personal details on file but also the addresses of places where his mother had part-time jobs.

He finally tracked her down to the very hospital where Kaori Hirakata had died hours earlier. She worked as a cleaner there and was crossing the parking lot, having finished the night shift. She was a scrawny woman in her early sixties with permed hair dyed yellow, and seemed more angry than worried when the officer confronted her, and she realized her son was a suspect in a murder investigation.

"My boy!" she said, shaking her head wearily and frowning. "I had no idea he even had a girlfriend, let alone that Hirakata girl. He goes his own way."

"I'm sorry, ma'am. But could you tell me where he might be?"

The gaunt, tired-looking woman sighed. "He was in Tokyo for a year and a half, then returned to Murota six months ago. Maybe he's gone back there. Mind you, I don't know where he stayed in Tokyo or even what he got up to. He told me he was heading off again, but didn't explain where or why."

She sat down heavily on a curb, passing a hand over her lined, sweaty face, looking up to speak to the officer. "Hiro-*chan* and I share a house, but we hardly meet, let alone talk. I'll admit, I haven't been much of a mother to him. With no husband to support us, I've been too busy working jobs at all hours for us just to get by. He was always in trouble as a young boy."

The woman smiled weakly, revealing stained, broken teeth. "When Hiro-*chan* got back from Tokyo, he had changed. It was like he'd finally grown up. Sometimes he even seemed happy! He'd been working at the car factory right after high school—till he took it in his head to try his luck in Tokyo—and the Nissan boss was kind enough to take him back on when he returned to Murota. I thought my son had turned a corner and was going to be okay after all." She sniffed. "Turns out I was wrong." She spat, a little globule landing on the asphalt. "He never said as much, but I think he got mixed up with a dangerous crowd in Tokyo. *Yakuza!* Like I said, I hoped he'd changed. But maybe the Nissan job is a front, and he's involved with gangsters here in Murota."

"You must visit the station as soon as possible to give a statement," Officer Fujii said.

"I promise," she said, staring grimly down at the road.

Upon reporting back to the chief inspector, the officer received instructions to take the bag holding Hiroki Sato's belongings to the Ishizaki forensics team, which was just winding up its operations at the Hirakata house.

Once it became clear the young man was nowhere to be found and hadn't been seen or heard of since Sunday evening, the chief inspector provided personal details and a photo in an all-points bulletin alerting the police throughout Japan that Hiroki Sato, aged twenty-eight and a resident of Murota in Kyushu, was a suspect in a murder investigation. He stressed Sato might already have fled the country, but that special vigilance was required at the nation's airports and ferry terminals.

Inspecting Hiroki Sato's picture made Ito feel melancholy. Even Japan wasn't exempt from deplorable trends current throughout the world, he thought. Lately, many young Japanese were as sulky and ill-behaved as their Western counterparts. There was something androgynous and disagreeable about Kaori's boyfriend. He looked out from his photo with a sullen expression; the mouth curled in what looked suspiciously like a sneer, his face shadowed by long hair gelled into a thick black crest. Had he killed his lover? If so, why?

Hiroki and Kaori
Sunday, 18 September

Hiroki visited Kaori in her bedroom a second time that day. Once more, he shinned up the clematis vine winding up the front of the house to her balcony, but this time he'd thought to wear gloves to protect his hands. It was eight o'clock in the evening, a good hour before their arrangement to meet on the street outside the Hirakata property and run away together. He wore jeans and a light hooded jacket and had on a large backpack.

He grinned, peeling off his gloves as he slid open Kaori's window and walked in. Then he felt dismayed. She didn't jump up and greet him with her usual smile and a kiss. She was sitting on her bed, and her green suitcase was open beside her as she idly toyed with its contents. He saw the yellow notebook she used as a journal. Looking up with reddened eyes, she said, "I hope nobody saw you."

"I don't think so," he said. "I'm glad it's already dark. It helps I moved out of my mother's house yesterday and spent last night at a friend's place. I think they're watching my home. Still, on my way here, just to be safe, I walked into two buildings by the front entrance and left by the rear exit. I don't think anyone followed me." He shrugged and took off his backpack, which fell to the floor with a thud, then sank to his knees before her, taking one of her hands as if he intended to kiss it.

Kaori withdrew her hand and stared at him dully. He wondered at her coolness but pretended not to notice, leaning near to inhale her perfume. "You smell so sweet. You always smell sweet."

Kaori stood abruptly, nearly causing him to fall backward. After locking her door, she sat at her dressing table, her back to him. Staring into the mirror, she dabbed at her makeup. "You're too early," she finally said. Then she turned to look at Hiroki, who was still sitting on the floor. "I was going to spend my last hours here writing a letter to my parents explaining about us and what we planned to do. But after what you said this morning, I'm not sure if I can go with you after all. So, I have written nothing! I've even thought of unpacking."

Hiroki sighed deeply, shaking his head. He rose and picked up his backpack. Placing it beside Kaori's case on the bed and opening it, he withdrew a white plastic bag that he put next to the pack. Then he walked over to Kaori and fell on his knees beside her stool.

After a silence, he said, "Kaori, I'm sorry. You're disappointed in me. I can understand that. But I was *afraid*, thinking I wouldn't have a chance if you knew. Remember, I could have just *not* told you. But this morning, it came to me you had to know, that it wouldn't be fair if I didn't tell you." He grabbed one of her hands and squeezed it tightly. "Believe in me. We can make a new life together. I can make you happy."

Kaori sniffed, pulling her hand from his grasp. "It felt like you'd hit me when you told me your secret. I'm giving up everything for you—my family, my friends, my home, my whole life here. And then you spring something like that on me at the last minute."

"Everyone thinks you're too good for me, and they're right."

She looked down at him, her eyes bright with tears. "What I find most unforgivable is you intended to *use* me!"

"I didn't want to. They asked me to. But like I told you, I refused because I love you."

"I'm not sure I can ever trust you again."

"Kaori, I'm through with that life. I hate myself for what I did as a *yakuza*."

"I thought of you as a gem—the lump of coal that's become a diamond."

"I know."

She turned around to look at herself in the mirror again. "But you're in danger," she said. "And you said I am, too."

"We should have a good start, and even if they find out where we've gone, I doubt they'll track us down. Busan is too far away. And we won't be staying there long. I want us to get to Seoul as soon as we can and disappear there. It's such a big city, it shouldn't be hard. Anyway, I'm not worth what it would cost them in time and money. I hope they'll realize I've gone for good and have no interest in ratting on them to the cops or anyone else."

Kaori still said nothing. She stared at her face in the mirror. Hiroki, watching, saw her take on a sullen pout and then massage her arms.

"You *hurt* me!" she moaned. "When you were here before. I have bruises where you grabbed me."

"I saw red when you said you might marry that man at your church. I lost control. Forgive me!" She swiveled around to look at him again, and then she slumped down on the floor beside him.

"Can I believe you? Can I trust you?" Kaori said.

Hiroki responded with a kiss. After initial reluctance, Kaori succumbed to his embrace. Sitting on the floor, they clung to each other and began murmuring endearments.

"I'll go with you, Hiro-*chan*," she finally said. "I wish you'd told me before, but we must move on if we're to have any future together."

Then she drew away from him abruptly and, fixing him with a stern glare, added, "You must promise you'll never do it again. We can't keep secrets from each other."

"I promise."

"You're not perfect. But I'm not either. For one thing, I'm selfish, selfish enough to agree to run away with you. I can't bear to think about how upset my family will be. And I've not even written them that note to explain."

Kaori lifted a hand to Hiroki's wet cheek. "You're crying!" she said with surprise.

Hiroki felt ashamed and stood, rubbing his face roughly.

Kaori rose, too, and that's when she registered the white plastic bag on the bed.

"What's that?" she asked.

"A present," he said. Picking up the bag and with the air of a conjurer taking a rabbit from a hat, Hiroki slowly withdrew a black box with gilt lettering. "Sweets for the sweet," he said, lifting the lid.

Kaori exclaimed with delight, "How beautiful!" The box included powdered truffles and dark, milk, and white chocolates fashioned into ovals, rectangles, and squares. Gilt paper covered some of the chocolates, while others had icing sugar depicting delicate patterns of flowers, trees, and clouds.

Kaori glanced up, looking surprised. "But some are missing."

"Never mind. There are plenty left."

"Let's have some," Kaori said. "They'll give us energy for our trip."

"You have them. I'm not hungry. I've been too terrified about how you felt about what I'd said to have any appetite." He smiled. "But haven't you just eaten?"

"Yes, but there's always room for candy."

Hiroki watched as Kaori ate two dark chocolates decorated with a cherry blossom design. "Kirsch," she said happily. Then she picked up one covered with gold paper and, unwrapping it, popped it into her mouth. After she'd chewed and swallowed, she said appreciatively, "Milk chocolate with chopped almonds." Finally, she tried what looked like a chocolate-covered pretzel.

Hiroki looked at his watch. "It's only 8:30. We can just sit here and relax for half an hour before we need to think of starting off. I can climb back down the vine. I suppose you'll be able to sneak down the stairs and slip out the front door."

He looked at her case and lifted it tentatively. "I can take that. It's small and light enough for me to carry down the vine. Anyway, we have lots of time. My uncle's not expecting us till nearly ten."

They sat on the floor, leaning against the bed, holding hands. Kaori lay her head on his shoulder. Minutes passed. Kaori straightened and took a few more chocolates from the box. Hiroki was nearly asleep when he heard it. The sound of a cough.

"Are you okay?" Hiroki asked. Kaori couldn't answer. Now she'd started coughing, it seemed she couldn't stop.

"I'll get some water." Hiroki went to the door, unlocked it, and looked down the hall. He'd been to the house once before and knew where the bathroom was. The coast was clear. He didn't notice a door slightly ajar or the small head that poked out to watch him. Focused, Hiroki found a mug next to the sink that he filled with water and hurried back to the bedroom.

Kaori was still coughing and now lay partially slumped on the floor. She began gasping as if she was having trouble breathing. Kneeling beside her, Hiroki held the mug to her lips. She took a sip but spat it out, seeming unable to swallow. Then she bent her head down and retched. Hiroki rushed to get a box of tissues on her dressing table.

It went on and on. Finally, still alternating between coughing and vomiting, Kaori pointed to the window and said, "Go! Go!"

It was obvious she couldn't go with him, that she desperately needed medical help. Hiroki kissed her on the forehead and gripped her hands. "Sayonara, my sweet," he said. "I hate to leave you like this. I can't believe this is happening, but you need a doctor. It's just for a little while, Kao-*chan*. I'll be back for you." Picking up his backpack, he hurried to the window to slide down the vine. As he stood on the balcony, preparing to make his descent, he looked through the window and saw a boy had entered Kaori's bedroom. He heard the boy shouting: "*Okaasan*! *Otoosan*! Come quick! Something's wrong with Kaori!"

Hiroki slid hastily down the vine, cursing he hadn't thought to put the gloves back on. His hands tingling, he ran to the front gate. That's when he noticed a dark figure standing across the street, well away from the light.

It was instinct. Hiroki took to his heels and ran. For a few minutes, he heard somebody behind him in hot pursuit. But he knew Murota better than any *yakuza* from Tokyo ever could. He avoided the roads and darted down alleyways, garden paths, and narrow lanes bordering rice paddies, somehow making it to the dock, where his uncle was waiting by his boat.

"We have to go now," Hiroki said.

He noticed his uncle looking behind him, the question etched on his face.

"She can't come," is all he said, unable to meet his uncle's gaze.

Chief Inspector Ito and Superintendent Takenaka
Monday, 19 September

Chief Inspector Ito felt his heart sink when his desk telephone rang. He guessed who it was. It was only to be expected that Superintendent Takenaka, the head of the Ishizaki police station, would be in touch. After all, Ito had requested the services of his forensics team. They must be back at their own station by now, and Ito was expecting the results at any time.

Ito thought of Takenaka as an individual with an uncanny resemblance to a rat terrier in appearance and character. He was short and wiry with beady black eyes and what Ito thought of as caterpillar brows. He always seemed to tremble with an eagerness to attack or criticize. Ito knew he wasn't the only one to find Takenaka difficult to work with. Other officers in the region had hinted as much. Still, Takenaka was the district's administrative head, and it was imperative to keep on good terms with him.

Ito picked up the receiver. It was Miss Hino from reception again. "A call from Superintendent Takenaka, sir," she said.

"Put him through."

"I've been expecting your call," Takenaka said in an irritated voice. "I've been waiting for it."

"Sorry, sir. I intended to ring once I had the autopsy results. I haven't received them yet, but the doctor who treated the victim in the emergency room has contacted me. He told me large amounts of thallium have been found in her blood and urine samples. She was poisoned."

"Murder," Takenaka said. "In fact, I expected it from your description of the girl's death. I first heard of thallium in a case in Tokyo a few years ago. A daughter impatient to inherit her mother's money poisoned her. The woman was old, and the authorities initially thought it to be a natural death. But then, a neighbor raised concerns, and the authorities conducted an autopsy. The woman's daughter had administered the poison in such small doses the symptoms were mistaken for gastritis. We never learned how she'd gotten hold of it."

"Of course, many people once used thallium as a rat poison," said Ito thoughtfully. "Or to kill ants."

"That daughter struck me as a perfect monster, devoid of any human feelings," Takenaka said, ignoring him. "She tried to make out *she* was the victim, painting her mother as heartless in refusing to keep on subsidizing her expensive tastes."

"Lacking any taste or odor, thallium is a perfect weapon in the hands of an unscrupulous individual."

"Still, from what I've heard, the Hirakata woman died so suddenly nobody could think it was natural."

"That's right, sir. I'm still awaiting the report from your forensics team, but one of your officers told me there was a box of chocolates on the victim's bed, only half full, and he speculated that might have been the source of the poison she consumed—a reasonable guess given nobody else in the family was affected. Naturally, we are exploring the possibility the boyfriend gave her the box. The victim was on the point of eloping with a local boy named Hiroki Sato."

"Yes, I heard about that from Officer Suzuki," the superintendent said.

"Maybe they quarreled, and she changed her mind about going away with him, and he got his revenge that way."

"It sounds implausible to me," Takenaka said. "Your theory depends on his knowing beforehand that she intended to call the whole thing off, and he injected the chocolates with poison to kill her. It would have needed time and planning to carry it off. My forensics team asked me to tell you that, having examined the items of Sato's from his work locker that you provided them, they've matched his prints to the ones on that box. So, perhaps it was him. I imagine he's your principal suspect."

Ito sighed. "Yes, but we haven't been able to question him. Hiroki Sato has vanished."

"Pity. But I hope you will actively pursue all other lines of inquiry while you look for him. We may be premature in assuming it was the boyfriend."

Ito frowned. "You're quite right, Superintendent. I mustn't jump to conclusions. In fact, I associate poisoning with female murderers. Also, we must entertain the possibility Kaori Hirakata wasn't the intended victim. And for that matter, Sato's prints being on the box don't prove he gave it to her. I'm just making that assumption since the two were to meet last night to elope. But if it was Sato who brought the chocolates, perhaps somebody had given them to him. Perhaps *he* was the intended recipient and didn't know some contained poison."

"That sounds rather fanciful," Takenaka said dismissively. "In any case, it's been established it was murder. I'm counting on you to send me the autopsy results once you get them. I'll ask my team for a copy of the forensics report. Also, we need to arrange a press conference as soon as possible. Journalists are always snapping at our heels in such cases, knowing a good murder sells papers, especially if the victim is young and pretty. No doubt the story will appear in the afternoon editions. In fact, the Ishizaki television station has already contacted me. They suggest we hold a briefing tomorrow morning at their studio to air on local channels. Can you make it?"

"Yes, of course," the chief inspector said. "Just let me know the time and place, and I'll be there."

"They've hinted NHK may even pick up the story. I think it's advisable to reassure everyone they're safe. The poisoning of a young woman isn't exactly something that happens on Kyushu every day. We want to quash any useless or inflammatory speculation. Nip it in the bud," Takenaka said decisively. "The sooner you can finger a suspect, whether it's that Sato boy or somebody else, the better."

The superintendent hung up before Ito could respond.

Lieutenant Miyagi and Chief Inspector Ito
Monday, 19 September

Although dusk was settling in, sufficient light remained for nearby objects to be visible, and Miyagi looked incredulously at the big white dwelling at the end of the garden. With one large block placed on top of one even larger, it had the simplicity of a child's picture of a house. Strange that it's a private dwelling, he thought. It could be a top-class hotel or a casino.

Miyagi allowed himself a feeling of sneaking satisfaction. He'd had to park the patrol car on the street. The Hirakatas were ostentatiously rich but seemed to have no car or, at least, no provision for one. He thought complacently of his own blue Toyota, neatly tucked in the tiny garage attached to his one-story house in a street near the train tracks.

On opening the front gate in the tall wall surrounding the property, he and the chief inspector made their way up a brick path that wound through a formal garden to the door. Miyagi looked around curiously. There was a fountain with a little naked boy pouring water from a jug. The front door was between an enormous tree and a thick vine twining up the wall to a balcony on the second floor.

The door was open, and a middle-aged couple stood just inside, holding hands. Miyagi felt a twinge of disapproval. He disliked public displays of affection. Whenever they were outside their home, his parents acted like acquaintances rather than husband and wife, and that seemed right to him. It was very much in line with Japanese custom and tradition. Then, seeing the strained, miserable look on their faces, Miyagi's heart softened. They'd lost their daughter and in a horrible way. No wonder they were trying to comfort each other.

He and the chief inspector bowed deeply. Taking off their shoes and lining them neatly in the *genkan*, they stepped up to don the slippers left out for them in the hall. Miyagi noticed a large vase of fresh flowers on the shoe cupboard, placed between a phone and a glass box holding what looked like an expensive Japanese doll. He felt a spurt of envy—the luxuries of the well-off!

Bowing again, he and the chief followed Mr. and Mrs. Hirakata down a passageway to a large room furnished in the Western style. It had a big gray sofa, two matching gray armchairs, a coffee table, and even a grand piano. Large French windows revealed a view of the garden.

Miyagi looked about the luxurious surroundings nervously, scouting for an unobtrusive place to sit. He audibly sighed with relief when he noticed the piano bench. Perching on the edge, he took a notebook and pencil from a pocket and gazed expectantly at Ito.

A sense of *déjà vu* overwhelmed the chief inspector. As he walked up the path with his lieutenant, everything looked just as it had when he'd visited the house twelve years earlier—from the outside to the inside. He recognized the trimmed bushes, the vivid patches of flowers, and the fountain with the statue of a naked boy pouring water from a jug. Once inside, the living room also looked exactly the same. Only the couple had changed—aged, although he supposed it was what had just happened to their daughter that accounted for their lined faces and bowed shoulders. As soon as the couple had settled side-by-side in the two armchairs, they beckoned him to the sofa opposite.

Ito sat and then rose slightly to bow to them, saying, "I'm sorry to meet you both again in such tragic circumstances. I find words useless in such situations, but my lieutenant and I wish to offer you our deepest sympathies." The couple inclined their heads and said nothing, although Mrs. Hirakata sniffed audibly.

In the brief silence that followed, that sense of *déjà vu* overcame Ito once more, seeing the handsome furniture, the reproductions of Impressionist paintings on the walls, the bookshelves, and the piano. He longed for any diversion—to be offered coffee or invited to stand and admire the view of the garden—because it was too painful to have to observe the man and woman sitting across from him. They looked not only older but gripped by suffering, with their faces pale and drawn. They'd already suffered one terrible blow over a decade earlier, and here was another.

In normal circumstances—if Mr. Hirakata hadn't been shot in that unfortunate incident and if their daughter hadn't just died—he could imagine that by this point in their lives, they would have resembled any similarly circumstanced middle-aged couple living in Murota's expensive Kitaguchi district. They'd have looked the picture-perfect husband and wife of considerable means, him with a new haircut and custom-tailored suit, her wearing pearls and a stylish dress, her hair recently waved.

But these two had been broken. Slumped in their chairs, heads bowed, staring at the ground, both clad in black, they looked disheveled and distraught. Kaori's mother was trembling, and her husband drew his chair nearer to take her hands in his. Ito wished he could somehow console them but knew it was impossible. The thought of losing his own daughter was unbearable. And now he'd have to compound their grief by telling them their child had been murdered.

Ito settled back in his chair and spoke in his customary calm and authoritative voice. He said the hospital pathologist had discovered traces of thallium in the girl's bloodstream and that, at the moment, they were acting on the supposition that she had ingested the poison through chocolates found in a box in her bedroom. They were still awaiting the results of the autopsy (and here he saw the couple shudder) and the report of the forensics team that had inspected not only the young woman's bedroom but also the rest of the house.

Ito thought again of Aiko and felt the familiar surge of anxious protectiveness. But duty forced him to press on. After a short pause to allow the woman's parents come to terms with what he'd said, he continued, "My apologies for bringing you this terrible news."

"Murder?" Mr. Hirakata said, while his wife moaned and sobbed. "It's a shock, although I guessed as much when your officer insisted on spending the night here, forbidding us from entering the kitchen and taping off our daughter's bedroom. At first, my wife and I thought it might have been a burst appendix. Kaori had been complaining earlier in the day of stomach pain."

"It's beyond belief," Mrs. Hirakata burst out. "Kaori had no enemies. Everybody loved her. She was the sweetest girl in the world."

"I'm afraid it's beyond doubt," the chief inspector said. "As I've said, it seems she ingested a highly toxic amount of thallium."

"I've never heard of thallium before," Mrs. Hirakata said. She turned to look at her husband, who said he hadn't either. "You've indicated it was in the chocolates," she continued. "I suppose that's possible. Otherwise, we had the same food last night. Seeing that box on Kaori's bed surprised me. I'd never seen it before. She loves...loved sweets, but she wouldn't have bought an expensive box of chocolates to have by herself in her room."

"We have to find out how the box came into your daughter's possession. If you knew nothing about the chocolates and she didn't buy them herself, we need to establish who gave them to her. Did your daughter have a visitor yesterday who might have brought them?"

"Not that we know of," Mr. Hirakata said.

The chief inspector paused again. "Forgive my bringing this up, Mr. Hirakata," Ito said, "but the doctor who attended your daughter told me you said, repeatedly, that it was your fault."

Mr. Hirakata paled, and his wife took his hand. "I just meant that, as her father, I naturally wanted to protect her. I failed. In that sense, I feel it was my fault."

Mrs. Hirakata lifted his hand to her lips and kissed it. Then she said, "I wish Yumi were here."

"I suppose you mean your daughter," Ito said, adding involuntarily, "your *other* daughter," then cursing himself for having done so.

Fortunately, Mrs. Hirakata either didn't notice or didn't mind. "That's right," she said. "Yumi has been living in London for the past four years. She's flying to Japan now and should be back in a few hours. She and Kaori are—were—twins. Kaori might have confided in Yumi, told her secrets she didn't want us to know."

"I'm looking forward to meeting her soon," Ito said, adding, "Please ask her to come to the station as soon as she can after her arrival back in Murota. Now, as for those chocolates..."

Suddenly the door opened, and a figure rushed into the room, stopping just short of Mrs. Hirakata. The chief inspector realized it must be Aki, the murdered girl's younger brother, and that he had been standing just outside the door of the living room and heard everything they'd said. Ito was not a fanciful man, but he saw in that long-limbed boy the gawky elegance of a young deer poised to bound away at the slightest hint of danger.

"There was a *man* here yesterday!" the boy said, standing beside his mother's chair. "To see Kaori. *He* brought the chocolates! I heard him say he was giving them to her as a present."

Mrs. Hirakata shook her head wearily. "Aki, Aki, you have such an active imagination. I've warned you not to tell tales."

"But it's *true*! He came twice, once in the morning and then at night."

"But we didn't know Kaori had a visitor," Mr. Hirakata said. "Nobody came to the door. How did he get in?"

"He crawled up that vine outside Kaori's room."

"Why didn't you tell us?" his mother wailed.

The boy sank to his knees beside her, looking mournful. "I wanted to, but Kaori made me promise to keep it a secret."

His mother, looking shocked, put one arm around his shoulders. He accepted her embrace momentarily, but then struggled from her grasp and walked over to Ito. "I was outside her door," he said in a defiant voice. "I was eavesdropping."

Miyagi rose from the piano bench and cast a questioning look at the inspector, who nodded.

When he returned in a few minutes, Miyagi said, "The vine shows distinct signs of damage. There are lots of leaves scattered at the base, near the roots. Unfortunately, the ground is hard-packed dirt. I can't see any footprints."

"We'd better contact Superintendent Takenaka when we get back," the inspector said. "See if he can send one or two forensics officers over to have a look."

While Miyagi scribbled away, the chief inspector had a few more questions to ask Aki. "You say you heard a man in your sister's room. Did you see him at all?"

"The first time he came, in the morning, I got a peep at him. I opened my sister's door without them noticing. And the second time, after Kaori began coughing..." The boy gulped, his eyes bright, and was briefly unable to go on. Finally, he continued. "I heard the man say he was going to get some water. I guessed he'd be going to the bathroom, so I hurried down the hall and hid in a room. I saw him then, too, getting a better look at him."

"Did you know him? Have you seen him before?"

Aki looked embarrassed and was silent for a minute. Then it came out. "I've always enjoyed following Kaori, sometimes spying on her," he said. "I don't know why. I just like—liked—to be with her or near her. A few months ago, I followed her to the bus stop and saw her talking to a strange man. I can't be sure, but I think he was the man I saw yesterday."

"When you saw her with him at the bus stop, did you have the impression they knew each other?"

Aki shook his head. "No. Kaori asked him something, and he looked at his watch, then they began to talk."

"Can you describe him?"

"That day at the bus stop, he wore jeans and a ripped T-shirt," the boy said. "Something was glistening in one of his ears, maybe an earring but he was too far away for me to be sure. He had that moony look on his face guys get when they see my sister for the first time." Suddenly, he gasped, "Kao-*chan*," with a ragged sob escaping from deep in his throat. He gulped and looked at the floor.

Miyagi glanced at Ito, and when the inspector nodded, he rose and approached Mrs. Hirakata. "Perhaps we could go into the kitchen and get us all some tea." He looked at Aki. "I'd be grateful if you could help."

Mrs. Hirakata and Aki followed Miyagi out of the room.

Once they had gone, the chief inspector gazed intently at Mr. Hirakata and said, "Again, I'm very sorry to disturb you. But we must. Time is of the essence if we are to catch the culprit."

Mr. Hirakata nodded his head. "Please go ahead, Chief Inspector," he said in a soft voice.

"Did you have any idea your daughter had a visitor yesterday? This man that your son says he saw and heard."

"None at all."

"Have you ever met the individual your son has described?"

"Not to my knowledge. No!" and his face twisted with disgust and rage.

"When did you last see your daughter?"

"About eight. We'd had our evening meal as usual, then she retired to her bedroom." He paused, considering. "I should tell you something that struck me at the time. Kaori was a loving daughter, but she was even more affectionate than usual last night. Now that I think of it, when she said goodnight to my wife and me, it was like she was saying goodbye."

"Well, you must have noticed the suitcase on her bed last night. And given the secrecy of her young man's visit, which I'm certain occurred, I think we can reasonably assume she intended to run away with him. His name is Hiroki Sato. Was your daughter in the habit of lying to you?"

Mr. Hirakata flushed and said indignantly, "No!" Then, after a pause, much more quietly, "Yes. Perhaps." He gazed at his hands, twisted in his lap. "*Children*! We try to give them everything—to love and protect them—but while we can clothe and feed them, we can't know what's in their hearts and minds. Until last night, I would have said I knew my dear daughter very well. Now I wonder if I knew her at all."

"Did your daughter mention she planned to take a trip soon?"

"No!"

Ito paused, reflecting. It had to be asked, but he was reluctant. Finally, he got it out. "Do you think what happened to your daughter has any connection to that incident twelve years ago?"

"No!" The two men silently looked at each other, and Mr. Hirakata said, "Of course, I remember you."

At this point the door opened, and Miyagi walked in, carrying a tray holding a teapot and cups. Mrs. Hirakata and Aki trailed behind, Aki holding a small plate of cookies. The boy looked pale and embarrassed. After laying the plate on the coffee table, he stared at the windows. Watching him standing there—remote, aloof—Ito thought, given the darkness outside, the boy could only see his own reflection.

Miyagi busied himself with the teapot, pouring out steaming green tea for everyone. Once he had distributed the cups and cookies, he resumed his perch on the piano bench.

"Mrs. Hirakata," Ito said, "your husband and I were just talking about that person your boy described. We believe his name is Hiroki Sato."

"I overheard a little of what you said. It's incredible. I can't believe my daughter was involved with this...*person!* That she was actually thinking of running away with him!"

Mrs. Hirakata took a few deep breaths as if trying to calm herself before continuing. "But maybe I was wrong. Of course, I saw that suitcase in her room. If it's true, it means I didn't know my own daughter. It feels like losing her a *second* time!"

As she burst out weeping, the boy suddenly rushed over to the chief inspector and kicked his leg, saying, "You leave my mother alone!" Then he leapt back, a furious look on his face. Arms crossed and stamping his feet, he shouted, "Just go away! *Go away!*"

The chief inspector darted forward with surprising speed and agility for one of his bulk, taking the boy's hands in his own. Aki was so shocked he stood perfectly still, silent and white.

"Aki Hirakata, I know you loved your sister. I'm going to ask for your help so we can find out what happened to her. I need you to tell me as clearly as you can what you saw and heard last night," the chief inspector said.

The boy's face got even paler, and his words came out slowly. "I promised Kaori I wouldn't tell, but now she's dead, I will. The first time he came—that is, yesterday morning—he told Kaori he'd been a *yakuza* in Tokyo."

The inspector heard Mr. Hirakata's intake of breath and his wife's gasp, but the boy went on.

"My sister was furious and said she might not go away with him. She said she might marry a man at church who loved her. He was upset and left. Then, when I went to her bedroom after dinner, I heard that man's voice again. He and Kaori were talking. After Kaori began coughing, I hid in the hall and saw him go to the bathroom. The man came back, carrying a mug of water." The boy gulped. "Kaori couldn't stop coughing!"

"Anything else?"

"I ran inside her bedroom and shouted for my father to come. Kaori couldn't talk, and the man was gone. He must have climbed down the vine."

"Aki, think. Can you remember any other details of what you heard?"

The boy trembled. "When he came back that second time, he had the box of chocolates, and Kaori was happy because she loves sweets."

"Did he say how he came by the box? Had he bought it for your sister?"

The boy couldn't answer. He shook his head, and another sob erupted with a harsh, painful sound. Aki hid his face in his hands, and his mother darted forward to hold him.

Seeing Mrs. Hirakata observing him reproachfully over the boy's shoulder, Ito beckoned to Miyagi. They bowed and left the room. A middle-aged woman with thinning hair pulled back in a bun, wearing an old black dress, was standing in the *genkan*.

"My name is Muraji. I'm Mrs. Hirakata's cousin," she said. "I'll see you out."

"How are they...taking it?" he asked her, surprised that this woman with her careworn expression and dingy clothes could be that wealthy woman's cousin.

"They'll never get over it," she said in a tone that sounded to the chief inspector like one of grim satisfaction. She bowed as she held the door open while they stepped into their shoes and left the house.

Back at the station, the chief inspector sat at his desk, reflecting on the curious twists of fate. How odd to be back at the Hirakata house, meeting those two in circumstances strangely similar to their first encounter, once again reeling after life had dealt them a heavy blow. He shuddered and touched a pocket of his tunic, feeling a bulky shape that reassured him. His wife teased him for being superstitious. It was true. He refused to sleep with his head to the north or cut his fingernails at night. He also kept a little blue and gold *omamori*—a lucky amulet—in his tunic pocket that he'd finger whenever he felt worried.

He couldn't help feeling the Hirakatas were *unlucky*—an ill-starred family. Coincidentally, he had been the investigating officer when Kaori Hirakata's father got shot. It had been his first assignment after being transferred to the Murota force twelve years earlier. Ito gave a wistful smile, remembering how anxious he'd been to justify the trust of his former boss, who'd arranged the transfer as a promotion for his favorite officer. Ito had had enough of temporary postings. With him pushing forty and their daughter almost ten, his wife demanded they move to what she called a forever home, a place where Aiko could grow up and they could grow old.

Because the attack on the businessman involved a gun, it was presumably a *yakuza*—yet to be identified—who'd attacked Mr. Hirakata, but it seemed a stretch to imagine they'd poison an innocent young woman. What would have been the motive? The only plausible one he could come up with concerned Hiroki Sato. In her statement, his mother had said she thought he might have joined a gang when he was in Tokyo and could still be involved in gang activities. What the little brother had overheard of the conversation between his sister and her boyfriend seemed to confirm that supposition. Ito decided to get in touch with his contacts in the Tokyo and Murota *yakuza* to see if there was a gang that claimed Hiroki as a member. *Had he done something that made the* yakuza *decide to warn—or punish—him by killing his girlfriend?*

The chief inspector began rubbing his eyes. The *yakuza*. Sometimes he thought of them as the bane of his life as a policeman. They spoke of honor and proudly boasted they were criminals with a conscience. They even had the nerve to call themselves *ninkyō dantai*—a chivalrous organization! But in his years on the force, what he'd seen was the weakest and most vulnerable in society falling prey to their wiles—Filipino women lured into the sex trade, troubled boys persuaded to be drug runners, small businesses intimidated into paying protection money. In his opinion, they were just thugs, unscrupulous gangsters leaving shattered lives in their wake. The attack on Mr. Hirakata bore all the hallmarks of a *yakuza* hit. He was shot—but only wounded, so it must have been meant as a warning.

Ito was proud of the fact that gun crime (apart from clashes between rival *yakuza* gangs) remains nearly unheard of in Japan, a country where only the police and military may own weapons. He paused. No, that wasn't quite right. A few hunters were granted licenses, but their activities were strictly monitored. Ito rubbed his chin and grinned. Foreigners, especially those from America, didn't realize this about Japan. That's why it made national news when a young man from Ohio employed to teach English at a Tokyo language school pulled out a gun one evening at a local convenience store and demanded all the money in the cash register. Of course, given the efficiency of the Japanese police, he was arrested almost immediately. It turned out he'd used a makeshift gun in his attempted robbery; he'd had its component parts sent in separate mailings from the States and then assembled the weapon in his tiny Tokyo flat. It went without saying he got a long prison term and, once he'd served it, was deported. He'd never be allowed to visit Japan again.

It was beyond strange that Iwao Hirakata should have had dealings with the *yakuza*. He was a local boy made good. Clever and ambitious, he'd married Megumi Inoue, daughter of Murota's richest family, whose wealth originated in their ancient recipe—a closely guarded secret—for manufacturing soy sauce. But that was the rumor after the attack—that Mr. Hirakata had exploited his position as director of finances at the Taniguchi real estate company to embezzle funds, aided and abetted by the local *yakuza* who then shot him after he'd failed to agree to all their demands.

The chief inspector frowned, recalling the frustration he'd experienced years before trying to find Mr. Hirakata's assailant. It had felt like his efforts were thwarted at every turn. There was old Mr. Taniguchi, Hirakata's employer, for example, a thin man who resembled a gaunt Santa with his pure white hair and beard and rosy cheeks. He'd scarcely been any help at all. In fact, the chief inspector had the suspicion he was being obstructive. Ito wasn't a man to rely on instinct in his policing, but he'd felt there was something not quite right about the man, despite his wealth and position.

That's why it didn't come as a complete surprise to learn that Mr. Taniguchi had quarreled with his only son and disinherited him. The son, rumored to be a scoundrel and wastrel, left Murota in his late twenties and became an alcoholic, living on the streets of Tokyo and dying there, leaving a wife and son and daughter in Murota. They'd ended up moving in with old Mr. Taniguchi, sharing his big house on the northern edge of Murota. It was situated in an exclusive neighborhood near the Kitaguchi district, where the Hirakatas lived.

Then there was Iwao Hirakata, who seemed unwilling to offer a single word in his own defense. Once he'd recovered from his injury, the chief inspector asked him to come in for questioning. He'd found a slim, erect man still holding himself proudly despite facing public censure for his alleged crime and being demoted within the company. But Hirakata-*san* offered such simple answers to his questions that the chief inspector toyed with the idea that the businessman was not nearly as intelligent or ambitious as he'd been led to believe.

When Mr. Taniguchi insisted the police drop their investigation, asking for it to be considered an internal matter for his firm to handle in its own way, the chief inspector had to close the case. Naturally, the Murota *yakuza* denied any involvement, leaving nothing to go on. The case had left a sour taste in Ito's mouth. He was certain some unsavory, undisclosed secret was behind it all. It didn't help that forensic science was in its infancy when Mr. Hirakata was attacked.

A tentative knock sounded, breaking Ito out of his musings, and a familiar head poked its way around the office door again. The chief inspector looked at his watch. It was six o'clock in the evening. It had been a long day, and he didn't expect it to end anytime soon.

"Sir," Miyagi said, presenting himself in front of the chief inspector's desk and bowing. His hands trembled slightly as he held out a sheaf of papers, retaining a folder that he hugged to his chest.

"These are the transcribed statements taken from individuals close to the victim. Unfortunately, the Hirakatas have only one neighbor living near enough to see who went in and out of their house. It's a widow named Mrs. Goto who rushed to the house when she heard the screams. She's the one who called for an ambulance."

"It's a pity it's a place of big houses and big gardens with no shops and little traffic," Ito said. "Meaning few witnesses to anything that might go on there. And the folder?"

Handing it over, Miygai said, "This holds the forensics and autopsy reports. We've just got them."

"Please fax a copy of the autopsy report to Superintendent Takenaka," Ito said, and then, placing the folder on his desk, he opened it and began reading, waving Miyagi away without looking up.

After sending the fax his boss requested, Miyagi wandered out to see his best friend at the station. "How's the Bear?" Miss Hino at reception asked, pushing a plate of rice dumplings filled with sweet red bean paste in his direction. She was plump and attractive, and she and Miyagi had struck up an unlikely friendship years earlier. It had started when she began bringing in treats for him, thinking he was too thin. Now it was based on their enjoyment of swapping anecdotes about the man they secretly referred to as the Bear—a nickname expressive of affection and respect. Chief Inspector Ito could be as endearing as a teddy, but equally as intimidating as a powerful animal in the wild.

"Shocked and sad," the officer said, picking up a dumpling and eyeing it with anticipation. He popped it into his mouth, chewed, and swallowed, smiling with pleasure. Then he winced. "Me, too. I'm shocked and sad. That poor young woman. What a way to go!"

Miyagi jumped when Miss Hino's phone buzzed. Lifting the receiver to her ear, she said, "Yes, sir, I understand. I'll tell him now."

"It was the Bear," she said. She bit her lip and shook her head. "Poor girl! He said the autopsy confirmed she was poisoned and that forensics found poison in the chocolates in her room but nowhere else in the house. Only half the chocolates in the box had the poison in them. It was just her bad luck that she ate so many of the bad ones."

"Any news on whether that missing boyfriend has been found?"

"Not that I know of."

They both jumped when the buzzer sounded again. The receptionist had just eaten a dumpling herself and had to swallow quickly. She spoke briefly, hung up the receiver, and said, "The chief inspector has arranged to interview the woman who called for an ambulance, the Hirakatas' next-door neighbor, Mrs. Goto. He must have found something in her statement he needs to investigate further. He wants you to bring the car around to the front of the station in ten minutes." She got a little plastic container from her drawer, put the remaining dumplings in it, and held it out to Miyagi, saying, "Take these for later."

Miyagi was striding toward the station parking lot when he heard footsteps running behind him and a voice calling out, "Sorry, I forgot to say. You're to take the unmarked car," Miss Hino said breathlessly. "Out of respect. To protect her privacy."

Miyagi parked just a little way down the street from the Hirakata house. As they strolled slowly down the sidewalk, the inspector said, "Thinking back to my interview with the Hirakatas, we might just have our motive. When Hiroki Sato visited Kaori Hirakata in the morning, she threatened to call it all off and even said she might marry a man at her church. Perhaps Hiroki Sato couldn't bear the thought of her with anyone else."

Mrs. Goto's place was almost as large as the Hirakatas', but it was close to the road, with no walls or gate. A garden was at the side of the house, and the driveway was at the front. The chief inspector pressed the front doorbell, and they heard it sounding loudly inside. Still, they needed to wait for a minute or two for anyone to answer. First, they heard a shuffling, scraping noise, then a stout old woman with a puffy and pale face slowly opened the door, holding a cane. She wore a thick pink kimono and a pale pink headscarf.

"I don't want to buy anything," were her first words, her frown succeeded by a look of annoyance when they produced their police IDs.

"I was expecting you," she said, shuffling back across the *genkan*, leaning heavily on her cane. She stepped up into the hallway, taking two pairs of slippers from a rack that she laid out for the police officers. "But it's late, and I'm missing my favorite TV show."

They left their shoes in the *genkan* and, stepping up into the slippers, followed her into the Western-style guest room, which was furnished with the requisite two armchairs and matching sofa. An ancient television was in one corner and faded family photos lined a shelf beneath the room's sole window. She beckoned them to the sofa and settled in one of the chairs, a disgruntled expression on her face.

The old woman said crossly, "I thought the statement I gave your officer this morning would have been sufficient." Then, as if she'd remembered her manners, she gave Ito an apologetic nod, saying, "But I'm honored you've come to visit me personally, Chief Inspector."

The chief inspector inclined his head in, saying, "The statement I read was thorough and satisfactory, but as you're our only witness, I wanted to come see you."

The frown was back. Mrs. Goto closed her eyes, sighed, and said, "I know why you're here. I'm an old woman. You want to ask me about the Hirakatas, but you also need to know if I still have my wits about me. Well, I do."

She opened her eyes again and looked at them with an expression of such keen intelligence that any doubts the chief inspector may have entertained about her acuity were instantly dispelled. "I may as well tell you I have a better memory than you." She said. "I remember your coming here twelve years ago, asking about the attack on Mr. Hirakata."

Ito smiled, and she went on. "I can see and hear perfectly well. It's walking I find difficult, what with my rheumatism. Last night, I'd just turned off the television and was heading off to have my bath when I heard screaming from next door. I grabbed my cane and made my way there as fast as I could. I tried the front door and found it unlocked. I called out, but there was no answer, just that horrible yelling from the second floor, so I opened the door and hurried in. It was a struggle to get up the stairs, but once I did, I found the poor parents bending over their daughter in her room. She was twisting and turning on the floor, clutching her stomach and vomiting. She seemed to find it hard to breathe. I guessed they hadn't called for an ambulance, so that's what I did. I'm slow, but did my best to get back down the stairs as quickly as I could to use the phone in the hall."

"Can you recall what you saw when you entered the girl's room?"

"An open box of chocolates was on the bed next to a small green suitcase and a white plastic bag on the floor."

The chief inspector rose. "You've been very helpful. It's late. I have just two more questions. When was the last time you'd seen Miss Hirakata?"

Mrs. Goto closed her eyes. "I can't remember. Perhaps several weeks ago. I slipped a leaflet through her door on Saturday but didn't see her."

"And what was your opinion of her?"

"She was sweet and innocent—too sweet and innocent." She added, unexpectedly, "It's dangerous to be that sweet and innocent."

CHAPTER TWO

Chief Inspector Ito
Tuesday 20 September 1988
Murota police station

Tuesday morning dawned hot, bright, and sunny, but that didn't please Chief Inspector Ito. He was tired of summer's sultriness. What he longed for was a typhoon that would bring rain and lower temperatures in its wake.

He was sitting in his office, feeling frustrated. It wasn't only the weather that irritated him. For dinner, his wife had made the fried vegetable and tofu dish she knew he disliked and later, when they'd all adjourned to the living room—he to do a crossword and his wife a sudoku puzzle—his daughter had flipped out when he complained she shouldn't waste her time watching stupid game shows on television. *Families!*

Then he paused, feeling angry with himself. He knew he should count his lucky stars that he had such a normal existence and such petty problems. He fingered the amulet in his tunic pocket and sent up a prayer that he would never be visited by the kind of tragedies that had crushed poor Mr. Hirakata and his wife.

Ito frowned. Takenaka had been in touch again, letting Ito know the press conference in Ishizaki was scheduled for ten. They'd need to set off from the Murota police station within a few minutes to be on time. Ito knew his attendance was compulsory, but it wasn't convenient. What he was longing to do was to plunge into his investigation into the murder. On the basis of the list of Kaori Hirakata's associates Miyagi had compiled, he was eager to talk to several individuals as soon as possible. They'd already had their statements taken, but Ito wanted to interview them in person. In particular, he wanted to meet Junko Nomura and Pastor Nakagawa and his wife—key figures at the Christian church in Murota which occupied such a central role in the Hirakata family life—and also a woman named Emi Tada, who'd been Kaori Hirakata's best friend since childhood. Naturally, Ito was also eager to question the victim's sister, and if they could manage to track Hiroki Sato down, that would be the icing on the cake.

The phone on the chief's desk rang. Miss Hino told him that Miyagi was waiting in a patrol car at the front of the station for their drive to Ishizaki.

The television studio was far more crowded than the chief inspector had expected. As they entered, Miyagi was just behind him, obviously feeling cowed. Superintendent Takenaka was already seated at a long low table in the front with Mr. and Mrs. Hirakata sitting to his right. On catching sight of Ito, Takenaka impatiently beckoned him forward, pointing to the seat on his left. Miyagi refused to accompany him up there, staying at the back of the room.

The half hour allotted for the press interview passed in a blur. There were flashing lights, angry questions posed by reporters and members of the public, and tears from the parents. Ito felt shocked that some people seemed to regard the Murota police force as culpable for the fact such a crime could be committed in its precinct. Aspersions were cast on its efficiency. Of course, it had quickly become common knowledge that a young Murota local named Hiroki Sato was the prime suspect, and that he was still on the run. Someone had even latched on to the possible *yakuza* connection and asked what the police were doing to tackle such a blight on Japanese society.

It was all a blur, a haze of criticisms and recriminations. Only one figure stood out as distinctly memorable for the chief inspector. Midway through the proceedings, a man in a gray suit had unfolded his tall lanky frame from his seat and stood, introducing himself as Koji Yanagihara, a reporter for *The Nippon Daily,* one of the largest dailies published in Tokyo.

"Of course, I'm aware this tragic case has attracted national interest," Takenaka said, leaning forward eagerly, his eyes alight.

"And it has drawn international attention," said Koji Yanagihara. "Not surprisingly, considering the rarity of violent crime in Japan. But my own interest is personal. My aunt lives in Murota and told me about it."

Here, he bowed to the parents and addressed his remarks to them. "I wish to offer you my sincere condolences. The tragedy of your beloved daughter has touched my heart, and I hope you won't consider it an impertinence if I write an in-depth piece that will allow her story to touch the hearts of my readers."

Mr. Hirakata shook his head. "I don't know if I can stop you, but I'd consider it an invasion of my family's privacy." He looked at his wife, who shook her head, too. He added, "I would only agree if the police advised it, if they thought the publicity might help them apprehend the monster responsible for our daughter's death."

Koji Yanagihara bowed again. "If that is your wish, out of sympathy for your recent terrible loss, I'll have a word with my editor. After all, as I've said, my aunt is a Murota resident, and that makes me feel personally connected to it and its inhabitants. I will limit myself to a short article stating only the confirmed facts."

The parents rose and bowed their thanks.

Takenaka leaned back in his chair, looking dissatisfied.

When the chief inspector got back to the station, he found Kaori Hirakata's twin sister Yumi had arrived. He instructed Miyagi to bring her to his office. After he'd risen and they'd bowed and were both seated, Ito scrutinized the woman opposite him. He'd heard she was Kaori's fraternal rather than identical twin. In fact, he could scarcely see any resemblance between the two. He'd met them both as eleven-year-old girls, but they'd grown up since then and changed beyond recognition. Recent photos of Kaori showed a beautiful young woman, but Yumi Hirakata was striking rather than conventionally attractive—a tall, slim woman with strong features and long, black, glossy hair caught back in a ponytail.

Miyagi had settled himself in a hardbacked chair at the back of the room. He had his notebook and pencil out, but Ito caught his gaze and shook his head. He preferred an official transcript of this interview. Ito indicated a tape recorder on his desk next to a stack of files, saying to Yumi, "I hope you won't mind if I make a recording."

"Not at all," she said, looking indifferent.

After Miyagi had switched on the machine, the chief inspector said, "I'm very grateful to you for coming in today. I hadn't expected to see you this soon, considering the length of the journey from London back to Japan."

"I never suffer from jet lag," she said. "I'm one of those people who can sleep anywhere, anytime."

"Lucky," the chief inspector murmured.

"I don't feel particularly lucky just now," she said. Ito's cheeks colored slightly.

"No, no, of course not," he said. "Not in these circumstances."

He straightened up in his chair and looked stern. "Miss Hirakata, I need to ask you a few questions, please. First, I'd be grateful if you could give me some idea about your relationship with your sister. Was she in the habit of confiding in you? Did she mention Hiroki Sato? I've heard such conflicting reports. I'm having trouble developing a clear picture of Kaori-*san*."

"Conflicting reports?" said Yumi, looking surprised.

"Yes. For example, your parents thoroughly trusted your sister and had no idea she planned to run away with the boyfriend she'd kept secret from them."

"Kaori was a wonderful girl and a dutiful daughter. She'd only have resorted to such desperate measures if she felt she had no choice. From what I've heard, our parents would have thought her boyfriend was very unsuitable. But it may be helpful if I give you some background on my sister. I'll try to be as honest as I can."

"That would be very helpful."

"As you probably know, I'm only a few minutes older than my sister. We were very close as children. Kaori is—was—very sweet and kind, even as a little girl. I wasn't and never have been. I'd describe myself as tough and cynical. I worried people might take advantage of her good nature, so I was protective of her. Especially after our father was shot."

She looked at him curiously. "I think I remember seeing you on that occasion. Weren't you the investigating officer?"

"Yes," he said. "My apologies for not having brought that case to a more satisfactory conclusion."

"I'm sure you did your best. We all knew it was a *yakuza* who shot *Otoosan*, but I still can't think why. I'll never believe my father engaged in wrongful behavior or had anything to do with gangsters."

The woman suddenly fell silent. He noted the grim expression on her face.

Finally, she shook her head ruefully and said, "In fact, it was my father who disappointed me, not the police. He'd been my idol, my ideal even, so I couldn't help wondering why he didn't defend himself more vigorously. Why he simply seemed to give up."

She sighed. "Oddly enough—after all this time—he's recently reconsidered. My mother called last week and told me *Otoosan* had decided to contest the accusations, that he couldn't stand living with that stain on his honor any longer. My mother is against it, she's worried about stirring up trouble."

Yumi smiled wryly and shrugged. "But fate has intervened. Our home holds too many unhappy memories now, and my parents are planning to move to Tokyo. That means, I suppose, that my father will simply give up on trying to clear his name. *Again!*"

"If you don't mind, I'd like to take a brief detour here. I'd intended only to ask about your sister, but as you've brought up that earlier— tragedy—that befell your family, can you give me your opinion of that?"

"My sister and I grew up loving *Otoosan*'s boss, old Mr. Taniguchi. He was like a grandpa, always dropping by and bringing us presents. But when we got older, he acted in ways that made us dislike him. He'd stare at us, insist we still kiss him on the lips, and give us big hugs. That didn't seem appropriate behavior after we'd become young women. I began to think of him as a dirty old man."

"I had no idea."

"And then, after our father's public disgrace, we disliked him even more because it seemed like he was bullying *Otoosan*. He demoted him in the firm, which was a terrible humiliation. Mr. Taniguchi didn't visit us anymore. I was glad. I never want to see him again, and I think Kaori felt the same way."

"I hear his grandson is being groomed to take over the company," the chief inspector said. "Apparently it's still very successful."

Yumi Hirakata frowned. "Pity! I'd be glad if it failed. After what happened to my father, I lost a kind of innocence. I became even more skeptical about other people, and distrustful. I'll admit that I was appalled when my parents became Christians. It seemed like their faith took over their lives. I hated seeing how they changed, how they became so pious and lost their sense of humor and fun. Kaori was so sweet she went along with it all. I'm not sure how much she believed, but she never liked to upset people. Also, I think she sensed that religion was our parents' way of coping. She never complained about having to go to church every Sunday or read the Bible or pray before meals. That's just the way she was."

Ito saw her smile sadly. "As for me, I made my opposition perfectly clear. Once we reached our mid-teens, I worried more than ever about Kaori, feeling she let other people push her around. I began withdrawing from her, hoping to make her tougher and more self-reliant. I know I hurt her." She paused, adding, "Finally, I couldn't stand the situation at home any longer. I had to escape."

Yumi glanced down at her hands clasped on her lap, and he saw a tear trickle down one cheek that she simply ignored. "I feel so guilty now about deserting Kaori and Aki. I'll never have a chance to explain—not to her. To apologize for deserting her when she needed me."

"I'm not sure I understand," said the chief inspector gently. "You thought she was too influenced by others?"

"Yes. By Emi Tada, her best friend. By Juno-*sensei* at church. Even by our parents. And maybe by that boyfriend I've heard about. Kaori wanted to travel the world but got a dead-end job here to stay with my parents. I was more selfish and got away."

"So, you think she might have been under Hiroki Sato's spell, too?"

Yumi finally wiped her cheek with one hand and sniffed. "Perhaps. I never met him, and Kaori only mentioned him a few times in her letters. Once I heard about him, I should have come home and checked out whether he was right for my sister. As usual, I consulted my own wishes. Now I'll never know why she loved him. Maybe he had some kind of hold over her. Or maybe she'd finally tired of putting everyone else first and thought he was her best chance of happiness."

"I appreciate your opinion on this. As I've indicated, it's something that has confused me. The picture I've formed of your sister from the accounts of her friends and family is of a saintly creature who always sacrificed her own desires to help others. It's been hard to reconcile that person with the young woman who secretly formed a relationship with a man she knew everyone would disapprove of."

"If Hiroki Sato was bad, I imagine she thought she could change him and probably also hoped to reconcile our parents to their marriage." Yumi looked thoughtful, then said, "The one thing that's surprised me is that she didn't leave our folks a message explaining what she intended to do. She was always considerate as well as kind. Maybe she preferred to present them with an accomplished fact. Begging their forgiveness, but as someone's wife."

"I see," said the chief inspector, feeling, in fact, that Yumi Hirakata's words had made the attack on her sister murkier than ever.

"It's what I wanted for my sister—that she become strong and independent." Her mouth twisted, and she moaned softly before saying, "But it's all ended so badly!"

The two sat in silence for a minute. Then Yumi stood. "My apologies. I hope I've answered your questions satisfactorily, Chief Inspector, but I should leave now. I need to be with my parents. We have preparations to make. As you know, Kaori's funeral is the day after tomorrow."

"My lieutenant will drive you home," said Ito. "Many thanks for your insights and information."

Emi Tada

It was just after noon on Tuesday and Emi Tada was pacing up and down the living room of her house when she got the call informing her to expect a visit from the police in an hour. She'd called in sick on Monday upon hearing about Kaori, then waking miserable and groggy on Tuesday, realized she needed to ring the bank again to beg for one more day to recover from the murder of her best friend. Luckily, her mother's only friend, a gossipy middle-aged housewife who lived just down the road, agreed to take her mother to a shopping mall a few miles away in her car. She said it was to give Emi some space, but Emi couldn't help wondering if the woman just wanted to pump her mother for tasty tidbits about the shocking murder. Everyone knew she and Kaori had been very close.

The cops! Coming here! Emi thought. It felt like the second of two knockout blows. The first was getting the terrible news about Kaori. The second was that call from somebody who'd introduced himself as Lieutenant Miyagi.

She'd given a statement the day before and hoped that was sufficient but, apparently, it wasn't.

Emi wanted to sink to the floor and weep. Instead, after replacing the receiver, Emi plumped down on the old sofa and looked around at the shabby surroundings. She thought longingly of the luxurious Hirakata home where she'd been treated like a member of the family, like a third daughter. But that privileged status was gone now that Kaori was dead. Despite the affection she knew they felt for her, it was unlikely Mr. and Mrs. Hirakata would ever want Emi to visit again. She'd remind them too much of their terrible loss.

Despite her wretchedness, Emi smiled, then gave a mirthless bark of laughter. Kaori! She was such a child. So naïve! She never had the slightest idea of how exasperating she could be. Kaori's innocence meant Emi's love for her was always tinged with a faint contempt.

Emi had needed to become an adult at the age of four when her father abruptly fled the family home, leaving her and her mother nearly destitute. Emi knew she was cleverer than Kaori and certainly much tougher. She'd had to be smart and mean just to survive.

Even as a little girl, she'd had the sense to don kid gloves with her sweet, innocent friend. Sometimes Emi thought Kaori had no idea what she was like or how she felt about things. Emi hadn't deliberately set out to mislead her friend. That she and Kaori had never argued was due to Emi's ability to hide her anger and envy, her bitterness at the unfairness of life.

Emi was used to keeping secrets. She'd hidden her true self when she was with Kaori—just as she'd hidden her knowledge of her friend's growing intimacy with that wretched boy she'd chanced upon at a bus stop. It was some consolation to Emi that she wasn't the only one who disapproved. Her chance encounter with Juno a week before had made that clear. Juno was just as appalled as Emi.

Standing at the old tin kitchen sink, Emi threw water into her face. *Kaori. Kaori!* she thought. She remembered the last time she'd seen her, only three days ago. She kept replaying the scene in her mind—what she'd said and how Kaori had reacted.

It was Emi's usual Saturday afternoon visit to the Hirakata house, a routine they'd adopted years earlier when Kaori returned to Murota after graduating from her university in Tokyo. Emi would turn up about two, bringing a small pink box filled with choux crème. Kaori would have pulled out the Royal Albert bone china tea set her mother had bought three years before in London when she'd visited Yumi there. Mr. Hirakata would be at work, and Aki and Kaori's mother would stay out of the way to let the two friends have their time together without interruption.

That Saturday was oppressively sultry. Cicadas as large as birds swarmed the bushes in the Hirakatas' garden, chirping out the melancholy chorus that signaled the approach of fall. The two friends sat on the plush gray sofa in the spacious living room, sipping tea and chatting, and from time to time, they'd turn around to gaze out the big French windows behind them.

"I love this view no matter how often I see it," Emi said, standing to take a better look. "It's so beautiful and so calming."

Kaori joined her. A narrow brick path bordered by clipped shrubbery and flowers ran the length of the garden, connecting the front porch and the gate. The windows were slightly ajar, and they could hear the faint splash of a big fountain in the center of the garden, featuring a chubby cherub gently pouring water from a jug. A stone bench was positioned next to a little carp pond shaded by a Japanese maple tree whose miniature green leaves were just beginning to turn an autumnal red.

They smiled, sat back on the sofa, and Emi poured more tea into their cups.

"How nice you're having *tea* for a change," Emi said. "That awful drink you like will rot your pretty teeth." Kaori's fondness for a sickly sweet peach nectar popular in Japan was a standing joke between the two, with Emi insisting it showed her friend clinging to childish habits.

Emi pointed to an enormous picture hanging on a wall—a reproduction of one of Monet's Waterlilies series. "I once saw a documentary on the artist, and the garden looked absolutely stunning," she said. "It was like a magical place from a fairy tale. Did you know you can gradually see Monet going blind by looking at his paintings of the lilies done over many years? How sad is that? I dream of going to Giverny one day and seeing that garden for myself."

As she spoke, she recalled something Kaori had once inadvertently let slip—that the painting concealed a safe hidden in the wall behind it. She wondered if Kaori remembered having told her.

Suddenly, Emi put on the look she reserved for saying something she knew her friend would find unpleasant. "Kao-*chan*, why are you hanging out with that boy?" she said. "He's bad and bad for you."

Of course, Kaori had looked horrified, but Emi had gone on.

"When you told me about meeting him at the bus stop, you laughed. I thought you considered him just the topic of an amusing anecdote. I never imagined you'd see him again. But you have. I've seen you with him, out and about, looking like a couple. Even from a distance, I can tell he's awful. Those clothes! That earring! He's just *bad*."

"His name is Hiroki Sato. He's poor, but that's no crime," Kaori had said. Emi was poor herself, so she felt the truth of her friend's words, but equally she felt she had to save Kaori from herself. And that's when she uttered the remarks that she would later feel so guilty about, saying, "If your parents knew, they'd be out of their minds with worry." Then, seeing Kaori's stricken face, she'd added, "Maybe they *should* know. An anonymous note would do the trick."

Emi had hardly ever seen Kaori angry. But she was furious then, standing over Emi and saying, "If you knew him, I think you'd realize how remarkable he is. But you won't give him a chance. I think it's time you went."

Emi remembered how sad she'd felt at being turned out. "We're not children," she'd said. "I'd hoped we could talk about this reasonably and calmly." Picking up her purse from the sofa, she'd risen, too.

"We shouldn't see each other for a while," Kaori had said. "But that's going to happen anyway," she'd added unaccountably.

Emi nodded. She wanted to be the adult in the room. But, after all, she couldn't help herself. "You know he's only after your money," she said as she opened the front door. "I'd rather see you dead than with that loser."

As Emi marched down the garden path to the gate, she looked back and gasped in horror when she noticed an old woman standing by the front door, gazing at her quizzically. Emi recognized her as old Mrs. Goto, the Hirakatas' nearest neighbor, and a notorious gossip.

Emi had been so distressed when taking her leave of Kaori that she had failed to notice the old woman standing there, and it was a jolt to realize Mrs. Goto must have heard her parting words.

Now, the front doorbell banished her musings. Emi hastily picked up a tea towel, wetted it, and rushed to the living room to give the sofa and coffee table a quick swipe.

A large man stood at the door with a thin one beside him, almost hiding behind him. They showed their police identification, confirming Emi's guess as to who must be the chief inspector and who the lieutenant. Despite her misery, she had to suppress a smile. They were like stock characters from an old comedy film.

"Gentlemen, please come in," she said, then realized she still held the damp towel in her hands. She bowed, and they bowed. She placed the towel on the shoe cupboard and put out slippers for them to step into. On impulse, thinking the tatami mat room housing the family altar was more presentable than the Western-style guest room, she led them there, saying, "Please sit wherever you like. I'll get us some green tea."

"Thank you, but no," the chief inspector said, following her. "We've just had coffee at the station," he explained as she hastily positioned cushions around the low table in the room's center. He sat cross-legged at the table while his thin, gawky lieutenant dragged a cushion to a corner of the room and, settling himself on it, took out a notebook. Emi sank down opposite the inspector, folding her legs beneath her.

"An officer has taken your statement, but I'd like to ask you a few more questions, Miss Tada," he said. "In person." He looked at Miyagi, who began scribbling away with a pencil. "I was interested to read that you saw Miss Hirakata on Saturday afternoon, the day before she died, that you'd visited her at her house."

"We are very old friends," Emi said. "We have been best friends since nursery school. I usually went to her house at least once a week, almost always on Saturday afternoons."

"As you must have heard, it's been established that Miss Hirakata died as a result of foul play. We're asking people closely associated with her whether they have any idea how a box of chocolates found in her bedroom—which, it turns out, included some that were poisoned—came into her possession. Do you have any idea?"

"Anyone who knew Kaori at all knew she loved sweets," said Emi. "She adored that awful syrupy peach nectar you can find in any drinks vending machine, for example. She was very fond of chocolates, but I never took her any. Whenever I visited, I'd take a box of pastries."

"I see. Of course, your statement included those details. But I'd like now to ask you a few questions to refresh my memory. Where do you work?"

"Mitsuo Bank on Murota's main street. I'm on the international transfers counter because I can speak English."

"Did Miss Hirakata seem her normal self when you met her on Saturday afternoon?"

"Exactly the same."

"There was nothing troubling her?"

"No, nothing. We had a pleasant chat. Everything was just as usual." She paused, briefly losing her composure, but then clenched her fists and went on. "That's why it's so hard to accept what's happened."

"Yes, it must be a shock to hear that the friend you've known so long and loved so well has not only died, but been murdered."

"I can't believe it! It's so shocking." Emi's lip was trembling again. She turned her head and wiped her eyes, then, recovering, said, "It's also very cruel. Kaori-*chan* loved sweets. It was a harmless indulgence. I'm horrified anyone could think of using that weakness to kill her."

The chief inspector paused briefly before resuming his questioning. "Did Kaori ever mention an individual named Hiroki Sato? Do you know him?"

"I've seen him a few times with Kaori—in the distance. I never got introduced to him. I think they were just friends. I can't recall her saying anything about him that afternoon."

"As you've probably heard, we now consider him a suspect in your friend's death."

"I'm horrified, but not completely surprised. I didn't think him a suitable friend for her. He was a factory worker who hadn't even graduated from high school. He didn't seem Kaori's type at all."

She paused again to regain her composure, then said, looking distressed, "I wonder if you've found him. If he's given you a convincing alibi."

"Naturally, we'd like to ask him some questions, but he seems to have vanished. He hasn't been seen since Sunday night. Miss Tada, I'd appreciate it if you contacted us if you hear anything about him."

"Of course."

The chief inspector and his lieutenant rose, looking grim.

"Sorry, Chief Inspector," said Emi. "Before you go, there's one other person you might want to question."

Miyagi whipped out his notebook and stubby pencil while the chief inspector stood, looking expectantly at Emi.

"There's a man at the church Kaori attended who was talked about as a future husband for her," said Emi. "The pastor, his wife, and a missionary helping them were very keen to promote a match. His name is Yuichi Motoki. I can't imagine he'd have had anything to do with the attack, but maybe he can offer more details about Kaori. I've heard he was quite excited at the prospect of marrying her. From remarks Kaori dropped about him, I doubt she reciprocated those feelings."

"I see. Thank you for that information."

"You might also want to interview Junko Nomura," Emi added. "She's a missionary working at the Christian church. She's known as Juno-*sensei*."

After the police officers left, Emi slumped on the sofa in the living room again, feeling a twinge of remorse. Had she landed her old friend Juno in the soup? But they weren't really friends, just acquaintances. They'd last met over a week earlier when Emi was walking in town and had noticed Juno stumbling blindly along the pavement, not looking ahead. Emi had needed to stand in front of her and touch her arm just to get her attention.

Because Juno had always been cool and standoffish, Emi was surprised when she looked up, grabbed her arm, and wailed, "Tada-*san*, I'm so worried about Kaori. What can we *do*?!"

Seeing bystanders looking at them curiously, Emi steered Juno by the arm to a nearby coffee shop that played non-stop classical music and always seemed deserted. She found them a booth in a corner by the window. As soon as they'd sat down, a Mozart symphony playing in the background, Juno put her big purse on the table and burst into tears.

"I saw her!" she said. "Kaori! Just now! She was with a boy with weird hair and awful clothes." Juno gulped and paled. "*Holding hands!*"

The waitress interrupted her story, coming up to take their order and bringing glasses of iced water and hot towels.

"You'd never seen him before?" Emi asked after she'd gone. Emi was surprised by how upset Juno was, noticing the trembling of her hand as she lifted her glass to her lips. After all, the woman was human, and Emi felt an unexpected stirring of pity.

"Never. Do you know him?"

"His name is Hiroki Sato. He works at the Nissan car factory in town. Kaori met him a few months ago at a bus stop. Said he was more interesting than he looked, that he's an artist, and they both have a sweet tooth."

"How idiotic!" Juno said. "I can't believe that awful boy has anything in common with Kaori. She's far superior to him, of course. Has she ever introduced him to you?"

"I've seen him from a distance a few times, always with Kaori, but they didn't see me, and I didn't make my presence known. Kaori never mentioned him again after that first time, so I guessed she didn't want to talk about it." Emi looked grim. "It's only lately I've realized she's been seeing him regularly. It's a fact she prefers to keep secret."

"He had an earring! He was wearing dirty jeans! The way they were standing so close to each other, looking like...like...lovers!"

The waitress came by with the hot drinks. Juno sighed and took a sip of her coffee. "It's unbelievable. Kaori can't be serious."

"She is. She thinks she's in love," said Emi, shaking her head. "But I wouldn't trust him an inch, either. Like I said, I've never actually met him, but I've heard about him. His mother is the talk of the neighborhood—dubious boyfriends, dyed blonde hair." Then she relented. "I feel sorry for him, in fact. People say he has been neglected all his life—his mother always putting herself before him. My next-door neighbor knows the family and told me that when Hiroki was just a kid, his mother gave him a birthday cake she'd already eaten half of."

At that point, Juno put her cup down so hard Emi couldn't help glancing to see if it had cracked. "He's had a tough life," she said dismissively. "But that's happened to lots of people. Our concern is Kaori. We have to *do* something, Tada-*san*. We can't let her throw her life away on a loser."

"But what can we do?"

"It can't go on. We can't *allow* it to go on." Juno shuddered.

Again, Emi felt sorry for Juno. She had never particularly liked her—she was too melodramatic and always talked about Christianity—but the earnest woman sitting opposite her in her drab black dress, looking so distraught, moved her. "I can't bear to lose Kaori either," Emi said. "What can we do? Do you have any ideas?"

"We have to keep an eye on her, make sure she doesn't do something foolish."

Emi found herself unexpectedly agreeing. "We should watch Hiroki, too," she said. "I know where he lives."

"How?!"

"I followed him once after I'd seen him and Kaori in town. Kaori walked off, and I trailed behind him, wondering what hole he'd crawled out of." Emi shuddered. "His house is one of those awful little places near Soaplands. With the trains running by at every hour of the night and day, it must be so noisy, so dirty."

After giving Juno the address, Emi was too ashamed to confess she didn't live far from him, in a house not dissimilar to his. But she knew Juno was so wrapped up in herself that it would never occur to her that Emi had as much admitted—in talking of mutual neighbors—that her house was near the Satos' place.

Juno Nomura

Back in the unmarked patrol car, Miyagi sat expectantly behind the wheel. "Where to now, sir?" he asked.

The chief inspector lifted his hand and looked at his watch. "Perfect timing. In ten minutes, we're due at the Murota church to interview the pastor and his wife and the missionary, Junko Nomura."

Although he'd never met her—only seen her about town—the inspector had often heard of the missionary who called herself Juno-*sensei*. Ito, a firm believer in the adage that forewarned is forearmed, had taken the precaution of asking his wife about her the night before, knowing her to be an avid connoisseur of local gossip.

"But why do you want to know?" she'd asked, looking up from her sudoku puzzle.

"Just interested."

It was a flimsy explanation, but it had satisfied his wife, and she'd told him what everyone in town knew. Juno Nomura was born Junko Nomura but demanded everyone address her as Juno because while Junko signified a weak and helpless Japanese woman, Juno was a goddess. Junko, already known as Juno, had gone to the States in her early twenties to improve her English. Along with achieving near-native fluency, she'd converted to Christianity and trained as a missionary on returning to Japan.

According to Mrs. Ito, Juno-*sensei* was fond of saying, "It was God's will that I was born in little Murota. Divine fate sent me to Spokane, Washington, and to its Methodist church, which has links to the single Christian church we have in this town."

Once she was back in Murota, Juno ended up sharing the living quarters of the church with the pastor and his wife, the Nakagawas. She held classes for the children in the congregation and prepared the lunch served on Sundays after the first service, basking in the glory of her elevation from a shy, bookish girl born and raised on a farm outside Murota to a local oracle on Christianity and all things foreign. She was also glad to have access to the pastor's extensive library.

Besides her work at the church, Juno assisted at a multi-faith center housed in a small room above a travel agency that held mid-weekly open-house sessions for foreigners temporarily resident in the town. Juno regularly visited the prison in Ishizaki, twenty miles from Murota, to give talks about Christianity to the prisoners. Additionally, she held a part-time job at the local college, where she taught a few English conversation classes.

Mrs. Ito told her husband Juno liked keeping herself busy, going on to conjecture that because (rumor had it) Juno had been such a timid child, it was like getting a new lease on life as an adult. Over forty now, the arrangement with the Nakagawas had gone on for almost twenty years and saved her from any regrets about remaining unmarried and childless. "I'm single because I don't want to lose my independence," she was fond of saying.

She was still a countrywoman at heart. Dressed in a broad-brimmed straw hat, exchanging her worn black dress for *mompei* or loose-fitting work trousers, she was a familiar figure in the fields and mountain slopes in the vicinity of Murota as she foraged for edible plants. It was a skill fast disappearing in a Japan becoming increasingly urbanized, and one she shared with the town's old people, the younger disdaining such pursuits.

When the chief inspector's wife reached this point in her story, she gave her husband a mistrustful look. "I have this feeling you're pumping me for information about your latest case," she said. "Does this have anything to do with that poor Hirakata girl?"

He'd shaken his head, but she wasn't convinced. "I'm sure I've told you any number of times how Juno-*sensei* had an unusual fondness for that girl because of what happened to her father." Luckily, Ito was spared having to make a reply because of the noise that suddenly emanated from their daughter's bedroom. Aiko was fond of K-pop, and they both grimaced at the dull thudding of drums and twanging of guitars while Mrs. Ito went on with her story.

Of course, Ito knew what had aroused his wife's suspicions. It was something else everyone in town knew about—the legend of how Juno-*sensei* had visited Mr. and Mrs. Hirakata after he'd been mysteriously shot in the leg twelve years earlier. The locals would relate, with a mixture of wonder tinged with amusement, how she'd begged the pair to welcome Christ into their lives.

At that time, Mr. Hirakata was the director of finances at the lucrative Taniguchi real estate company in the heart of Murota. It was his habit to cycle to and from work, a journey taking about twenty-five minutes one way. He'd never got a driver's license and extolled the benefit of cycling to stave off middle-aged spread. Then one day, after he'd dismounted and propped his bike against the wall to open his front gate, he'd got shot by a mysterious assailant, a wound in his leg that left him with a slight limp.

Mrs. Hirakata had been raised a Christian but lapsed after marriage. Mr. Hirakata, like most Japanese, said he had no religious beliefs even though, like most Japanese, he was a Shinto Buddhist, keeping a *butsudan* altar in his living room used for memorial services for dead relatives. He and his wife appeared at the Murota Methodist church the following Sunday with their twin daughters, Yumi and Kaori, and became regular attendees.

Mrs. Ito reiterated this story and finished by saying, "Juno-*sensei* means well, but if she buttonholes me one more time, I'll scream! The way she boasts, taking all the credit for the Hirakatas' conversion and even for their son's appearance. She always says the Hirakatas spent hardly any time together before they became Christians because he was out playing golf and she was shopping, but after finding God, they became inseparable, and that's how Mrs. Hirakata got pregnant when nobody thought they'd ever have more children."

Ito thought he'd heard enough. He asked his wife to fetch him a whisky to forestall further revelations.

Now, as a dingy building made of corrugated iron with a two-foot white cross on its roof came into view, Ito found himself wondering whether Juno-*sensei* would regale him with this tale as well. But he forgot all about it when Miyagi surprised him with an unexpected remark.

"I feel uncomfortable in this kind of place," he said.

"This kind of place?"

"A church. Or any hall devoted to the worship of any sect."

"But why?"

"I have nothing against Christians. Or Buddhists, or so on. It's religious fanatics I distrust," Miyagi said, astonishing Ito even more. "They're so sure they're right."

There was a pause as Miyagi skillfully maneuvered the car into a narrow space between two parked cars. "Sorry, sir," he said once he'd brought the car to a halt. "I don't suppose you know. Several years after my father died, my mother got involved in one of the new religions springing up all over Japan these days. I'd prefer not to say which one."

Ito kept quiet, and his lieutenant heaved a great sigh. "She's spending all her weekends at services. She's donated a lot of money, too."

"It must be a great worry," said the chief inspector, reflecting on how little he knew about the personal life of his second-in-command. His knowledge of his lieutenant was limited to his work as a policeman. Miyagi was a man he trusted, liked, and relied on, and his skill as a stenographer at interviews conducted outside the station was invaluable. He'd note down details in his notebook and type them up to present to the chief inspector later. But what he did in private was beyond Ito's power of imagination. It was impossible, for example, to picture his lieutenant brushing his teeth or having a bath or wearing pajamas.

They were getting out of the car when the church's opaque glass doors slid open, and a couple appeared. The man was short and slim, wearing a black suit and tie and wire-rimmed glasses that glittered in the sunlight. The woman beside him was at least a foot taller and many pounds heavier, clad in a black dress, her only ornament a large gold cross. She had thick lips and an earnest expression. Stubbing her feet into sandals, she rushed to the car to greet the visitors.

"We have been waiting for you, expecting you," she said. The chief inspector was taken aback. Instead of bowing, she grabbed his hand to shake vigorously, then Miyagi's.

"My name is Nakagawa," she gushed. She was doughy-faced with two bright black eyes protruding like raisins. Flakes of dandruff adorned her shoulders. She proudly pointed at the man in the doorway. "And that is my husband, the pastor of this church."

The chief inspector said, "We're hoping to interview you both, and the missionary, Juno-*sensei*."

"Of course. She's inside."

After the disconcerting enthusiasm shown by the pastor's wife, the chief inspector was relieved when the pastor contented himself with a short bow. As he and Miyagi followed the couple into the church, he was amused to see how the pastor's wife towered over her husband as she walked respectfully behind him.

Stepping up to the hallway and into the slippers provided, the chief inspector looked curiously about him and sniffed. Permeating the air was the odor of boiled Japanese radish with undertones of miso paste he associated with visits to his grandparents when he was a child. It seemed to emanate from the tiny kitchen he glimpsed to the left. A closed door faced him, which he presumed led to the church, but the pastor and his wife opened a door on the right that led to a small room with an armchair in each corner and a coffee table in the middle.

The chief inspector had seen Juno-*sensei* walking about Murota, but she was always at a distance. Up close, he found her a plain-looking, angular woman with sharp features and hair pulled back into a bun. The sight of her simple black dress made Ito wonder if she was in mourning for her dead friend. She rose at his entrance, bowed, and introduced herself, then sat back down, propping a big black leather purse against her chair while Mrs. Nakagawa hurried out of the room, returning with a folding wooden chair that Miyagi appropriated.

"Please have a seat, Chief Inspector," said Pastor Nakagawa, exchanging a meaningful glance with his wife. "And you, too..." he added, looking uncertainly at Miyagi, obviously unsure how to address him.

"I'll fetch us some refreshments. It'll just take a minute. Everything is ready," Mrs. Nakagawa said, rushing out of the room.

"Thanks for agreeing to meet us at such short notice," said the chief inspector. "I'd like to offer you my sincere condolences," he added, bowing to the pastor and the missionary. "On the basis of statements you have given, I understand you two, as well as Mrs. Nakagawa, had a close relationship with poor Miss Hirakata and her family. Purely as a formality, we're asking her family and friends about a box of chocolates found in her bedroom. As you may have heard, some chocolates were laced with thallium. Do any of you have any idea how that box came into her possession?"

"Thallium?" the pastor echoed.

"It's a poison that's hard to detect," the inspector said. "It used to be used to kill rats, but its sale is prohibited now."

"Put into chocolates?"

"Yes, forensics has established some contained poison."

"As for chocolates, I'm diabetic, and my husband is pre-diabetic," Mrs. Nakagawa said, just catching the inspector's words as she returned with a tray carrying five cups of steaming green tea and small saucers with slices of *yokan* and tiny forks carefully positioned on top.

As she passed around the cups and saucers, she said, "We never have sweet treats normally. I only serve them when we have guests."

"I love chocolate myself," said Juno, "but as a missionary, I feel I must act as an example for others, so I rarely indulge in them."

She frowned and added, "Dear Kaori adored sweet things. Peach nectar. Cake. Any kind of candy. But I have no idea how that box of chocolates might have got to her bedroom." She paused and then said, "Unless, unless..."

"Please go on, Miss Nomura."

Juno leaned forward, and the chief inspector involuntarily wrinkled his nose. This ugly but eager-faced woman with her rough red hands let out a whiff of something that smelled unpleasant. Mothballs? That was a detail that his wife had omitted in her description of the woman, although he imagined it was one that could scarcely have escaped the notice of anyone who spent more than a few minutes in close proximity to her.

"Excuse me, Chief Inspector," Juno said, speaking in a voice breaking with emotion. "Murota is a small town. Gossip travels fast here. We've all heard a certain young man named Hiroki Sato mentioned as a suspect—a local boy who somehow managed to worm himself into dear Kaori's affections, despite being completely unworthy of her. It's also common knowledge he seems to have disappeared. I'd have thought *he* took those chocolates to her. May I ask? Have you tracked him down yet?"

Seeing the chief inspector shake his head, she sank back into her chair with a disconsolate expression. "I'm sorry to hear that," she said. "He struck me as a very suspicious character."

"Did Kaori talk about him to you?"

"Yes, of course. Kaori and I were very close. But I only actually met him once." Her nose wrinkled. "As I've indicated," she said, "I didn't particularly care for him. He couldn't appreciate her." She leaned forward eagerly while he tried not to draw back from that unpleasant smell she exuded.

"Kaori Hirakata was clever! She graduated from Aoyama Gakuin with a degree in English, for heaven's sake!" she said, rapping out the words for emphasis. "She wrote an honors thesis on philosophical references in Iris Murdoch's last novel. How could that ignorant boy, that factory worker, even begin to understand her?" She sat back, looking indignant. "What

Kaori saw in him is a mystery to me. She was infatuated. It's a perfect illustration of the proverb 'Love is blind.'"

Nonplussed, Ito looked at the pastor. "And how about you?" he asked. "Did you ever meet Hiroki Sato?"

"Never. And I never knew anything about him," said the pastor, sadly shaking his head. "If I had, I would have warned the dear child against him." His wife nodded vigorously at every word he said.

"When did you last see Kaori Hirakata, Miss Nomura?"

The corners of Juno's mouth drooped. "I'd hoped to see Kaori on Sunday," she said. "She always comes to church with her parents and her younger brother who's now..." Her brow puckered as she tried to recollect. "Oh, yes, Aki must be eleven now." She smiled confidingly at the chief inspector. "He was born a year after that terrible incident with his father."

Juno sighed. "But Kaori didn't turn up. She told her parents she had a stomachache. I was very disappointed."

The pastor leaned forward. "You've said Kaori may have been poisoned. Do you think her stomachache that morning was a symptom? Had she already ingested some harmful substance?"

"We're exploring every avenue at present," the chief inspector replied dismissively. "As you can understand, I'm not at liberty to discuss the details of the case."

Juno put her saucer on the table, straightened in her chair, and looked brightly around, even triumphantly, as she spoke. "I feel so grateful I could help the Hirakatas when they suffered that earlier tragedy. I played my little part in it all. When I heard Mr. Hirakata had returned home from the hospital, I rushed to his house to pray with him and his wife. I convinced her to return to her childhood faith and to bring her family to this church, too."

"That is all...quite wonderful," said the chief inspector, unsure what to say. He hated it when people gushed, and he had reservations about Christianity. He wound up the interview shortly after. As Miyagi drove them back to the police station, Ito asked his opinion of Emi Tada and Juno Nomura.

Miyagi's voice was soft and trembled slightly as he replied, a sure sign, the chief inspector knew, that he worried the opinion he was about to venture might be considered controversial.

"I didn't fully believe what either of them said, sir," said Miyagi. "I had the feeling they were hiding as much as they were revealing."

The chief inspector was impressed. He'd thought the same. Still, he put on a brusque voice as he said, "Well, well, we shall see. And Miyagi, please slow down a bit. I don't like being bounced about on the back seat like a bag of potatoes."

"Yes, sir. My apologies, sir!" said Miyagi, as he slowed down and began driving with exaggeratedly solicitous care.

The chief inspector indulged in a silent chuckle while also feeling a twinge of remorse. Miyagi was a treasure, but it was as well he didn't get egotistical about it. Also, the chief inspector felt it his duty to quash what he'd seen as his lieutenant's unnecessarily sentimental side. He'd once seen him shed tears over a tiny black kitten that a patrol car had inadvertently run over as it entered the police station parking lot.

Like Miyagi, he thought both Emi Tada and Juno Nomura were lying. But why? What did they hope to conceal?

CHAPTER THREE

Koji Yanagihara
Sunday 25 September 1988
Chuo Dori, Murota

He wondered how the local tourist board had the temerity to describe it as a thriving and attractive mid-sized town well worth a visit. In Koji Yanagihara's opinion, Murota wasn't much more than a small collection of boring high-rise buildings at its heart surrounded by equally undistinguished two-story buildings housing shops, restaurants, supermarkets, pachinko parlors, and snack bars—a depressing urban landscape of buildings of glass or stained concrete or corrugated iron relieved by only a little greenery. He thought the town's principal asset of proximity to the coast was under-exploited. The train station was next to the ferry port, but little else of interest was there, a waste given its potential for development into an inviting area filled with charming cafés, boutiques, and bars.

Still, Murota was tidy. Koji had often been abroad, and the graffiti and litter he encountered in many countries always startled him. None of that could be seen here: the streets and pavements were almost painfully clean. He'd also heard Murota boasted one of Japan's most famous formal gardens and hoped to visit it at some point. But when he asked a local about the town's attractions, he was told its best feature was its extensive maze of covered shopping arcades.

He'd only been in Murota a few hours, but Koji already felt homesick for Tokyo. Now that was a city! The bright lights! The bustle and buzz! The daring architecture! The quaint little neighborhoods tucked away in unlikely corners—secluded, private, a world away from the skyscrapers and bustling intersections and streams of endless traffic.

Koji Yanagihara was a Tokyoite through and through, rarely venturing to other parts of the country. This meant his friends and colleagues were astonished when, two days after the Kaori Hirakata's murder, he took a plane to Ishizaki, the prefectural capital, to attend a televised police briefing about the case, returning to Tokyo that evening.

They were even more surprised when he announced, less than a week later, that he'd be going back to Murota to spend several nights there.

"It's my job!" he'd protested when they teased him. "I'd be fired for insubordination if I didn't go."

They imagined that was an exaggeration. Koji Yanagihara was a high-profile journalist of such standing that other newspapers regularly tried to poach him from *The Nippon Daily*. He'd even been able to get away with posting a short neutral piece about Kaori Hirakata's murder after that first visit to Murota, telling his friends he'd refrained from including more electrifying details because of a promise he'd made to the murdered girl's parents.

Naturally, his editor wasn't pleased, particularly as the other Tokyo dailies were boosting circulation figures by printing all the juicy details. Koji's boss was a journalist but also a hard-headed businessman. When the story first broke, he was content to placate his most valuable writer. But his patience soon wore thin, and he told Koji to return to Murota, instructing him to write an emotive piece on the town's atmosphere a week after a sensational murder had been committed there. He urged Koji to concentrate on the fear factor. The fact that no arrests had been made meant that the culprit was still at large and free, presumably, to kill again. He should convey the enormous pressure the police were under to solve the case while also portraying the pathos of the victim's grief-stricken friends and family.

The editor rubbed his hands at the prospect of the increased sales. It was a tall order, but his star reporter had showed time and again that he could come up with the goods. What was dubbed the chocolate box murder mystery had captured Japan's collective imagination, gripped by the improbable murder method and by photos of the victim—the beautiful young woman killed the very night she planned to elope. There was also the enticing detail that the boyfriend, rumored to be a *yakuza,* was on the run, and the unsettling coincidence of the girl's father having been shot, possibly by the *yakuza,* twelve years earlier. A brief news segment on the Hirakata case was aired on NHK two nights running.

After all, Koji wasn't completely averse to going back. He was only slightly troubled by qualms of conscience. The story, with its improbabilities and coincidences, fascinated him. He thought the details sufficiently thrilling to confirm the truism that truth is stranger than fiction.

Koji's aunt had offered to put him up, but he told her all his expenses were being paid and that his editor had insisted he stay at the town's best hotel, the Excelsior, in the center of town. In fact, he was stretching the truth. The paper had agreed to cover his train fare, but not his living expenses. But he scarcely knew his aunt and preferred to stay somewhere he could keep his own hours and enjoy his own company.

Besides, his aunt lived on the outskirts of the town, far from the action, and there was also the fact she was a traditionalist who believed modern amenities sap moral fiber. He doubted she even had air conditioning. No, he would refuse her hospitality. Finding a place with all the conveniences positioned in the heart of the town, midway between the station and the ferry port to the north and the business and entertainment districts to the south, was worth the cost. Koji spoke English fluently, and a phrase an American friend was fond of popped into his head: "It's a no-brainer."

Koji noticed he attracted curious glances as he strolled around the town, trying to soak up the local ambience. It was no wonder. He stood out. He was unusually tall for a Japanese and, having gone gray as a young man, refused to follow convention and dye his hair black. He was also wearing a gray suit when all the businessmen hurrying to their offices wore only black or blue ones. He had a theory that Tokyoites are distinguished by a cosmopolitan air unachievable by Japanese who lived anywhere else.

Koji decided he would first present himself at the Murota police station, dipping his toe in the water to see if anyone there was willing to be interviewed. If not, his aunt had helpfully provided names and addresses of people who'd known the murdered girl.

He asked directions of a woman who looked as out of place as he felt. While the clothing worn by the people scurrying around Murota was dowdy, or at least a good year behind what was fashionable in Tokyo, they showed the locals had made an effort. This woman reminded him of a Greek peasant with her angular body, pulled-back bun, and rusty black dress. Despite her ugly clothes and face, Koji guessed from her proud bearing she demanded respect, so he bent down in an exaggerated bow before asking her the way. She looked irritated but told him and then, somehow, intuited his reason for going there.

"You're a reporter," she said, adding, flatly, "here about the Hirakata case." It was an accusation rather than a question. She shook her head in disgust and marched off, saying, "The press—despicable vultures preying on people's pain."

The police station—a large anonymous-looking building constructed from cement that was aging badly, with cracks and stains marking its walls—was located in the center of town. A plump and attractive young woman whose badge read Hino was at the reception desk. She took in the lanky figure approaching her with a quizzical glance. Once he'd shown his credentials, she made some phone calls as he sat in the lobby, flipping through a newspaper somebody had left on a chair. Then she beckoned him over. "The chief inspector has agreed to see you," she said, pointing to a door behind her. "Go through and somebody will direct you to his office."

Koji was amused at how closely Chief Inspector Ito conformed to his stereotypical image of a senior police officer. He was a heavy magisterial figure sitting behind a desk covered with papers who kept running a hand through thick black hair streaked with gray as he spoke. Koji imagined it was a nervous habit the policeman wasn't even aware of.

"I rarely speak to reporters," the inspector said, after he'd beckoned Koji to an armchair in front of his desk, taking a seat on the sofa opposite. "I take part in press conferences reluctantly. But as you've come all the way from Tokyo, I've agreed to see you."

He lifted a hand and looked at his watch. "I can give you five minutes."

"I'm sure my readers would agree that the most pressing issue is whether the culprit generally mentioned in this case—Hiroki Sato—has been found and detained." Koji waved his hand at the window. "Even as a visitor to your fair town, I've noticed a certain tension in the atmosphere—a kind of fear—understandable with a murderer on the loose."

The chief inspector involuntarily grimaced.

That touched a nerve. It must not be going well, Koji thought. He suddenly felt sorry for the stocky, impassive man. "I can imagine you're under a lot of pressure to solve this case," he said.

"We're busy pursuing several lines of inquiry," the policeman said. "You'll understand I'm not at liberty to divulge details."

"I wish you the best of luck," Koji said and meant it.

The inspector leaned forward. "In fact, Yanagihara-*san,* I think I should admit that the real reason I've agreed to see you is to ask a favor. One that I have reason to believe you will grant."

He stood and walked to the window, gazing out at the solitary green hill surrounded by a sprawl of buildings. When he turned to look at the reporter, he smiled, saying, "I remember you from the press conference Superintendent Takenaka held last week in Ishizaki. That's why I've agreed to see you. I recall how, on that occasion, you promised Mr. Hirakata you wouldn't publish personal details of the case because you wanted to respect the family's wish for privacy at this difficult time."

"And because I have an aunt who lives in Murota," Koji said, smiling, too.

"Of course, I have no power over you. I can't prevent you from seeing any of the individuals connected to the Hirakata case, however much I'd discourage it. But I appeal to you not to try to meet the victim's family. I doubt they'd agree to such a meeting—they've turned down all requests for interviews—but they might make an exception for you because of the courtesy you showed on that occasion."

"I'm back here because my editor insists I submit an emotive piece," Koji said. "Something that will tug at the heartstrings."

"I think the facts are sufficiently tragic without the family being dragged into it any more than is necessary. This case has attracted far too much attention, which muddies the waters and makes it all the harder for those investigating it."

Koji swallowed and sat up straighter. "I'm sorry, sir. I've come all this way. My job may be on the line. My editor demanded I come back with a scoop."

The chief inspector sighed heavily, rose, and bowed stiffly. "I can't stop you. But I feel I should warn you. You might not only jeopardize our investigation, but also put yourself in harm's way. As you've pointed out, it appears people with murder on their minds may be strolling the streets of our fair town." Tight-lipped, he glanced at his watch. "And now I'm afraid you must excuse me."

Koji Yanagihara left the station rather less jauntily than he'd entered it. He noticed that the receptionist failed to match his smile as he walked toward the door. She even bent her head, ignoring him as if suddenly preoccupied by a pressing task. Stopping at a street corner, he rummaged in a pocket for a notebook. Opening it, he scanned a page of names and addresses, reflecting on the adage that blood is thicker than water. Although he scarcely knew his aunt, his call to her begging for information on individuals who'd known the victim had resulted in her generously sending an email whose contents he'd shortened as follows: Makoto Taniguchi, grandson of the current owner and young heir apparent to the real estate firm where the victim's father had worked; Emi Tada, bank clerk and childhood friend; Juno Nomura, missionary at the church attended by the Hirakatas, presided over by Pastor Nakagawa and his wife.

Now Koji checked his watch. It was just ten o'clock. He needed to sit down and get organized, to make a list not only of people he wanted to talk to but also places he wanted to see, including Kaori Hirakata's family home and the boutique where she had worked, the Taniguchi real estate firm, the church where the Hirakata family spent so much of their time, and Emi Tada's and Hiroki Sato's houses. Koji looked across the busy street and saw a coffee shop just opposite. Koji was superstitious. He thought of it as serendipity. He was meant to go there. Walking to the intersection, he waited for the green light for pedestrians.

Chief Inspector Ito

After the reporter left his office, Chief Inspector Ito sat at his desk again and slumped over it, holding his head in his hands. He felt depressed. The case of the murdered girl was going nowhere.

There was the matter of Hiroki Sato, for example. As that reporter observed, it seemed everyone knew that the police hadn't apprehended the prime suspect yet. Within a few days of Kaori Hirakata's murder, it was common knowledge not only in Murota but throughout the country that this factory worker, her boyfriend, had disappeared, and that a suitcase and a box of poisoned chocolates had been found on her bed. It added to the piquancy of the case that this attractive young woman had planned to run away with her questionable suitor while managing to keep her family completely in the dark.

The poor Hirakatas, the chief inspector thought for the umpteenth time. Well, at least he'd saved them from the undoubtedly unwelcome attentions of that reporter.

What wasn't public knowledge—and the inspector hoped wouldn't be for a while—was *how* the couple planned to elope. It was information the inspector had been keeping close to his chest for nearly a week, ever since late last Monday, when Hiroki Sato's mother had come to the station to give her statement. An hour later, Ito had instructed Miyagi to pick up her brother for questioning but to keep it hush-hush. The lieutenant was told to go in an unmarked car and wear civilian clothes so his visit would go unnoticed.

On that Monday evening, after Miyagi had rapped at the door of the fisherman's house—a small, shabby building with a blue-tiled roof near the port—a man with the wiry, muscular body and the ruddy, deeply furrowed face of someone who has spent most of his adult life in hard physical labor out in the open air appeared. He opened the door abruptly, glaring and demanding to know who was making such a racket. Miyagi was so startled he was speechless until, coming to his senses, he took out his identification and explained he was there on police business.

As he followed the man into his house, Miyagi smelled the reek of alcohol, meaning it came as no surprise to see a half-empty bottle of whisky on a low table near a sofa covered by a ragged blanket. The skipper bent down, poured some in a glass, tossed it off, and then glared even more fiercely at the policeman.

"What do you want?" he said, scowling as he squared off threateningly, putting up his fists as if he intended to land a few punches. "You're lucky you caught me in. I should be at work today, but couldn't face it." Then his face lost its defiant look, succeeded by one of despair as the man slumped down on the sofa. "No, I know why you're here. In fact, I was expecting you. My sister rang to say you'd probably be paying me a visit. It's true. I took Hiro-*chan* to Busan. I have no idea where he is now. He had his passport and some local currency. Once I pulled into the port, he jumped onto a pier with his bag and disappeared. Some guards shouted—he hadn't shown his papers—but I couldn't stop him, and neither could they. The guards let me off with a warning and, as far as I know, they're still looking for him. I got back a few hours ago. For your information, I don't believe he hurt that girl. True, he had a quick temper. True, he could be violent and unpredictable. But I think he loved her. From what I've heard, that was a planned murder, not a crime of passion."

He poured another glass of whisky and swigged it down. "But what do I know?" he said. "The boy joined the *yakuza*—and I would never have expected that of him." Then he emptied the contents of the bottle into the glass and drained it in one gulp. A glint of that former defiance gleamed fitfully in his eyes as he added, "I'd offer you a drink, but there's no point. For one thing, there isn't anymore. For another, you're on duty." He sighed and stood up, all fight gone out of him, even holding out his hands obediently. "I'm ready to go with you. Do you want to handcuff me?"

At the station, Miyagi ushered Hiroki Sato's uncle into Interview Room One, where the chief inspector was waiting. It was a small windowless cubicle with scuffed beige walls that held only a table and two chairs on either side. Miyagi beckoned the skipper to the chair opposite the inspector's while he sat next to Ito. A cassette recorder was on the table that Miyagi switched on when the inspector nodded.

"The date is Monday, September 19th, 1988, and the time is half past eight in the evening. Lieutenant Miyagi is speaking. Chief Inspector Ito and Itsuki Beppu are in the room with me." He enunciated each word loudly and slowly.

"Tell me about your relationship with Hiroki Sato," Ito demanded.

"Hiro-*chan*, that is, Hiroki Sato, is my nephew, the son—the only child—of my sister, Megumi Beppu."

"Why is his surname different from yours? I understand your sister is unmarried."

"When she got pregnant, she told everybody she and her boyfriend—a scumbag named Kenji Sato—had got hitched. It was a lie. That came out after the birth when she had to register the child at the town office. Still, she insisted her boy take that bastard's surname. Maybe she hoped his family would cough up some dough for the boy someday, or he might inherit something. Fat chance!" The tough-looking man looked disgusted and said, "Can I have a smoke?"

Ito pushed an ashtray, a full pack, and a lighter across the table.

"Your sister has indicated her belief that your nephew joined a *yakuza* gang in Tokyo. Do you know whether your nephew had any connections with the local gangsters here in Murota when he returned?"

"He hated working on the assembly line at that car factory. I can tell you that," the old man said before taking a long drag on his cigarette. "Whether he went back to his bad old ways, I don't know." He fixed the inspector with an earnest look. "But what I do know is that once those creeps have a hold of you, they don't like letting go. Bastards! I hate thinking the boy had anything to do with them."

After his interview with Hiroki Sato's uncle, Chief Inspector Ito immediately contacted the South Korean police authorities. After giving details of the suspect and faxing his photo, he requested them to detain Sato if found for extradition back to Japan.

As of now, six days later, there were no reported sightings of Hiroki Sato. A warrant for his arrest had been circulated throughout South Korea, but nothing had come of it. Not yet anyway. The boy's uncle had imagined the police might arrest him for facilitating his nephew's escape, but Ito didn't have the heart to charge him. He did, however, extract Beppu's promise to let him know if his nephew contacted him. Ito's long years of service had honed his instincts. He felt sure the skipper was a man of integrity who'd keep his word.

The disappearance of the main suspect was a loose end in a case that seemed to have too damned many of them. Ito wanted to get his hands on the boy—literally and figuratively. He was desperate to grill him, to get a confession, by force if necessary. He didn't have to admit to killing her. Ito just wanted to determine whether he had *anything* to do with his girlfriend's death.

Given his disappearance, Ito was left with questions he couldn't answer. If Hiroki Sato had killed Kaori Hirakata, what could have been his motive? Granted, her little brother had told them Kaori had got so furious at Hiroki's *yakuza* connection that she might be tempted to accept the proposal of a man at her church. Still, she and Hiroki were on the point of eloping and despite her understandable hurt and sense of betrayal, from what the boy had heard, it seemed they planned to go through with it.

Then Ito needed to consider the *yakuza* connection. After Kaori Hirakata's father had been shot, the police had finally found the gun, hidden at the bottom of a public rubbish bin, with ballistics confirming it was the one used in the attack, but they'd never identified the shooter. Was he still in Murota, a member of the local *yakuza*? Or had he been brought in from Tokyo to do the deed? And was there some connection between the father's getting shot and, over a decade later, the daughter poisoned?

He pondered the timeline. Someone shot Mr. Hirakata in 1976 when he was thirty-nine years old. He'd been hired by the lucrative Taniguchi real estate firm in his late twenties and quickly won the president's trust and respect with his energy and abilities, rising to become director of its finances while Mr. Taniguchi's own son was embarked on a self-destructive course of behavior that would end in his dying a homeless alcoholic on a Tokyo street. But after Mr. Hirakata got shot in his left leg, the company demoted him due to his alleged involvement with the local *yakuza*.

It was common knowledge old Mr. Taniguchi had disinherited his son and promoted Mr. Hirakata in his place—although, years later, he ended up stripping him of his directorship. Could a festering sense of guilt and shame have developed in the man Ito thought of as a skinny Santa? Could he have been at fault but forced Kaori's father to take the blame? If that were the case, was he also somehow responsible for what happened to Kaori? But the manner of Kaori's murder argued against a *yakuza* connection. They generally employed more rough and ready ways of dispatching anyone they considered a foe or simply inconvenient. The knife and the gun—those were their preferred methods.

The inspector wanted to find out whether Hiroki Sato had bought the box of chocolates or if somebody had given them to him. If it was the latter, perhaps he'd guessed it was a potentially lethal gift from the gangsters he'd chosen to part ways with. Had he taken it to his girlfriend by way of an experiment? Had he had any of the chocolates himself? Presumably not. Forensics had established Kaori must have eaten at least seven or eight chocolates heavily laced with thallium. When the police had arrived on the scene, twelve chocolates were missing from the box—and Kaori's brother said he'd heard his sister remark, on opening the box, that it was missing a few.

But this would mean Hiroki Sato didn't care whether Kaori lived or died. All the evidence pointed the other way, indicating he'd loved her and intended for them to begin a new life in another country. On the other hand, while he might be capable of love, he'd also proved himself capable of violence. He'd joined the *yakuza* of his own volition and presumably done horrible things in their service. There was no established evidence that he had left the gang he had belonged to in Tokyo. Ito also thought of the significant bruising on the victim's arms—presumably caused by her boyfriend during their disagreement the morning of her death.

Ito knew he had to keep open the possibility somebody else had killed Kaori Hirakata. It was obvious she was loved, attracting devotion from friends and family. Maybe she was hated by somebody in equal measure.

If not Hiroki Sato, who? Of course, the murdered girl's sister could have had no hand in it. She'd been in London when it occurred. Ito felt he could also discount any involvement by her parents and younger brother. Who were the other significant figures in her life? Ito held up one hand and counted them off on his fingers. One, there was her childhood friend, Emi Tada. Two, the suitor proposed for her—Yuichi Motoki. Three, four, and five, the pastor and his wife and the missionary at the church that played a prominent role in the Hirakatas' family life.

Ito considered them. If Emi Tada knew her friend had fallen in love and was going to elope, she might feel frustration, envy, and rage. She presumably knew where Hiroki Sato lived—his house was a short distance from hers. If he ate the chocolates, her friend couldn't elope with him. He could take them to Kaori, but perhaps Emi had dismissed that as unlikely. Or maybe that's what she wanted, if only subconsciously. Was anger seething below that calm, even dull, exterior? Life had showered her friend with bounty, but she had been condemned to drudgery and hardship through no fault of her own. It was Emi Tada who'd told him Kaori was especially partial to chocolates.

As for the pastor, his wife, and the missionary, they seemed to have hoped Kaori would be tempted to marry Yuichi Motoki, the wealthy and ambitious young man who attended their church. Perhaps any complicity they might share for the girl's death only extended that far. The chief inspector had invited Motoki in for questioning a few days earlier. He'd been away at a conference in Nagoya the weekend when Kaori met her end. Miyagi had checked the timetables and confirmed it would have been possible for him to return to Murota by a late-night train on Saturday, leave a bag holding the box of chocolates on Sato's door, and return to Nagoya in time to attend the Sunday morning meetings. But Ito had his doubts. Unless Motoki was a skilled actor, Ito was inclined to believe the shock he'd exhibited on learning Kaori had been murdered was genuine. He was also so obviously a stolid and successful businessman that Ito found it hard to believe he'd risk everything to kill either the woman who'd spurned his advances or the boyfriend she'd preferred to him.

Now Ito held up his other hand. Six and beyond might be individuals whose existence the police had yet to discover. Ito heaved a deep sigh. He knew himself to be in the hot seat. As that gray-haired, trendily dressed reporter had correctly guessed, the Murota police were under tremendous pressure to solve the case. Superintendent Takenaka was on the phone at least daily, demanding results. He'd even hinted at taking over the case himself or finding a replacement for Ito within his own force. Ito hated admitting it, but his officers had begun to feel demoralized. The eagerness his team used to show at their morning sessions when he issued orders and summed up progress on the case was visibly dissipating as one lead after another dried up.

It was humiliating. But Ito was Japanese, taught from childhood to endure the unendurable stoically, without complaint. He could only do one thing, and that was his best.

Koji Yanagihara

"Irrashaimasei," the staff chorused as soon as he opened the café door, which was equipped with a tinkling bell to alert them of customers. *Welcome!* When he sat down, a waitress immediately brought him a glass of iced water and a hot towel wrapped in plastic.

The café was nearly deserted. It was a cat-themed place with photos and paintings of felines everywhere and even a furry white one sunning itself on a window ledge. Only one other customer was inside—an elderly man wearing glasses and a tracksuit who occupied a booth in the corner, reading a newspaper as he slowly sipped from a white cup. Koji had chosen a table for two by the window, and for a few minutes, he occupied himself while he waited for his coffee by looking out at the passersby.

Then he took a map of Murota he'd picked up at the train station from one jacket pocket and a pen from the other. Smoothing the map out on the table, he beckoned the waitress over to ask for their current location, marking it with a large black X. She also helped him find some of the other addresses jotted down in his notebook, which he labeled on his map. They included the high-rise building that housed the Taniguchi real estate company where Mr. Hirakata worked and Kaori Hirakata's boutique. Koji sighed with pleasure. It was all working out perfectly. Both those places turned out to be just around the corner from the coffee shop, and Mitsuo Bank, where Emi Tada was employed, was only a few blocks away. The church the Hirakata family attended was near Murota's famous garden park, a twenty-minute brisk walk south, down Chuo Dori, its major thoroughfare.

As he marked out an itinerary, numbering each destination, Koji saw he could make a loop that would take him to all the places he wanted to visit and then return him back to his hotel. The café where he was sitting was in the town center. He'd go to the real estate company, the boutique, and the bank first, then walk south to the garden and the church. After that, he'd need to head east to what was obviously the poorest part of town where Hiroki Sato once lived and Emi Tada continued to live—a place bisected by railway tracks that included factories and industrial parks and houses and an area called Soaplands, with the fishing port nearby. Finally, he should head back north to the Kitaguchi district, which the waitress had described as the most exclusive neighborhood in town. That's where the Hirakata family had their house. Heading back south from there to the town center would complete the loop.

Koji returned his pen to his pocket, drained his water glass, and smiled. Although he'd compared Murota negatively with Tokyo, in one respect, the town held the advantage. Tokyo was so huge he'd have needed to rely heavily on its extensive subway system to get around. Murota didn't even have a subway—just buses and trams. He could get to all the destinations on his map on foot, and it would probably only take a few hours. Paying for his coffee, which he'd barely touched, he set off.

The tall, impressive building where Mr. Hirakata worked was on Chuo Dori, the broad and leafy main avenue in Murota lined by the town's biggest and most successful businesses. It looked like an attractive brick structure, but Koji knew it was a façade. Murota was frequently visited by earthquakes, just like any place in Japan, and a building made of real bricks would collapse like a house of cards if shaken hard enough. He walked into the lobby, noticing how expensive and new everything looked, then scrutinized a notice board that informed him the Taniguchi real estate firm was on the tenth floor. Koji whistled. At the top, the most desirable spot in the building—it must be doing well. Below were insurance companies, travel agencies, lawyers' offices, and dental clinics. The building obviously attracted a well-heeled clientele—and must, he thought, charge a hefty rental fee from its tenants.

While he waited for the elevator, Koji wondered how to play his visit. Should he be truthful and admit he was a journalist from Tokyo researching the Kaori Hirakata murder? That would probably get him thrown out on his ear. No, it would be better to give a fake name and pose as a visitor contemplating a move to Murota. His byline on *The Nippon Daily* featured a small photo of him. It was unlikely anyone would recognize him from that, but he'd just have to take the chance.

Koji hoped he could meet Kaori's father there but thought it unlikely. He'd heard rumors Mr. Hirakata was going to resign and move his family to Tokyo. He might see Mr. Taniguchi, the president who'd demoted Mr. Hirakata from his directorship when the *yakuza* scandal had broken. Like the good investigative journalist he knew himself to be, Koji had researched people involved in the Hirakata case and found the backstory unexpectedly gripping.

He wondered if the old man had seen in ambitious and hardworking Iwao Hirakata a substitute for the son who'd proved such a disappointment. Perhaps he even blamed himself for what had happened. He'd probably spoiled and indulged his son as the heir apparent to the family business, while Iwao Hirakata had risen from the humblest of beginnings. His father owned a tiny bicycle shop in Murota, but he had managed to graduate with honors from Tokyo University and become a successful businessman. Making the comparison even more acute was that Taniguchi's son and Hirakata were the same age and had been classmates in high school. Hirakata's only idiosyncrasy—according to an article on him Koji had come across—was that he never learned to drive, saying Japanese people had become too soft and needed to walk or cycle more.

When the elevator doors softly whooshed open on the tenth floor, Koji found himself in a large, dimly lit, wood-paneled space with deep green carpeting and a receptionist behind a desk. He gave her a meaningless smile as he approached and bowed. Making a show of patting the breast pockets of his suit, he expelled a loud, exasperated sigh, saying, "Pity! I forgot to bring my card case."

The pretty young receptionist smiled. "It doesn't matter. Can I help you?"

"I'm from Tokyo, visiting my aunt here in Murota. I've found myself charmed by your fair town," Koji said, lying with the easy fluency he had acquired as a journalist. "It's so...quaint, so accessible. I was passing by your building and noticed your real estate firm and thought I'd just pop in to see what properties were available and at what prices."

"We're grateful for your interest," she said. "I'm sure we can assist you in your search." Waving at three or four armchairs arranged against the wall beside the elevator he'd not noticed on entering, she said, "Please just sit over there, and I'll see who's available to talk to you."

At that moment, a thin elderly man with a trimmed white mustache and beard and red cheeks opened a door, accompanied by a much younger man who bore a striking resemblance to his companion. The older man appeared to be giving instructions and admonitions to the young man, who kept bowing and saying "I understand" in hushed, respectful tones. They glanced over at Koji Yanagihara, who'd just sat down. As he rose slightly and bowed, they didn't deign to bow in turn. Instead, flicking a haughty hand in Koji's direction, the old man draped an arm around the younger man's shoulders and led him to another room.

Koji looked askance at the receptionist, who was casting an indulgent, amused smile at the pair as they disappeared through the doorway. "Mr. Taniguchi and his grandson," she said. She added apologetically, "They're very proud, but they have reason to be."

"Mr. Taniguchi?" Koji said, feigning ignorance.

"His father founded this company," she said. "And now he's teaching the boy all about the business. Keeping it in the family."

Koji didn't imagine that the younger Taniguchi who, despite his age and good looks, had something thuggish about his bearing, would relish being called a boy. Still, he gave the receptionist an appreciative smile and nodded. Koji didn't like people looking down their nose at him. Both men were nasty, he concluded. They were dismissive of their own potential customers, and the thick brows prominent on a small forehead that marked both the grandfather's and the grandson's faces seemed to signal not only their kinship but a predisposition for unpleasant behavior.

The receptionist spoke into the telephone on her desk, and a third man appeared, carrying a thick file and a folder. Bowing, he introduced himself as the chief salesman of the firm. After giving Koji his card, he seated himself beside him. The file contained photos and descriptions of all the housing stocks managed by the firm. Placing it in Koji's hands, the salesman leaned over as he flipped through the pages, offering remarks on the various features of the real estate pictured. When Koji asked about any particular property, he searched through the folder for a photocopy of its price and features for Koji to take away and consider.

After fifteen minutes, Koji found himself clutching a manila envelope containing the details of two flats and three houses he had no intention of buying. He rose and, thanking the salesman and the receptionist profusely, summoned the elevator. On leaving the building, he found a waste bin conveniently located outside the front door and stuffed the envelope into it. *How lucky!* he thought as he strolled down the street toward the boutique where Kaori Hirakata had been employed. He'd been able to meet the man who'd demoted her father as well as his grandson. Makoto Taniguchi seemed to bear his grandfather no animosity for the harsh treatment meted out to his own father. Koji had been impressed by the naked ambition obvious in the young man's face and the obsequiousness apparent in his behavior. Perhaps he was even glad his father—a potential rival, ultimately, for the firm's presidency—was out of the picture. As for the grandfather, Koji thought Mr. Taniguchi might look genial and radiate old world charm, but he undoubtedly had a ruthless, unpleasant streak.

The boutique was only two blocks down the wide avenue that ran through central Murota. Koji contented himself with looking in the window, noting the expensive look of the clothing on the mannequins on display and the snooty expressions on the shop assistants' faces. He could see no price tags. *If you need to know how much something costs, you can't afford it*, he thought. He had no wish to go inside and chat with the staff. He was sure they'd look askance at his gray suit and hair.

Emi Tada's bank was another two blocks along—a seven-story building of dark plate glass that exuded stability and prosperity. In the research he had done on Murota before his visit, he had learned that they had erected this structure in the early fifties. The original bank, like most of Murota, had burned to the ground after an Allied bombing carried out several weeks before the end of the Second World War.

Koji looked up admiringly. Unlike the undistinguished buildings around it, the bank headquarters, at least, was aging well. It wouldn't look out of place in any of the best districts of Tokyo.

A middle-aged woman wearing the bank uniform for its female employees—a beige blouse with a bow at the neck and a brown pencil skirt, her hair neatly caught back in a ponytail fixed with a plaid ribbon—bowed as he entered. When he told her he was looking for the international transfers section, she pointed to an escalator leading up to the second floor.

Koji's luck was holding. Three employees were manning the counter, but he was approached by one whose badge identified her as Emi Tada. She was a plump young woman with spotty skin, slightly reddened eyes, and a wistful expression. She smiled as she bowed, but it was obviously an effort.

Koji told her he needed to send money to a friend in London. Despite her air of misery, Miss Tada impressed Koji with her well-informed and efficient explanation of the current exchange rates, the bank's method of sending Japanese yen as English pounds, and the speed at which such a transfer could be completed. While they were talking, a foreigner approached, asking for assistance, and Koji was also impressed by Miss Tada's excellent English.

Koji decided to risk detection. Once Miss Tada had finished explaining the transfer system, he said, "By the way, even in Tokyo, we're hearing about Murota these days. Something about a young woman dying after eating poisoned chocolates." He shook his head and smiled sympathetically. "I couldn't believe it at first. It sounds like something out of a novel."

He watched the woman's eyes redden and fill with tears she tried to blink back. "Yes," she said, bowing her head, obviously trying to avoid his gaze. "Poor Murota has been in the news lately—but it's not a fame any of us locals would desire."

Koji knew he needed to change the topic. He told her he'd consider what she'd told him and return soon to make the transaction, citing his lack of a passport as his excuse for delaying. Bowing and thanking her for her help, he went down the escalator, pursing his lips in a silent whistle. *She's taking her friend's death badly.*

Koji glanced at his watch as he exited the bank. It was nearly noon, and he realized he felt hungry. He spotted a long line forming outside a noodle shop nearby and decided he was willing to wait twenty minutes for lunch at a place whose popularity attested to its quality.

Half an hour later, wiping his lips with a handkerchief he'd taken from a pocket, he felt sated and satisfied. He rose and, balancing his chopsticks on his bowl, carried them to the man in a white coat in a corner who was hastily washing a steady stream of dishes and glasses brought to him by customers on finishing their meals. Looking around, Koji noticed it was a utilitarian restaurant—just simple tables with benches—but that it was packed with people slurping their noodles loudly in every available space. He also acknowledged the truth of the adage that slurping was an essential part of the *udon* experience, heightening the flavor. It was no wonder the place was so crowded and still had a long line of people waiting outside. The broth had a rich savory taste, the noodles were of a wonderfully chewy firmness, and the slices of lotus root and pumpkin tempura he'd bought as an accompaniment had been crispy and warm.

Koji blinked as he left the shop, the brightness he encountered as soon as he was outside making an almost painful contrast to its dusky interior. He strolled down the long, broad, and leafy avenue crowded with buses, taxis, cars, and scooters, as well as pedestrians on the sidewalks. Despite the noise of the traffic, he could hear the loud thrum of cicadas. It was hot! He took off his jacket and slung it over a shoulder.

He decided to visit Murota's top tourist attraction—its famous garden—before going to the Hirakatas' church. He was so close it would be a shame to miss this place celebrated for its trimmed topiary, ornamental lakes, waterfalls, and teahouses. Reading the plaque by the ticket office, he learned it had been designed in the eighteenth century for the entertainment of the local feudal lords and was opened to the general public in the late nineteenth century. Koji walked down its paths slowly, admiring the subtle beauty of the park's manicured greenery, its bridges spanning ponds swarming with huge yellow, white, and red carp, and the shops selling traditional toys as well as ice cream and cold drinks and even fish food. Koji decided he needed to revise his estimate of Murota. The garden made it worth a visit.

At this time, Koji noticed a man wearing a suit, hat, and sunglasses behind him. Visitors thronged the park, but this man stood out because of his odd behavior. He seemed to stop to admire a view whenever Koji did. He kept the same distance between them, no matter how quickly or slowly Koji walked.

I'm just paranoid! Koji thought. But he hastened his pace and left the garden.

The abrupt transition from a space whose every detail and vista bespoke tradition and attention to beauty to the area where the Hirakatas' church was located came as a shock. It was only five minutes away, but it felt like another world. Suddenly, Koji found himself in a cramped, smelly neighborhood where dingy houses were crowded inches from each other, their gardens consisting of tiny strips of compacted earth, and greenery provided by a few shrubs. The church stood out from the surrounding houses due to its even shabbier appearance compared to most of them, and it had a large white cross perched on its tiled roof.

Koji toyed with the idea of just looking at the building and taking in the atmosphere. But he'd come this far, so he thrust back his shoulders, crossed the dusty courtyard in front of the building, and knocked. A big woman with a pale, doughy face slid open the door. When he explained—lying again—that he was from Tokyo, thought of moving to Murota, and was a Christian, she eagerly invited him in after introducing herself as Mrs.

Nakagawa, the pastor's wife. As he slipped out of his shoes in the *genkan*, she hurriedly put out a pair of slippers for him in the hallway. A familiar odor assailed his nostrils, and he realized the church smelled like his grandmother's poky little home in Tokyo. It was a musty odor, a mixture of the scents of boiled daikon radish and miso and green tea.

The hallway had three doors. After Koji stepped up and into the slippers, he saw the one to the left was ajar and glimpsed a small kitchen. The woman opened the middle door, proudly pointing out the features of the large chapel—its pulpit and organ fronting seven or eight rows of pews. Then he followed her through the door to the right into a room with several armchairs and a coffee table.

As a woman sitting in one of the chairs stood up, and he registered her sharp, angular body enveloped in an ugly black dress, Koji felt dismayed to see it was the person he'd asked directions of that morning—and who had guessed why he was in Murota.

"You're that reporter I met a few hours ago," she said accusingly before the pastor's wife could introduce them. "You wanted to go to the police station."

For once, Koji's facility for coming up with fluent lies deserted him. He was startled into telling the truth. "I'm Koji Yanagihara," he said, "a journalist for *The Nippon Daily*."

"I *knew* it!" the woman exclaimed, looking simultaneously triumphant and contemptuous. "When I saw how you were dressed, how you didn't look like a local, I guessed you might be a reporter. I also thought your face looked familiar. I often buy your paper."

"He's a Christian," the pastor's wife said, surprised. "He's moving to Murota and is looking for a church to attend." She turned to Koji, saying, "This is our resident missionary, Juno-*sensei*. She lives here and helps out. But please sit, you two, and I'll get us some tea."

The woman in the black dress failed to reciprocate Koji's bow. She plumped herself down on her seat and turned her head away. The two sat without speaking for a minute after the pastor's wife had scurried out, studiously ignoring the other's existence. Koji registered an odor emanating from her he thought might be mothballs.

Finally, the woman called Juno-*sensei* broke the silence. "I know why you're here, of course," she said, her voice dripping with scorn. "You're like a hungry junkyard dog hunting through dirt and muck for a juicy bone to chew. You're sneaking about trying to get details about that poor girl's death you'll print to entertain people who never knew or cared for her. You like being paid for your dirty work. You get a kick out of it. You must know about the unsuitable boyfriend. Well, I can tell you Kaori Hirakata was much too good for him. I think she changed her mind about him, and that's why he killed her. You can put *that* in your paper!"

As a writer, Koji admired the woman's unexpected poetic flair. As a journalist, he was used to heckling. He answered calmly, "I'm just doing my job."

"If you really are a Christian—which I don't believe for a moment— you'd know that your job is to *pray* for the girl and leave her family and friends to mourn in peace. I shall warn all my friends and contacts to have nothing to do with you." She smacked the table with one hand. "Heartless! That's what you are!"

It was at this awkward moment that Mrs. Nakagawa came in, bearing a tray with a teapot and cups. Just as she laid it on the table with a clatter, Juno sprang up and said, "Sorry, Mrs. Nakagawa, I can't stand being in the same room as this man. I'm going up to my room."

It would be charitable to say she closed the door with force. Koji winced as she slammed it.

Mrs. Nakagawa looked upset and confused. "But what's happened?" she said. Her forehead creased as she added, looking around helplessly, "I'm sorry, my husband is out."

"An errand of mercy?" Koji asked, then regretted his flippancy. But Mrs. Nakagawa hadn't even noticed. "He's taken our program for next Sunday's service to the printers," she said innocently.

She sat down heavily, then seemed to recall the missionary's parting words. "Excuse me, Mr. Yanagihara," she said, looking embarrassed. "Can you explain why Juno-*sensei* left us in such haste?"

Koji decided to make a clean breast of it. "I'm sorry. I've deceived you. I've taken advantage of your kindness. I *am* from Tokyo, but I'm not a

Christian and have no intention of becoming one or of moving to Murota. I work for a Tokyo newspaper. My editor sent me here to write a piece on Kaori Hirakata's murder."

"Oh, oh, oh," said Mrs. Nakagawa, flinching as if she had been struck. Still, she remembered her manners. She automatically poured them cups of tea and took a sip from her own, bowing her head.

"My editor insists I write a piece on Kaori Hirakata as a *person,* not simply a victim, to give our readers a sense of who she was and of how her friends and family and Murota itself are coping with this tragedy."

"A tall order," Mrs. Nakagawa said, looking up and speaking with an acuteness that surprised him. "I liked her but was certainly never very close to the girl, never taken into her confidence. But I can tell you how she struck me." She held her teacup in her hand, gazing at the steam. "If you're interested in the human angle, what you have to understand about Kaori is that she was kind. Too kind perhaps."

Koji left the church a few minutes later, feeling—unusually for him—ashamed. He strode quickly down the avenue, making his way southeast to look for Emi Tada's and Hiroki Sato's houses. He could have taken a bus—it was over a mile there—but he wanted vigorous exercise to efface the previous half hour from his consciousness. Koji felt slightly nauseous.

As a fluent English speaker, Koji was aware of the saying "the wrong side of the tracks," but once he got to his destination, he found himself questioning whether there was any "right side." After passing factories constructed of corrugated iron with chimneys belching smoke and then an area of brothels and pachinko parlors near the docks known as Soaplands, he came to a residential area. The houses were poky dark dwellings, some no better than shacks, inches away from the tracks. Such flimsy structures must shake and be filled by a deafening din whenever the trains thundered by, as they did with great frequency. Koji wondered how the people inside them could stand it. But maybe they got used to it and didn't even notice.

The neighborhood was smelly and noisy. Koji sniffed. He detected an odor, not initially unpleasant, but which became noisome the nearer he got to the tracks. Human waste! This neighborhood must lack connection to a sewer network. Koji had heard a few such places still existed in rural Japan, serviced by little blue trucks that periodically emptied the pits below the toilets.

Hiroki Tada's house was a one-story structure of iron and wood so dilapidated that it looked like it might collapse at any time under its heavy tile roof. Koji shuddered, standing outside and inspecting it. He couldn't imagine having to spend an hour in a place like that, let alone a life. He saw no garden, just trodden-down dirt at the front that probably turned into a sea of mud whenever it rained. In retrospect, he regretted he'd made his interest in that specific house so apparent. It attracted its occupant, a wiry middle-aged woman with dyed blonde curly hair and a wrinkled face who suddenly popped out the front door, cigarette in hand, and confronted him.

"Press, right?" she said, hand on hip, looking at him defiantly, taking a puff and blowing it angrily in his direction. "You're not the first and won't be the last. Still, better a reporter than the *yakuza*. They've been sniffing around, too. Well, my son isn't here, and I don't think he's coming back. So, you can get lost. Beat it! *Scram!*"

Koji hesitated, but when he saw her drop her cigarette and wave a threatening fist, he walked away quickly while trying to preserve his dignity. Then the woman's words sank in. He looked around and thought he saw the man in a suit, hat, and sunglasses loitering in the doorway of a derelict building nearby. He disappeared as soon as Koji stopped.

Paranoia! Koji thought, scolding himself. Shaking his head, he began walking again. Once he had rounded a corner and was out of sight of the Satos' house, he got out his map again. Emi Tada's house was a short distance away. Surrounded by a breeze-block wall, and with a few shrubs planted in the narrow space between the wall and the house, it was marginally better than Hiroki Sato's. He'd wondered about her economic status and how close her place was to the missing boyfriend's. Now he knew.

Koji heaved a sigh, suddenly feeling extraordinarily lucky to live on the eighth floor of an apartment building in central Tokyo. He enjoyed a good view, and the rooms were clean and spacious. Looking at the map again, he decided to head to the port.

The sight of the boats, large and small, bobbing up and down on the choppy blue waters, cheered him. He threw back his head and sniffed the fishy smell of the brisk breeze, welcoming it. He felt the gusts washing him clean of the memory of such dirt and squalor.

Then he headed back to Murota's central avenue and went north. After twenty minutes, he found himself back at the entrance to the park. He had to walk another two miles through central Murota to get to the Kitaguchi district where the Hirakatas' home was located. The contrast between the victim's home and those of her boyfriend and best friend couldn't have been greater. Koji whistled, feeling impressed. *Whew!* He lived in a so-called *mansion* in Tokyo—but he was sufficiently well-traveled to know that the designation was misleading. It was Japanese English for a condominium. The Hirakatas lived in what was a *real* mansion—a luxurious place like the ones he'd seen in rich neighborhoods in America and Europe. It was a huge white house surrounded by high walls.

On impulse, he tried the handle on the front gate and was surprised when it swung open. He pursed his lips together again, this time giving a whistle of disbelief. It was astonishing the family hadn't locked it given what had happened to their daughter. It made him wonder how the box of chocolates had made its way into the house. Did someone deliver it? Was it left on the front door? Or had somebody—either a family member or a friend—brought it? As far as he knew, the police hadn't yet divulged any information on that point.

Surveying the bonsai trees in pots and the carefully clipped topiary of the huge garden bisected by a curving brick path, taking in the fountain and well-tended flower beds stretching from the front gate to the door of the house, Koji wondered about Hiroki Sato and Emi Tada. Had they envied Kaori Hirakata? It wouldn't be surprising if they did. Or had they harbored resentment, comparing their own circumstances with hers? Could either of them have felt sufficiently aggrieved to kill her?

But it didn't make sense. Kaori Hirakata was going to run away with Hiroki Sato. By marrying her, he'd probably come into some of her money. That is, unless that unpleasant woman at the church was right, and the girl had changed her mind about the elopement. Maybe Hiroki felt he'd rather see her dead than with anyone else.

Koji had heard that poison was a woman's preferred method of murder. But as for Emi Tada, what conceivable motive could she have had to kill her best friend? Presumably, she benefited from having such a wealthy friend. The only motive he could think of was fury if she had discovered Kaori intended to leave her—forever, by running away with a boy she no doubt thought unsuitable. Her anger would be understandable. Koji had heard the two friends were nearly inseparable, and that Emi spent much of her free time at the Hirakatas' place. She'd be losing not only her friend but a second home far preferable to the one she had.

Koji was glad he'd made his brief excursion around sites in Murota associated with Kaori Hirakata's murder. A conscientious journalist, he always found that it was a good idea to check out the lay of the land and see with his own eyes where events had happened when composing a story. He never knew when something might click or what information he might glean.

Now, standing just outside the Hirakatas' garden, Koji noticed a curtain twitch in a downstairs room and, hastily closing the gate, strode down the road. On impulse, he looked around. No, nobody was following him. In fact, hardly anybody was around. The neighborhood was so exclusive that it was nearly deserted. There were few houses and almost no traffic on the road that passed in front of the Hirakata property. Even the nearest neighbor was a good five hundred meters away in a traditional Japanese house but one with no walls around it, hiding it from public view, and its driveway just off the road. As he passed, he read the name on the postbox: Goto. He paused, remembering what he'd heard about the case. It was a Mrs. Goto—an old woman troubled by rheumatism—who'd heard screams that night, gone to the house to investigate, and called for an ambulance.

Koji paused by the gate, debating whether he should try to get an interview. He crossed the drive, had his hand up to the bell, and was just about to press it when he noticed a figure loitering on the other side of the street. It was a shock to see it was the man in the suit he'd noticed earlier.

He still had the hat and sunglasses, but now he also wore a black mask. Koji stopped, and lowering his hand, waited. He watched as the man slowly approached. When he was a few feet away, he bent from the waist in an exaggerated bow Koji could only describe as insolent, tipped his hat, and took off his sunglasses. It didn't matter. With the mask on, Koji knew he'd never be able to recognize him in a police line-up. The only identifying feature was his lack of a pinky finger on his left hand.

"I won't bother telling you my name," the man said. The mask muffled his voice, but he had what Koji thought of as the typical *yakuza* drawl, with each syllable weighted by a tone of menace.

"And I won't show you my face," the man added.

He came even closer, lifting the pinky-less hand as if he intended to shake Koji's. Instinctively, Koji raised his own. But the hand suddenly darted forward and made contact with Koji's body. He found himself pushed with sufficient force he fell flat on the ground. The blow came so unexpectedly and hard that he found it hard to catch his breath. As he lay gasping and shocked, the man approached him and began kicking him. Hard. Relentlessly. Some blows landed on his head, others on his abdomen and legs.

Koji noticed the bright polish on the man's shoes while he twisted back and forth on the hot pavement, trying to dodge them. This intense activity had, as its soundtrack, loud yelping and moaning. He even heard himself say, in a piteous voice he didn't recognize, "Stop! It hurts! Stop! Please, please, please. Stop!"

Finally, the man stepped back. He looked down at Koji and said, "You don't know me, but I know you. You're that damned reporter, and you're here for the same reason I am. You're trying to find that bastard, Sato. You don't know where he is, and I don't either. Not *yet*!"

A smile that was more like a grimace twisted his face, and then one of his legs jerked out in a kick that landed squarely on Koji's abdomen, once more depriving him of breath; then he bent over and slapped Koji so hard his nose bled. "But he's screwed us over, and if I find you know anything about him—anything you don't care to tell us if we get around to asking you—we'll be dealing with you, too."

As he strolled off, he said cheerily, "Like I told you, be seeing you!"

In the dead silence that followed the sound of steps fading away, Koji heard something awful. It was an unearthly moan, and he was the one making it.

The Police

Inspector Ito looked up from his papers when he heard an unusual noise. Somebody was pounding on his door. He was even more surprised when the door was thrown open, and he saw that it was Miyagi. He was normally timid in their relations and would give the most tentative of knocks before poking his head around Ito's office door. But the man who was facing him now was almost unrecognizable as his lieutenant. He was panting, his face was flushed, and he only got his words out with difficulty.

"We've just had a call, sir," he said, clasping the doorframe as if to keep himself erect. "It's Mrs. Goto. She's reported an emergency."

"The Mrs. Goto living next to the Hirakatas?! *Again?!* She seems to attract disaster. I'd hate having her as a neighbor."

"It's not a Hirakata, sir. It's a journalist from Tokyo named Koji Yanagihara. Somebody attacked him right in front of her house. She called an ambulance, and he's on his way to the hospital."

Ito jumped to his feet, about to issue a command, when Miyagi preempted it by saying, "The patrol car is waiting for us in front of the station."

They were in the car in a matter of minutes, with an officer driving them down streets quickly cleared of traffic by the loud wailing of the siren that sent cars hastily pulling to the side to let them pass.

"As I've said, it's an unlucky neighborhood! Was he shot?" the inspector wanted to know.

"Beaten, sir."

"Any idea of his condition?"

"I've been told it's not serious."

"But undoubtedly, it was a very unpleasant experience. Just what we need. More adverse publicity. Tomorrow morning all of Japan will hear about how unsafe Murota is. *Again!*"

The inspector hit his window with a fist and then let his hand drop to his lap, rubbing it with the other as if it was sore, saying, "What is Murota coming to? A shooting, a murder, and now an attack in broad daylight. And all on my watch! I despair. I expect Superintendent Takenaka will be on the phone demanding action."

Miyagi was wise enough to keep silent.

The receptionist wasn't content to tell the policemen where Koji Yanagihara's room was. She sent a nurse to accompany them there.

Inspector Ito found the victim with a bandage circling his thatch of gray hair and bruises on his face. Pillows propped him up in bed and, as the visitors entered his room, he tried to sit up straighter, an effort that brought a grimace to his face.

The nurse glared at the inspector accusingly and rattled off a description of the patient's condition as if Koji Yanagihara were incapable of speaking for himself—and as if what had happened to him was Ito's fault. "Four cracked ribs, extensive abdominal and facial bruising, bruising also to the legs, and a slight concussion," she said, closing the door behind her hard as she left the room.

"She makes my injuries sound worse than they are," said Koji, although he had winced when the nurse slammed the door. "They told me that I'll be discharged tomorrow. The doctors have done all they can. Now I have to rely on time to heal me." He lifted a hand to his head and rubbed his forehead, touching the bandage rather than his own skin, wincing again as he added, "But I don't know if I can face the flight back to Tokyo. I'm in pain, and I must look a sight. I may have to stay here a few days longer."

He gestured at two chairs in the corner. "But please sit down, inspector. And your officer, too."

Miyagi dragged the chairs to the side of the bed. As soon as the inspector had seated himself on one, he perched on the other, taking his notebook and a pen from his pocket.

"I warned you off investigating this case, Mr. Yanagihara," the inspector said.

"You tried. But I felt I had to do a little snooping around to satisfy my editor."

"Any idea who attacked you? Or why?"

"He was a *yakuza*. Ostentatiously so—the way he dressed and acted, the fact he was missing a little finger on one hand, and when he finally had a few words to say, the way he spoke. It was almost comical how he resembled a stereotypical Japanese gangster, like a character in a film. I'd spent several hours walking around Murota, visiting places associated with the case. Midway through, I began to wonder if I was being followed. I noticed the man at that point. He wore a suit, a hat, and sunglasses. By the time he'd decided I needed a beating, he'd put on a black mask, too. I imagine you know the spot where I was attacked. He chose it well. Nobody was within sight. I wouldn't be able to identify him. He knew who I was and why I was here. He said he was looking for Hiroki Sato and wanted me to give him any information on his whereabouts I might dig up." Koji Yanagihara sighed.

"But you're going back to Tokyo."

There was a pause as the journalist looked at the two policemen. Then he said, "We have *yakuza* there, too."

At the station reception desk, Miss Hino stood as Miyagi and Ito entered the building.

Bowing, she said, "Superintendent Takenaka arrived a few minutes ago, sir. He's waiting in your office."

Making a muffled exclamation, Ito rushed off.

"The Bear looks upset," she said.

"No wonder," Miyagi said. "The superintendent wants an arrest, and we haven't been able to oblige him with one yet. That girl was killed, her boyfriend has disappeared, the *yakuza* are snooping around, and now one of those thugs has attacked a journalist from Tokyo. What a mess!"

"Somehow, I don't think Superintendent Takenaka's visit is going to cheer the Bear up."

"Me neither," said Miyagi, hurrying off.

Miyagi found the superintendent in the inspector's office. The short, slender man in his mid-sixties had his hands clasped behind his back and was pacing up and down impatiently while Ito, standing by the window, looked on impassively.

"We were waiting for you," Ito said. "The superintendent wants to be updated on our progress. Let's go to the incident room."

Three uniformed officers were tapping away on typewriters in a room lined with filing cabinets and glass-fronted cupboards filled with books and folders. Strips of fluorescent ceiling lights brightly illumined a space crowded with tables, chairs, phones, and a fax machine. The men stood as Ito, Miyagi, and Takenaka entered, bowing as the inspector introduced the superintendent and ordered them to offer him any assistance they could.

"They are collating all the data we've collected," Ito explained.

A large whiteboard in the corner bore photos of Kaori Hirakata and her family and one of Hiroki Sato, with pertinent information about the individuals scribbled beside the pictures, as well as a timeline of events. Another whiteboard had significant locations marked on a map of Murota, including the location of the Hirakata's house in the wealthy Kitaguchi district to the north of the town, Mrs. Goto's house nearby, and a black X marked the spot where Kaori Hirakata's father was shot twelve years earlier. Mr. Hirakata's firm, Emi Tada's bank, and the boutique where the victim had worked were at the center of town. Hiroki Sato's house was to the south, along with Emi Tada's, in the vicinity of the insalubrious district known as Soaplands.

The superintendent approached the two boards and studied them, the overhead light glinting on his thick, black-rimmed glasses.

Ito instructed Miyagi. "Get the inspector a desk. Then give him all the statements."

"Statements?" said Takenaka, pricking up his ears and looking eager.

"Once you've read them, I'll expect you back in my office, sir, so that we can discuss the case," Ito said, bowing as he exited.

Ito returned to his office, feeling restless. Even the routine paperwork he needed to finish couldn't calm him down. Miyagi brought him a large mug of black coffee, but the inspector couldn't drink it in peace. He'd just taken his third sip when he heard a brusque knock on the door, and the superintendent burst in, carrying a stack of files.

He can't have read them all! the chief inspector thought, irritated at being disturbed so soon.

Takenaka settled himself heavily in one of the chairs in front of the inspector's desk, his thick black brows vivid against the pallor of his face. Clutching the files, he gave the inspector a gloomy look.

"I see you and your team have been hard at work, Inspector Ito. Before I comment on these statements, I'd like to hear your own ideas about the progress of this case."

"First, I need to apprise you of the most recent development, sir. My apologies. I should have told you about it before I took you to the incident room."

The superintendent raised one of those eyebrows that reminded Ito of black caterpillars.

Ito looked at his watch. It was four o'clock. It felt like the day had been going on forever, but every day seemed endless since Kaori Hirakata was pronounced dead of thallium poisoning. It was one task after another—people to question, avenues to explore. And none of it had brought them any closer to finding her killer.

"Sir," Ito said, now regretting his omission keenly, "at approximately 2:30 this afternoon, a journalist from Tokyo named Koji Yanagihara, employed by *The Nippon Daily*, was attacked near the Hirakata household, badly beaten by an individual he identifies as a probable member of a *yakuza* gang. You'll remember him, sir. He was at the press conference you held."

Ito nodded at Miyagi, standing in the corner. "My lieutenant and I have just returned from questioning him at the hospital."

Surprised, Takenaka loosened his grip on the files, and they tumbled to the floor, with Miyagi rushing over to pick them up. "Astonishing!" Takenaka said. "Then we need to explore the possibility of a link between the murder of Kaori Hirakata and the *yakuza* attack on her father twelve years ago."

"It's not necessarily a direct link, sir," said Ito. "As you've doubtless noticed, sir, the file on Hiroki Sato details how he joined a gang in Tokyo—whether he ever left it is unclear—and it's rumored he may have hooked up with the *yakuza* in Murota on returning here. As I've mentioned before, I think it's possible someone may have anonymously given the box of chocolates to *him*. How or for what reason, I don't know. Perhaps the *yakuza* got wind of his plan to run away with his girlfriend and wanted to stop him. Or maybe they worried he'd divulge secrets if he got away from Japan. If that was the case, he would appear to have been the intended victim, and it was a matter of chance he gave them to Kaori Hirakata as a present."

"Chance? I'd say it was luck," the superintendent said. "Terrible luck for that pretty young woman." He paused. "Yes, I remember you proposing that theory. I thought little of it then, and I'm not sure I think much more of it now." He shrugged, adding, "Please refresh my memory. Were any fingerprints on the box retrieved?"

"Only Kaori Hirakata's and Hiroki Sato's."

"Did you have Sato's on file?"

"No, sir, but as you'll recall, your forensics team got them from objects we took from Sato's work locker." The inspector swiveled restlessly on his office chair and, lifting a hand, rumpled his black hair threaded with gray into a crest. "As for the box of chocolates, it's one of the most expensive brands currently on sale. Two shops in town stock them, but it has proved impossible to determine who might have purchased the box in question or when. The bag the box of chocolates was in was one of the plain white plastic bags used in every store in town."

The superintendent took the files Miyagi had picked up and was holding out to him.

Tapping them, he said, "I see you've interviewed the victim's family, her friends, her co-workers, and people at the church she attended. Based on those accounts, it seems she was universally liked. I can see no motive for her murder."

"I agree, sir," said Ito.

"That's why I'm inclined to think there must be a *yakuza* connection. That attack on the girl's father. Coincidence? Or perhaps it's as you've suggested—that Sato was the intended victim." The superintendent paused and added, "In any case, I'll confess there was something about Iwao Hirakata's case that didn't ring true."

Ito felt his face redden. Every word the superintendent uttered was like a stone dropping on his heart, crushing his spirit. He agreed. The memory of it had long haunted him. He considered it his greatest failure.

Relief from his gloomy reflections came from an unlikely source. The door suddenly burst open. "There's been another attack," an officer said, rushing in. "Hiroki Sato's uncle has been found on his boat, stabbed. He's been taken to the hospital."

The inspector dispatched two officers to the fishing port to secure the crime scene while Miyagi drove him and Takenaka to the hospital. The same receptionist he and Miyagi had met an hour earlier greeted them at the desk. But then the scenario changed. Rather than summoning a nurse to take them to the patient, she rang a doctor, who appeared in a white coat splattered with blood.

"You can't question him," he said, looking distraught and waving aside the police identification the officers showed him. He pointed to the accident and emergency room down a narrow hall. "He's in there, fighting for his life."

"Will he make it?" the superintendent asked.

The doctor shrugged and rushed off.

The officers got back in their car and hurried to the port. One of the two officers dispatched earlier was keeping guard over the uncle's boat. The other was standing on the pier, speaking to a wrinkled, white-haired man in a yellow fishing jacket and a peaked cap, who introduced himself as Shinosuke Fujiwara. He explained his boat occupied the berth next to Hiroki's uncle and that they were old friends.

"Someone attacked him!" the old man burst out, unable to restrain himself when he saw the inspector. "I sensed trouble as soon as I saw that creep wearing a suit, sunglasses, and a mask. He strolled down the pier, as cool as a cucumber, and boarded Itsuki's boat. A little while later, I heard a scream."

Shinosuke Fujiwara walked to the edge of the pier, leaned over, and spat into the sea. "I'm old! Too slow, too weak to stop that thug who then got off the boat and walked off as slowly as if he had all the time in the world. I ran over to the boat and saw Itsuki on the deck in a pool of blood. I hurried ashore and rang for an ambulance, then called you. Meanwhile, I could still see that creep. He was at the end of the pier. Like I said, he was in no hurry. He even stopped, looked back, and gave me a wave. The nerve!"

"Do you have any idea why Itsuki Beppu was attacked?"

"Revenge! Because he took his nephew to Busan a week ago, after that girl got killed. Itsuki told me he was going to do it, then he did. But I suppose you know that already. He mentioned his police interview to me."

Fujiwara puffed up his reddened cheeks and let out a loud exhalation. "That means you also know Hiroki Sato had *yakuza* links. I imagine those thugs wanted to hurt my friend for the fun of it—and as payback for him helping his nephew escape their clutches."

Noticing the old man was tottering as if in shock, the inspector escorted him back to his boat and insisted he sit on the sole chair on deck.

"I've known Hiroki Sato since he was a boy," he said, looking up at the officers standing in front of him, Miyagi scribbling as usual in his notebook. "He's a good kid, but took a wrong turn when he went to Tokyo. I can tell you his uncle was horrified when he learned the boy had joined a gang. But the kid's not stupid. It didn't take him long to realize he'd made a mistake. Still, it wasn't soon enough for those horrible goons he'd mixed up with. Once they get their claws in, they don't want to let go. I knew that the jerk on the pier was a *yakuza*. Knew he was trouble."

The old man sighed. "But I didn't think that he'd hurt my friend so bad." He looked up piteously. "How is he? I tried to stop the bleeding, but it just kept pouring out."

It was only when the old man lifted a hand to brush off his jacket that Ito noticed red speckles gleaming on its yellow surface: blood.

In the patrol car, Ito heard the news he'd been dreading but expecting. He and the superintendent sat in the back, remaining silent while Miyagi drove them to the station. It was already getting dark, and the thick lenses of Takenaka's glasses glinted in the light from the streetlamps they passed. He looked thoughtful, as if trying to make up his mind. Finally, he spoke.

"Inspector Ito, I need to inform you—most reluctantly—that I have decided I must take charge of this case myself. It's taken on dimensions that I think are beyond the reach of a local police force like yours. I know you've already contacted the South Korean police. But I have international contacts I can draw on to widen our search for Hiroki Sato. I also plan to lean on local informants and ones in Tokyo with links to the *yakuza* to identify the individual or individuals who attacked the journalist and Hiroki Sato's uncle. Conceivably, it was the same person."

Takenaka laid a consolatory hand on the chief inspector's arm. "Don't blame yourself or your officers. Naturally, as the head of the prefectural force, I have a greater range of influence and greater resources at my disposal." He paused, adding, "I'm very sorry. As I've indicated, I appreciate the hard work you and your team have put in on this case so far. It will be invaluable to us as we proceed."

A depression so intense he couldn't manage a word in response seized Ito. He gazed, unseeing, at the blur of shops, pachinko parlors, and gas stations passing by and wondered if he should submit his letter of resignation that night or the next morning. The timing wasn't important. The result would be the same. He'd lose the job he loved.

But he was too young to retire. He wondered if he could get a position locally that would utilize his talents. Perhaps he could head a security firm in Murota. Maybe the authorities would promote Miyagi and appoint him as the chief inspector in his place. Ito couldn't bear speculating about that possibility. He liked and respected his lieutenant. Miyagi was competent and loyal, but he wasn't leadership material.

Ito looked over at the superintendent. Takenaka had gone silent again, staring out the window, also lost in thought.

Ito felt he'd arranged his life badly. He'd married late and waited too long to have his first and only child. Now he was already nudging his mid-fifties and too old to begin again in a police force located anywhere else in the country. Ito knew he also needed to consider the financial angle. If he retired from the force in ten years, as he had always planned, he could expect a good pension. But leaving earlier would jeopardize all that, and he doubted that a security firm job would pay as well.

Shikata ga nai. It can't be helped. Then the car phone rang, rousing him from his reverie. Miyagi handed it to him.

Takenaka was looking at him expectantly when Ito finished the call and returned the phone to his lieutenant. "Itsuki Beppu—that is, Hiroki Sato's uncle—has just died."

"I was wondering about him," Takenaka said. "Wondering if I should charge him with aiding and abetting a fugitive from justice." He paused and looked out the window, adding coolly, "But now I needn't do anything about him at all."

A young woman's murder. The beating up of a hot-shot big-city journalist. A fisherman's pointless death. The spoiling of a police inspector's career. All in a day's work and none of it matters, Ito thought, looking out the window and seeing his own reflection in the glass. It's darkness for us all in the end, anyway. No, he'd have to stay on as chief inspector of the Murota police and get used to being thought a failure. That was the darkness he personally faced. *Shikata ga nai!* None of it could be helped.

Interval
September 1988-September 1998
Naturally, Ito did not know ten years would elapse before he'd get a second crack at solving the twin tragedies involving the Hirakata family.

After the Ishizaki force took over the case, Ito tried to stop thinking about it, relying on a monotonous routine to dull the pain. One day followed another, turning into weeks, months, and years. The Hirakata family moved to Tokyo after selling their house—which was left empty and neglected. The police never managed to trace Hiroki Sato. The man who attacked the journalist Koji Yanagihara slipped under the radar. Similarly, Hiroki's uncle's killer was never identified. The *yakuza*—both in Tokyo and the home-grown variety in Murota—had closed ranks, pulling up the drawbridge behind them.

As it turned out, Superintendent Takenaka, even with his superior manpower and resources and contacts, made little headway. Although Chief Inspector Ito had once felt he could never fully recover from the indignity of having his case taken from him, the periods of time in which he scarcely gave it a thought became longer and longer. Being human, he couldn't, however, help indulging in a guilty satisfaction—*schadenfreude*, he learned, was the German expression for it—that the Ishizaki police had done no better than his own, much smaller force in solving the mystery of the young woman killed by poisoned chocolates.

No arrests were made. Gradually, people stopped talking about the case.

The chief inspector occasionally heard news of the Hirakata family. Aki had joined his sister in London, and the parents were alone and lonely, suffering from ill health in their small flat in the big city. Years later, he learned Aki had returned to Japan, the parents died, and eventually Yumi came back as well to work as a journalist in Tokyo.

The bad luck Ito felt they'd introduced into his life seemed to dissipate with their departure from Murota.

He was only occasionally reminded of the Hirakatas' existence. Once, he happened to be in the exclusive Kitaguchi district and couldn't resist peeping over the wall at the property. The house needed painting, and the garden was an overgrown wilderness. The cousin who'd bought it was letting it go to ruin, but perhaps that was for the best. Ito deplored his superstitiousness but couldn't help feeling it was an ill-omened place.

Other cases occupied Ito's mind. Miyagi proved invaluable in helping him curb the activities of a local *bosozoku* gang who'd made central Murota unpleasant and potentially dangerous with their threatening behavior and noisy bikes thundering down its streets every night. The receptionist, Miss Hino, resisted her parents' attempts to persuade her into an arranged marriage. Declaring she valued her independence and enjoyed having a career, she bought her own apartment and seemed happy enough, working at the station and baking pastries for Lieutenant Miyagi, who continued his trajectory of premature aging by developing a stoop. Ito's wife found a new lease on life by joining twice-weekly tea ceremonies at a local community center, and his daughter got promoted at work and moved out.

A decade after the chief inspector felt at the lowest point of his professional life, Ito was anticipating the prospect of retirement. But he found that he still had unfinished business with the Hirakata family. And they had some with him.

CHAPTER FOUR

Aki Hirakata
Sunday 20 September 1998
Tokyo

"Damn!" Aki Hirakata said, slamming down the phone. He stared blankly into space, trying to take in what he'd heard when nausea seized him so suddenly and acutely that he just made it to the toilet in time. The vomiting came in bouts spaced two or three minutes apart and seemed to go on forever. He knelt, clinging to the toilet, racked by spasms. Finally, it was over, and he could breathe again. He stood shakily and tottered to the sink, splashing water over his face. Upturning a glass that he kept next to the sink, with the toothbrush and toothpaste that it held falling into the basin with a clatter, he filled it with water and drained it in great thirsty gulps.

He sighed and wiped his mouth with a towel hanging from a hook on the wall. Then he looked at himself in the mirror.

Aki supposed that, at twenty-one, others might describe him as a successful young man-about-town in Tokyo. He was self-employed, free-lancing as a commercial web designer. His services were highly sought after and lucratively remunerated. He kept a bachelor's flat in Shinjuku.

Still, it wasn't unusual for the string of casual girlfriends he attracted to tell him he had a haunted look. It's something that often happened after sex. Lying in bed, having post-coital cigarettes, Aki would feel relaxed and sated, as near happy as he ever got, and then the latest girl would spoil it all by looking at him with concerned eyes, asking if he was okay.

He'd laugh it off. Make a joke of it. He didn't bother telling them that no, he wasn't okay and probably never would be. This self-diagnosis was reinforced whenever he looked in a mirror and saw his own twitchy eyes, the pallor of his face and its faintly lined forehead, his anxious expression. But it was no wonder if he looked like he'd just seen a ghost. He'd been living with one for the past ten years, ever since he was eleven, and his big sister Kaori had ended up dead, poisoned by some chocolates she'd eaten.

What a stupid way to die! And, as the saying goes, it couldn't have happened to a nicer person. As far as Aki was concerned, the wonder was what girls saw in him, how they could be sufficiently attracted (as many seemed to be) to engage in intimate relations with a man who seemed to have the ability to see things—spirits, wraiths—that were invisible to their own eyes. When he felt depressed, Aki wondered if he attracted girls drawn to the broken and the damned. He believed he could never find peace or happiness until he found his sister's killer and understood the reason behind her murder. Was it Hiroki Sato, the principal suspect, who hadn't been seen since the night Kaori died? Everything pointed to his guilt, but sometimes Aki had his doubts. Kaori had been sweet and kind, but she was no push-over. It was hard to believe she could have fallen in love with a man capable of murdering her.

Aki turned away from his reflection. He hated looking at himself, seeing that gaunt face dominated by haunted eyes. And that phone call had made it all worse. It had brought everything back. No wonder he'd had to puke his guts out. Aki slumped down on the floor, overwhelmed by memories.

Aki could say in all honesty that he'd thought about Kaori every day since he'd run into her room and found her writhing in agony on the floor, coughing as if she'd never stop. His parents had added to the horror as they pounded up the stairs and made ineffectual attempts to help Kaori, looking at each other aghast.

They'd been so caught up in the drama they hadn't even thought to summon help. Mrs. Goto, the neighbor he'd pitied and patronized as a little boy, had performed that important function. He'd dismissed her as a fluffy old woman but had to revise that estimate that night. Once she'd thrown open the front door, stumbled up the stairs, and seen Kaori, she'd kept her wits admirably, hurrying back down as fast as her rheumatism allowed to make a beeline for the phone in the hall and call for an ambulance.

A scenario along the lines of what had happened that night often figured in his dreams—nightmares, rather—which he had on a disturbingly regular basis.

Aki sighed. It wasn't right to think only of the bad things. His memories of Kaori weren't always terrible ones. He smiled weakly, remembering his many happy moments with the sister he adored.

As a toddler and little boy, she'd been his second mother, one often preferable to *Okaasan,* who never seemed to have time or inclination to play with him and rarely showed him affection. He loved how Kaori looked and even how she smelled—she seemed to give off the sweet perfume of the peach nectar she was so fond of. It was Kaori who read him stories, applauded his first steps, taught him how to tie his shoelaces, and helped him with his homework.

Aki loved Yumi, too, but he knew she was like him—not an angel but a selfish human being—imperfect and flawed. He guessed it was an urge for self-preservation that had led to her leaving the family in her late teens to seek a new life in England, becoming an au pair with a family who lived in Golders Green and growing so close to the parents she even called them Mum and Dad. She never returned to Japan in the four years between her departure and Kaori's murder, although her mother paid a brief visit to London once. Yumi returned for her twin sister's funeral, but Aki thought that did not excuse her abandonment of family responsibilities for all those years.

He could barely bring himself to speak to Yumi during her brief visit home.

Shortly after interring Kaori's ashes in the family grave in the cemetery on the outskirts of Murota, Aki and his parents moved to Tokyo. Aki hated the thought of having to settle into a new school where he'd need to make new friends, but that was preferable to staying in the family home with its associations. He also wanted to escape from little Murota, where people pointed at him and gossiped about his being a member of an ill-fated family.

The place near Ueno Park *Otoosan* bought for them was nice enough. After the unwelcome notoriety in Murota, they craved anonymity, and that's what they got in a small flat in a high rise in a city of thirty-four million. But Aki missed Murota's easy access to the sea and the mountains, the luxury of having a huge garden on the doorstep and open countryside only a short walk away. His Tokyo bedroom was small, and he felt claustrophobic. Sometimes he'd go out on the balcony just to take deep breaths.

He got into an excellent school, one that placed such an emphasis on academic achievement that his classmates were too busy trying to keep up with homework and exams to take any interest in the new boy's previous life. Aki felt he was coping. But six months into his new life, he stopped sleeping at night, lost his appetite, and then fainted one morning on the subway. The doctor diagnosed post-traumatic stress disorder and advised a complete change of scenery.

That's when Yumi came back into her brother's life. After receiving distressed calls from her parents, she flew to Japan and urged them to let her take the boy back with her to London. Her English hosts would take him in for a few months. They had a spare bedroom, and would welcome him warmly.

Yumi! Making his way to the living room to collapse on the sofa after he'd spewed up everything he could have eaten in the past week, Aki thought of the great debt of gratitude he owed her. When Kaori died, he thought he hated Yumi. But she ended up saving him. Yumi carried out all her promises to their parents. She arranged his enrollment in a local school and the Japanese one he'd attend on Saturdays. She tutored him in English and helped him make friends. Most importantly, she became his best friend, just as he became hers.

The two or three months originally envisaged for his stay in London spun into six years. Aki occasionally returned to Tokyo for a visit, but he was so fervent in begging to return to England that his parents conceded. Sometimes, his mother would weep, saying, "I've lost all my children!" while his father tried to comfort her.

Aki grimaced as he walked to the fridge to get a beer. Guilt. Remorse. Those feelings seemed to sum up his life since his sister's death—apart from the idyllic time in England, where he found liberation in living somewhere entirely different. Having to speak in an unfamiliar language and adjust to different customs helped him feel like a new person, one released from the grip of the past and its unhappy memories.

But the guilt! Aki blamed himself for his parents' untimely deaths. When he was seventeen, he'd returned to Tokyo for good, having left Japan as a child and come back as a self-reliant young man. His parents wanted to spoil him, but he felt too old, independent, and cynical to play along. Then, they'd both died within two years, and there was no chance left to make amends.

"Damn! Damn! Damn!"

Aki slumped onto his sofa. He'd never wanted to see Murota again, but now it seemed he had to. The call that had made him so sick was from the woman he'd grown up calling *Obachan*—his cousin Mrs. Muraji—in which she insisted he come back to collect his belongings from his old house. Aki decided to call Yumi. But first, he needed to fortify himself. He knew it would be an ordeal.

"Damn. Damn." Aki drained his can of beer and went to the fridge to get another.

Aggie Snow and Rhoda Ellison

As Aki Hirakata was agonizing over the prospect of returning to his old family home, the American girl his cousin had rented it to was just moving in. Her university had enlisted a Canadian part-timer to show her around.

"I hope Mrs. Muraji had the courtesy to tell you somebody died here!" Aggie Snow said to Rhoda Ellison as they stood in the overgrown front garden of a large white house surrounded by high stone walls. It was a two-story dwelling with a long balcony on the second floor and a large camphor tree standing to the left of the front door. On the right was a thick vine that wound up the wall to a balcony on the second floor. It looked like a child's drawing of a house—two enormous blocks piled one on top of the other, demarcated by the balcony, and a flat roof topping it all.

"Somebody was *killed!*"

Rhoda gasped but the wiry little Canadian woman in her late fifties plowed on: "I mean, I hope she told you before she asked you to sign the rental contract."

There was a pause. Rhoda felt unable to speak.

"Ten years ago somebody gave Kaori Hirakata some chocolates that were laced with thallium."

"Thallium?"

"It is a lethal poison that's colorless and tasteless and can dissolve in water."

Another pause.

"I signed. I didn't know," Rhoda finally said. "Nobody told me. Did they find out who did it?"

"There was a suspect named Hiroki Sato, but he vanished. If you want to know what he looks like, go to any post office. They'll have a picture of him posted prominently on a wall along with the other unsavory individuals on Japan's 'Most Wanted' list. Of course, that photo was taken a decade ago. Maybe it's not a good likeness now."

Rhoda looked curiously at her new home, the large white building that loomed up behind the overgrown garden, thinking it resembled Sleeping Beauty's castle—neglected and smothered by weeds and brambles.

"But I've heard Japan is very safe," Rhoda murmured.

"It is. *It is!*" Aggie said. "That murder was very unusual."

"Why didn't anybody tell me?!"

"I knew Mrs. Muraji wouldn't say anything, but the college should have."

Rhoda looked around and whistled. "I can't understand how Mrs. Muraji can even *own* this place!" she said, thinking of the woman who had given her the key only half an hour before. She was an exhausted-looking old woman with thinning dyed black hair fixed into a tiny bun who lived in a shabby place a few blocks away. "The house has seen better days, but somebody rich must have lived here," said Rhoda. "And it must still be worth a lot."

"Somebody rich did," Aggie said. "Mr. Hirakata. He had the house built to his own specifications." She frowned. "But all that money didn't do him or his family much good."

The sun was beating down, and Rhoda felt beads of sweat trickling down her back. She was relieved when Aggie said, "Let's sit for a minute before we go in the house. Steel ourselves for the ordeal."

A stone bench was beside a dried-up fountain in the center of the garden. Rhoda lifted a hand to shade her eyes. It was so bright! Luckily, a Japanese maple gave some shade.

"I think this is where the carp pond used to be," Aggie said, peering at a dusty circle on the ground.

Once they were seated, Rhoda asked, "So, what's the story? What's the link between Mrs. Muraji and the Hirakawas? I can't imagine she could have afforded to buy this place from them."

"Hirakatas. Mrs. Muraji was Mrs. Hirakata's cousin. After the tragedy, the Hirakatas left Murota, never to return. Went to Tokyo, and both parents died a few years ago. From what I've heard, they sold the cousin this place for the proverbial song, wanting nothing more to do with it."

"Because..." Rhoda said.

"I thought you understood. Remember? I said the victim was a young woman named Kaori Hirakata—one of their daughters. I think she was in her early twenties. The other daughter was in England, and they had a boy who went to Tokyo with them."

Aggie pursed her lips. "It's just what I expected," she said. "They wouldn't have told you anything because they were desperate to get you accommodation. This is near the university and cheap. Maybe they even told Mrs. Muraji to keep quiet, too."

"She doesn't seem to speak any English, so she couldn't have warned me even if she wanted to."

Rhoda stared at the statue of the little boy at the center of the fountain. His handsome features and stone curls were grimy. Two tiny plump hands clasped a large urn with a fountain nozzle inside, poised to pour its contents into the basin below. But the basin was cracked, and instead of water, it cradled a nest of dead leaves and twigs.

The occasional slap of hands hitting arms and legs broke the silence as the two women tried to ward off the cloud of mosquitoes that enveloped them as soon as they'd sat down. The buzz of cicadas sheltering in garden bushes and in the big old camphor tree at the front of the house filled the air.

"How do you know all this?" Rhoda finally asked.

"I know the poor murdered girl's best friend. Her name is Emi Tada. I got friendly with her when I needed to transfer money to Canada. Emi works at the bank and speaks excellent English. We're friends. Emi is one of the few Japanese friends I have who speaks English so well it doesn't feel like I'm being used as a teacher."

Aggie pulled her hat brim down further to shade her from the blazing sun before continuing. "That girl's murder happened ages ago. Like I said, ten years. This place has been unoccupied ever since. The family, understandably, moved away soon after. It's a mess, but poor old Muraji-*san* doesn't have the dough to keep it up."

Rhoda looked around. "Can't she sell?"

"Nobody would want to buy. This place has an evil reputation. The Japanese are superstitious. I've even heard local kids claim it's haunted by the dead woman's ghost."

Rhoda shuddered again. "But there's such a lot of land," she pointed out.

"Land's dirt cheap in this part of the country. Haven't you noticed all the orange groves gone to seed? All the derelict houses? If we were in Honshu, near a big city, a place like this with an enormous garden would be priceless. But here, it's got nearly no value at all. And like I said, people think it has bad karma."

Aggie smiled, obviously feeling it was her duty to cheer Rhoda up. "But you're lucky. You're only a short walk from campus and from the center of town."

Rhoda didn't reply. She couldn't imagine feeling lucky to live in a place that now reminded her of a mausoleum.

Aggie stood. "Let's go in. Get it over with."

Aggie insisted Rhoda open the front door with the key Mrs. Muraji gave her. "It's rusty. We need to make sure it works. And you need to be capable of using it." On entering the *genkan*, they saw a shoe cupboard on the right with an old rotary dial phone on top and a glass case housing a Japanese doll.

Stepping up, they took the first door to the left of the hallway and entered a large, dark room. Aggie went to the floor-length French windows and pulled back some thick drapes.

"The living room," she announced. When she poked one wall, a cloud of dust rose, then trickled down to form a tiny sand pyramid on the carpeted floor.

"It beats me why the Japanese like interior walls made of this stuff," Aggie said. "I guess it's nostalgia. It's a material that mimics the finish of the old traditional Japanese house, made of wattle and mud. But it's so damned dusty!" She took off her hat and threw herself into a large gray armchair, her body so small she looked swallowed up in it, Rhoda thought. Aggie fanned her face with one hand and looked around. "The place time forgot," she said.

Rhoda shuddered, half expecting a ghostly Hirakata to enter and demand they leave. The room contained a complete set of furniture, featuring a plush gray sofa that coordinated with the two big gray armchairs on the other side of the low coffee table. Reproductions of Impressionist paintings covered the walls. Rhoda inspected two fancy glass-plated bookcases, noting a few English books inside. A piano was in one corner and a big old TV in another.

Then she strolled over to an imitation marble fireplace. A bouquet of dried flowers in a large vase stood on the hearth. Another vase, empty, was on the mantelpiece. She blew on the mantelpiece, stirring up a cloud of dirt that made her sneeze. Apart from the heavy layering of dust on the furniture, carpet, curtains, and cobwebs in the corners of the ceiling, the room could scarcely have changed since the family had abandoned it all those years ago, she thought. Decades-old magazines were scattered on the coffee table, looking faded and limp.

"Let's open the windows," Aggie suggested. Standing, she unlocked the big French windows with their view of the front garden and slid them open, letting in a blast of hot air and amplifying the volume of the cicadas singing outside.

"Wait, it was a wealthy family that used to live here. They probably had an air conditioner," she said. Aggie looked around, then darted over to a large brown boxy machine above the piano and pushed a few buttons. It creaked and groaned but suddenly whirred into life. Some tattered red ribbons tied to its vents trembled and then fluttered in a brisk current of cold air.

"*Thank God!*" Rhoda thought, positioning herself directly in front of the sudden gush of wind while Aggie closed the windows.

When they went off to inspect the rest of the house, they closed off the living room to keep it as a cool sanctuary they could return to. Next to the living room was a large space occupied by two tatami mat rooms partially divided by paper walls. Rhoda felt ill. It was dark and almost suffocatingly hot. Aggie rushed over to yank open the heavy drapes covering floor-to-ceiling windows. Once she'd got the windows open, bright sunshine and the chirping of cicadas flooded the space, and Rhoda noticed the room they were standing in was almost empty apart from a pile of cushions next to a low table in one corner. In the other room, a row of portrait photos hung high on a wall beside a large piece of furniture whose purpose she couldn't fathom. Curious, Rhoda wandered over to examine it. About six feet tall, it was a large, black lacquered cabinet that had its gilt-lined doors thrown open. A huge statue of a golden Buddha presided over two lower shelves crowded with lanterns, urns, incense burners, bells, and candles. A third shelf held a few cans of peach nectar.

"What's this?" she asked.

"A *butsudan*," Aggie said. "A Japanese Buddhist altar. But I'm surprised they had one. I've heard the parents converted to Christianity."

Rhoda inspected the photos. The women were tiny and wore kimonos; dressed in formal black jackets, the men had shocks of white hair and weather-beaten faces. The picture of a beautiful girl looked incongruous in such company. She was young, and they were old. She looked like a modern woman, while they seemed to occupy a distant past. With thick black hair that framed a heart-shaped face, her lips curled in a smile and her eyes gleamed as if gazing at a vision of happiness.

"That must be Kaori," Aggie said. "The young woman who was killed. The others must be grandparents."

"She was so gorgeous!" Rhoda said. "How awful!"

Aggie knelt on a large red and gold cushion positioned in front of the altar. Steepling her hands, she bent her head and prayed. Rising, she pointed to the cans of peach nectar. "That's the tradition," she said. "Putting out offerings of the dead person's favorite food. Kaori must have liked that drink." She wrinkled her nose. "Peach juice. It's too sweet for me. It tastes like liquid sugar."

Next, they inspected a huge, tiled bathroom with a tub sunk into the floor and a basin and stool positioned below a shower. "You know how to use a Japanese bathroom, don't you?" Aggie asked.

Rhoda nodded even though she didn't. She prided herself on being self-reliant and hated having to ask for assistance or explanations. Still, she couldn't suppress a shriek when she saw a huge black spider darting up the wall of the adjacent utility room, with its washer and dryer, and disappearing behind a ventilation fan.

"That spider was as big as my *hand!*" she stuttered, shocked.

Aggie laughed. "You'll get used to them," she said. "They're completely harmless, as afraid of you as you are of them."

Rhoda shook her head. "Never."

After examining the kitchen, they made their way upstairs.

"When do you actually move in?" Aggie asked once they'd ascended the narrow staircase to inspect the four bedrooms and smaller bathroom on the second floor.

"The day after tomorrow. That means just two more nights at the university guesthouse. I'm glad. I hate the lack of privacy there. Two secretaries in the office have been friendly. They said they'll drive me here with my luggage and bring a vacuum cleaner, mops, brushes, and rags to help me clean this place."

"It's very kind of them," Aggie said. "But it really is too bad! Muraji-*san* should have warned the Hirakatas ages ago that she planned to rent out the property, and that they needed to remove personal items before the first tenant moved in. *You!* She should also have cleaned and aired this place thoroughly. She has done none of that."

Standing in the largest of the four bedrooms, Aggie looked around appraisingly. "Have you heard if the family intends to come back? Collect some of their things?"

"One secretary told me somebody might come in a few days," Rhoda said. "I'd get to keep the furniture and kitchen things."

Aggie walked down a long hallway and through a door into a large room, noting that it was at the front of the house. It shared a balcony with the adjacent bedroom, which had apparently belonged to Kaori, and was shaded by the big camphor tree beside the front door. "I suppose this was the parents' room," she said.

The room gave the impression that it had only recently been vacated, except for the dust and strong musty smell. A yellow quilt decorated with embroidered flowers covered a double bed, and a framed picture sat on a handsome chest of drawers. Rhoda picked it up and held it to the light.

It was obvious that the photo was taken at a professional photographer's studio. A middle-aged couple sat on a sofa with a boy between them. Behind them stood two young women Rhoda guessed were in their early twenties, with a noticeable disparity in their heights and attractiveness. The girl with a calm expression on a plain but intelligent-looking face towered over the other, the pretty one Rhoda recognized from the funeral picture near the family altar downstairs.

Aggie appeared beside her, peering at the photo. "It must be the Hirakata family," she said. "They had twin daughters and then, over ten years later, a boy."

"The girls don't look alike," Rhoda said.

"Fraternal twins, not identical."

"An attractive family," Rhoda said.

"And they look happy!" Aggie said. "The good old days. Before the tragedy." She unlocked the latch of the big window opening onto the balcony.

"This place is so secluded!" Rhoda said as they stood holding the railing, looking down at the thick vine twisting up the wall and at the garden. "There's only that one big house nearby."

Aggie squinted at the place Rhoda had pointed out. "It belongs to an old woman named Mrs. Goto," she said. "She must have been in her early eighties when Kaori Hirakata died. It's possible she's still alive, still living there. She gave evidence at the inquest."

Aggie sighed. "As you say, this place is secluded. It's a rich, exclusive neighborhood. That old woman didn't see the attack, just heard screaming and hurried over to help."

"You say the case was never solved?"

"They thought her boyfriend, a local boy named Hiroki Sato, killed her. A complete loser from all accounts. But he went missing that day and no one has seen him since. Rumor has it he fled to South Korea. And that he had links with the *yakuza*."

Aggie grimaced. "Or maybe he just felt guilty and threw himself off a cliff!"

Reentering the house, they chose the smallest of the four bedrooms as the most suitable for Rhoda. With its baseball pennants on the wall and large posters of Japanese football players, it must have belonged to the son.

"I like this one best because it's the most impersonal," Rhoda said. "No knickknacks. No dressing tables. No mirrors. I also like the fact it doesn't have a balcony. I'd worry about some intruder climbing up that huge vine into my room."

"You've watched too many stupid American crime dramas," said Aggie. "I'd choose the son's because it's near the upstairs bathroom. Anyway, it needs a good cleaning, like the rest of the house."

"Do you think I should ask Mrs. Muraji if it's okay if I make changes?"

"Not if you're just moving furniture and things. You'd only confuse and worry the poor old woman. Anyway, as I've said, you don't owe her any favors."

After Aggie had gone, Rhoda wandered about the house. "Home sweet home," she said half ironically.

Aki and Yumi Hirakata

"Aki!" Yumi said, picking up her phone. She'd said his name brightly, but then her voice descended half a scale and took on a note of exaggerated sadness as she added, "I've been expecting your call."

"Aren't you being a bit melodramatic?" Aki said, surprising himself with a laugh. He'd felt depressed ever since his cousin had rung, asking him and Yumi to return to Murota to help clear out their old home.

"But it's too awful that you have to go back to sort out our things," Yumi said. "I feel guilty. I'm so glad you've agreed. I should go with you, but..." And then she laughed, saying, "I don't want to!"

As she spoke, Aki had a disloyal thought that shocked him. If one of his sisters had to die, perhaps it was better it was Kaori. His relationship with her would always have been one of subservience—he adored her while always feeling daunted because she was so kind and good. She'd permitted him to act childishly. Maybe if he'd stayed so attached to her, he'd never have grown up. Perhaps it was as well she was an angel who'd returned earlier than expected to her home in heaven. With Yumi, it was a bond of equals. One of the unexpected bonuses of the time they'd spent together in England was Aki's discovery they had a similar sense of humor. Another was that the sister he'd always found distant and unapproachable when he was younger had become his soul mate. Yumi criticized and teased him. She wouldn't permit the selfishness he'd indulged in with Kaori.

"How long will you stay?"

"I'll take a train there on Sunday morning and stay three nights," Aki said. "Any advice?"

"Only take a few things," Yumi said. "Let's move on. The past is past."

"But it's so odd to think of a stranger living in our house and using our things," Aki said.

"Better to have somebody. It's pointless to have the place molder away."

"I suppose I thought *Obasan* would sell it. Or that she'd have the building demolished and something new put up."

"All that would require much more energy and enterprise than our cousin has ever possessed," Yumi said. "Anyone who could have married the loser she ended up with can't have the slightest bit of get-up-and-go."

"Why did our parents ever sell it to her?" Aki said. "And for next to nothing?"

"I've told you a million times. I don't know why you can't take it in. They wanted to forget everything about their old life in Murota, break any ties with it," Yumi said. "Understandably."

There was a pause, and then Yumi added, "Which is what we need to do now. And why I want you to be completely ruthless. Of course, leave that poor American girl anything useful. But throw away our old clothes, any furniture that looks dodgy, things like that. Just save a few mementos—photos and letters. Box them up and send them back to Tokyo."

Another pause.

"Can you forgive me for not going with you?"

"Yes, it's a hassle, but I've just finished a big project and have a little space in my schedule before I need to begin the next one. Being a freelancer has its advantages. I can work anywhere. You're the one who has to turn up at an office every day." He sighed. "When *Obasan* called me this morning, I got the distinct impression she was enjoying herself. There was a horrible satisfaction in her voice when she said I had to come and collect anything we wanted, or she'd throw it away."

"It's her revenge. We patronized her all those years as the poor feckless relative who married a loser. She finally has the upper hand."

"I never liked her."

"Me, neither."

"I'm so glad you've come back to Japan to live."

"Me, too."

"And by the way, I'm your brother. Remember? You can't hide anything from me. You've got a new boyfriend. Right? That's why you're so cheerful and so reluctant to leave Tokyo, even for a few days."

"I'm not talking to you. You're too ridiculous," Yumi said, hanging up.

Yumi smiled, startled at Aki's perceptiveness. It was true. She had met somebody who made her happy. But no, that wasn't quite accurate. She'd recently got in touch again with somebody who'd once made her happy and might do so again. They'd first met in England four years earlier, and now he had moved to Tokyo.

His name was Tetsuya Kataoka, and she'd got to know him shortly after Aki had returned to Japan for good. Yumi had accompanied her brother to Heathrow and then spent a few days in London, staying with her old host family in Golders Green. She'd gone to the National Gallery and was loitering in a room devoted to the Pre-Raphaelites when she noticed a young, good-looking Asian man standing near her.

"Do you admire this kind of painting?" he'd asked in curiously accented English.

"Yes, very much. Even though all the women have such long, thick, wavy hair and dreamy expressions that they don't look quite human," she said automatically, her mind preoccupied with the question of his nationality. Taiwanese? Korean? Chinese?

"I agree, but they're beautiful. In case you're wondering, I'm Japanese."

Yumi sighed with relief. "Me, too," she said in her own language. Sometimes she hated having to speak English.

It turned out he was a manga artist. His work hadn't reached mainstream status, but he already had a devoted following in Southeast Asia and the States. She was glad he was talented and ambitious. A year into her studying for a journalism degree, she'd realized she was, too.

Yumi later wondered if it was loneliness that led to her falling for the first suitable man she met once Aki was gone. Maybe, but she knew it was probably also a desperate longing for the consolation of love to assuage the pain of imminent loss. On arriving back in Tokyo, Aki had found both their parents seriously ill. *Okaasan* had breast cancer and *Otoosan* was diagnosed with heart disease. They were both dead within two years, with *Okaasan* going first.

Aki had asked her to help him take care of their parents, but Yumi made one excuse after another for not returning—she was busy writing her journalism dissertation, she was getting to grips with the job she'd got at a local newspaper, she was preoccupied with her new romance, she was short of money. *No, that won't wash*, she later realized. It had been selfishness, an aversion to suffering. She'd gone back for the funerals, but that wasn't good enough. She should have returned for a visit while her mother was still alive. Of course, she'd spent time with her father after *Okaasan's* funeral, but he was too stricken with grief at the loss of his wife to register her presence fully.

It was poetic justice. Or karma. Yumi had tried to avoid pain in her personal life, but destiny caught up with her after she'd met that compatriot—the manga artist who shared her admiration for Rossetti's paintings. She came to love Tetsuya, and the two spent most of their free time together, juggling the logistics of his living in London and her in Manchester. Still, Yumi began to chafe at his secretiveness. She hated how he could be so mysterious, giving so little of himself. He refused to speak of his past. He was multilingual, speaking several languages besides Japanese, but wouldn't explain when or how he'd learned them. He had odd quirks like insisting on complete darkness when they made love, explaining— improbably, she thought—that one of his little idiosyncrasies was that he was abnormally shy, reluctant for her to see him naked. The lovemaking was mutually satisfying, but she grew increasingly frustrated by his reserve.

After being approached by a good newspaper in London that wanted to hire her, Yumi knew she needed to decide about her future. She decided she wanted to return to Japan. Putting an ocean between her and Tetsuya felt like a means of self-preservation, a way to escape the anguish she'd begun to feel in his presence. At least she now had a means of supporting herself. She initially got a job at a small, locally run daily in Tokyo, but her work soon attracted the attention of the national papers. She had her heart set on *The Nippon Daily*. One of her heroes, Koji Yanagihara, a tall and distinguished gray-haired man in his fifties, interviewed her. He admitted he knew her family circumstances and had even written articles about her father and sister. He offered her a job on the spot.

Yumi Hirakata and Emi Tada

Emi Tada came to visit Yumi in Tokyo two days after she and Aki had been called by their cousin, insisting they clear out their old house. Emi had heard the news from Mrs. Muraji and rung Yumi, saying she needed to see her and her brother. She announced she'd got a day off work and would arrive at about one.

Yumi felt touched by Emi's intention to travel hundreds of miles to see her. It was obvious Emi understood she never wanted to return to Murota. Still, Yumi was surprised that Emi was taking the trouble. Emi had always been Kaori's friend, not hers. Also, she'd come by the bullet train, so her journey would not only take a considerable time—four hours one way—but cost a lot, too.

When Yumi opened the door, the appearance of the woman she had last seen ten years earlier at Kaori's funeral dismayed her. Although she was still in her early thirties, Emi dressed like a woman twice that age in an unbecoming long skirt and matching jacket. A bad cut gave her thick black hair a stiff, helmet-like appearance, framing her round face. She'd applied makeup so lavishly her face looked like a mask, leaving Yumi struggling to remember what Emi had looked like as the young girl who'd come so often to their house in Murota to play with Kaori.

Emi bowed deeply. Shuffling off her shoes, she stepped up into the slippers Yumi had left for her and placed a bag on the shoe cupboard and a big black purse. She turned to Yumi and bowed once again. "My apologies, dear Yumi-*san*," she said. "I'm so sorry I couldn't attend your parents' funerals. That's why I've come. To pay my respects."

Emi's tears inspired Yumi's. They silently processed through the large flat to the tatami mat room dominated by the *butsudan*. Yumi turned on the overhead lamps as Emi reverently gazed at three photographs hanging just above the big, elaborate wooden structure, its doors open to reveal shelves occupied by gilt ornaments, small statuettes, vases of fresh flowers, candles, and sticks of incense. The photos were of a distinguished-looking man in his early seventies, an attractive woman of roughly the same age with hair elaborately waved, and a young woman, unusually pretty, with a radiant smile on her face. Emi dropped to her knees, kneeling on the cushion in front of the shrine. She bowed her head, steepled her hands, and prayed. Meanwhile, Yumi lit the candles and the incense, then took her place beside Emi and prayed, too.

After several minutes had passed, Emi dropped her hands and rose slowly, smoothing down her skirt once she was standing. Yumi sighed, stood, too, and pointed to a can of peach nectar on the altar. "For Kaori."

Emi stifled a sob, then gazed up again at the funeral portraits, her eyes glistening with unshed tears. "Darling Kaori-*chan*. And your parents were always so kind to me, treating me almost like a daughter." Taking a handkerchief from a jacket pocket, she dabbed at her eyes. "I longed to come to Tokyo to see them, especially after I was told they'd both become ill. It was a great shock to hear of their deaths."

Her lower lip trembled as she gazed at Yumi. "Please forgive me. I should have come to at least one funeral. It's my mother. She began to suffer from dementia around that time, and I felt I couldn't get away. I only managed it today because a kind neighbor has promised to care for *Okaasan* while I'm gone." She grimaced. "For a fee, that is."

Emi looked at her watch. "You must remind me I need to leave by three. I'm booked on the four o'clock bullet train from Shinjuku Station. I promised I'd be home by nine."

Then she glanced around as if imagining Aki was hiding somewhere. "And your brother? Are you expecting him?"

Yumi felt a pang of compunction. She should have insisted Aki come. When she'd mentioned Emi Tada was intending to visit and wanted to see him, too, he'd refused. "Tell her I'm working that day," he'd said. "But give her my regards. Kaori loved her and Emi was always nice to me. Maybe I'll see her when I'm back in Murota next week."

"I'm so sorry," Yumi said. "He couldn't make it."

Emi's face fell. "How disappointing," she said. "I really hoped to see him."

Yumi felt she needed to offer comfort. She was relieved to see Emi brighten when she mentioned that her brother intended to visit her during his trip to Murota.

"Let's have tea," Yumi suggested, and she led the way to the living room, inviting Emi to sit on a sofa.

"Oh, dear, I'm afraid I'm going the way of my mother," Emi sputtered, looking upset again, glancing down at her empty hands. "Forgetting things! I left the little present I brought for you in the hallway. And my purse."

Yumi rushed out, found a pretty little pink bag holding a box on the shoe cupboard next to Emi's purse, and carried them to the living room. They seated themselves and Yumi slowly and carefully unwrapped the box. It was from the most expensive pastry shop in Ishizaki and contained individually wrapped butter sandwich cookies.

"I love these!" Yumi said, her face alight with anticipation. "I'll just get the tea."

She returned in a few minutes, bearing a tray weighted with delicate teacups and saucers decorated with flowers, a matching teapot, tiny spoons, sachets of sugar and a small jug of milk that she laid on a low table in front of the sofa.

Once they each had a steaming cup of tea and a cookie, Emi leaned back and gave a sigh of satisfaction.

"I'm so glad to see you again, dear Yumi-*san*," she said. "It's been far too long."

"I agree. I was away from Japan for so long. And now I'm here, it's inexcusable that I haven't returned to Murota to see old friends like you."

"I can imagine you dread the very thought of going back there," Emi said. "Considering what happened."

Yumi looked solemn. "You're quite right. But I don't have that excuse for Tokyo. I came back here for my parents' funerals, but I only managed a few days both times. My greatest regret is that I didn't return to spend time with them when they were alive. I will always feel guilty about shirking my family duties. You are admirable. I'm sure you're taking excellent care of your mother under what must be challenging circumstances."

"Sometimes, she doesn't even recognize me. She looks at me like I'm a stranger."

"Couldn't you put her in a care home?"

"I can't afford it. But even if I could, I'd find it hard to take that step. *Okaasan* took care of me when I was a child, making all kinds of sacrifices so I could have nice food and clothes. It's my turn to take care of her."

"As I say, I admire and respect you," Yumi said. "More tea?"

After they'd finished their second cup, Emi looked at her watch and said, "Now I must tell you something. It's the other reason I've come. But I'll have to hurry to catch my train."

"What is it?" Yumi said, curious.

"I wanted to warn Aki about what to expect when he returns to your old house. You probably know Mrs. Muraji simply shut it up after you left all those years ago. I imagine everything will be just as it was inside, but very dusty. I went by to have a look yesterday. When I peeked in at the front gate, I saw the garden is a wilderness, the windows are dirty, and the front wall of the house is cracked and stained."

"I'll tell Aki," Yumi promised.

"Another thing he should know is that Murota isn't the place it used to be. The mood has changed. Sometimes the town feels dangerous. Parents are more careful about sending their children out to play nowadays."

Yumi was looking down, her hands clasped on her lap. "Is that all?" she asked in a quiet voice.

"No, there's more! There was an attack on a young woman two months ago. She was jumped after she got off a bus near her home in the south of town. It was late at night, and the woman was walking down a deserted street. A man grabbed her and started dragging her towards some bushes, but she got away. She ran toward the first house she saw that had lit-up windows, banged on the door, and her attacker fled."

Yumi pressed her lips together, then repeated, "Is that all?"

"There's one more thing," Emi said, her face pale. "In the past six months some of us—people you know, like Juno-*sensei* and even the pastor's wife, Mrs. Nakagawa—have got poison-pen letters. We find these big white envelopes in our letter boxes. Inside are threatening messages made up of words cut from magazines and newspapers."

"Threats?"

Yumi watched as Emi's cheeks flushed. "And accusations. The ones I received said I hated my mother, that I mistreated her, and that I wanted her to die. They threatened to report me to the police if I didn't put money in a brown envelope and leave it in my letterbox. Juno-*sensei* wouldn't tell me what hers said, but I gather she was accused of some sexual perversion. I have no idea what the one the pastor's wife got said. Nowadays, whenever I see one of those big white envelopes in the post, I just crumple it up and put it with the other ones I got, hidden away in a drawer."

"Did you ever pay?"

"Once. One evening, I put a ten thousand yen note in an envelope like I'd been told to and left it in my letterbox. It was gone the next morning."

"The police don't know who's doing it?"

"No! After all, I did go to the station to report it, but they've been unable to find the culprit."

Yumi watched in horror as her old friend suddenly burst out crying. She sat helplessly as Emi sobbed and gasped, and finally recovered her composure. Holding a tissue to her reddened eyes, Emi said, "The terrible thing is, it's true. I *do* want my mother to die. I don't know how much more of it I can stand. She's like some whining child—always complaining, always demanding my attention. But a child will grow up and learn to behave. My mother will only get worse and worse."

Emi sniffed. "Fortunately, one accusation is incorrect. I haven't mistreated her." Then she rose, picking up her purse, suddenly in a hurry to leave. She stepped down to the *genkan* and slipped on her shoes, turning back to bow to Yumi. "Many thanks for your hospitality, Yumi-*san*."

Once Emi had gone, Yumi, who could scarcely be persuaded even to have a glass of wine with a meal, took a dusty bottle of whisky from a cupboard that she kept for visitors and poured herself a large drink. She had emptied half her glass when the phone rang.

"It's me!" Aki said. "I presume your guest has left already."

"Half an hour ago. And she was bitterly disappointed you weren't here because she had a few things she'd wanted to say to you."

"Such as?"

"She wanted to warn you about the state of the house. It'll be like entering a time capsule. Apparently, our dear cousin has done the bare minimum of clearing or cleaning up. The place is a wreck."

"That poor American girl!"

"Americans are tough. She'll cope."

"And what else?"

"Murota, it seems, has gone downhill. People are being attacked, and parents are worried about their kids."

"But that's happening everywhere these days."

"She also said Murota has its own sick, twisted individual who's sending off poison pen letters, accusing residents of awful crimes and misdemeanors and demanding money to keep quiet."

"Wow! Now you have surprised me!"

Yumi took another large gulp of her whisky.

"Yumi, are you okay? What are you drinking?"

"Whisky! I'm upset!"

"But why?"

"Of course, I felt sorry for her when she told me about having to take care of her mother. I admire and respect her. I could never act so unselfishly. But what got me is that Emi is so tactless. She was babbling on and on about how she felt she had to warn me that Murota's become dangerous. *Me!* Someone shot our father outside our house. Someone murdered our sister with poisoned chocolates. Then there was that boyfriend, Hiroki Sato. His uncle supposedly took him to South Korea on his fishing boat, and he was killed, too."

Yumi poured more whisky into her glass before continuing. "And...and! Somebody I work with, Koji Yanagihara, got beat up badly ten years ago when he went to Murota to write up a piece on Kaori shortly after her death. He's been a great help since I got back to Japan. It was his recommendation that landed me the job at *The Nippon Daily*. Koji's assailant must have been a *yakuza*. He wore a suit and black sunglasses and had no little finger on the left hand. The horrible experience is still vivid in Koji's mind. He's warned me not to go back, thinking if the *yakuza* cared then, maybe they still do. They have long memories."

"Got it. I'll watch for anyone who looks like a creep. Sunglasses. No left pinky." After a pause, Aki added sarcastically, "But you aren't even going."

Yumi gasped. "Aki, I'm a complete idiot. You're right. It somehow hadn't occurred to me it's you who'll be putting yourself in harm's way. Don't go. Let's just write to *Obasan* and say she can throw away anything she likes."

He laughed. "Are you kidding? You know I'm stubborn. Once I've decided something, it's hard to change my mind. I'm going! I can take care of myself." But then his voice turned serious. "What you say is worrying. I didn't know about the journalist being attacked, but that was ten years ago. And as for Emi, she was always tactless. She's awkward and plain, and she talks too much! You shouldn't let yourself be upset by anything she's said."

"But I am. And I'm going to have some more whisky."

"I'm on my way," Aki said. "Empty that bottle down the sink!" Then he hung up.

CHAPTER FIVE

Aki Hirakata
Sunday-Monday, 27-28 September 1998
Murota

Aki Hirakata arrived in Murota exactly a week after rushing to his sister's flat to wrest a whisky bottle from her. He'd poured the two inches remaining in the bottle down the sink before making a pot of strong coffee and forcing her to drink two cups of it.

Once he'd got Yumi sober and settled on the sofa, he said, "You're too silly." Sitting beside her, Aki took one of her hands. "You shouldn't let Emi get to you! I'm sure that wasn't her intention at all."

"No, and that makes it all the worse. She blunders in, hurting people when she imagines she's being kind."

"She is kind, but I could never understand her friendship with Kaori. They didn't seem to have much in common."

"Kaori was kind, too. Too kind! She took all kinds of lame ducks under her wing. Emi was just the most conspicuous example. Juno-*sensei* was another. Maybe Hiroki Sato was one, too. When Kaori mentioned him in her letters, he sounded like just the sort of good cause she'd adopt—raised in difficult circumstances, everything against him."

"Hiroki Sato," Aki muttered, remembering the dim silhouette of the man he'd glimpsed on the night his sister was murdered. "I still can't make out who he was. A monster who tricked my sister and cold-heartedly killed her? Or maybe he's a good man out-maneuvered by the actual killer."

"I know!" said Yumi. "He's a mystery to me, too."

"About Emi, she has her good points," he said. "She was like another big sister."

Yumi frowned. "Taking the place of the one who escaped to London," she said.

"You did what you had to do," Aki said. "Anyway, Emi used to help me with my homework. I think it was her tutoring that got me through math. I feel sorry for her now. Having to take care of her mother while holding down a full-time job must be a nightmare. I met her mother a few times when I was a boy. She was unpleasant then, and having dementia has probably made her even worse."

Yumi grimaced. "You're right. Emi's a dutiful daughter, and conscientious, and good at math. She'd have to be to keep that job at the bank."

"You have to forgive her."

"She's had a hard life," Yumi said. "You're right, and I forgive her. And, Aki, you must see her when you're in Murota. I told her you planned to look her up: it made her day."

"I'm glad somebody loves me."

"Idiot," Yumi said, leaning forward to rumple his hair affectionately.

Contrary to expectation, Murota favorably impressed Aki when he arrived the following Sunday afternoon. The town had changed, and mostly for the better. The train station was a perfect example. He'd last seen it through a haze of misery ten years earlier, boarding a train for Tokyo with his parents after Kaori's funeral. He remembered it as a dusty old wooden building surrounded by a few scrubby shrubs. Now, after surrendering his ticket to a white-gloved official with a peaked hat, Aki cast admiring glances at the gleaming new structure that had replaced it. The new station was at least twice the size of the old one and housed a convenience store, a bakery and an *udon* shop, with a garden out front awash with colorful flowers and bushes and even a few bonsai trees in pots.

Similarly, on exiting, he found that a broad avenue lined by poplar trees had replaced the narrow road that once connected the station to the town. Strolling down it, he marveled at all the changes. The ferry port was to the left. Aki wanted to see it but decided to postpone that pleasure. For now, he just wanted to see the town he'd once called home.

Smart boutiques had succeeded shabby old shops, and once he was near the town center, he saw that the wooded hill that once had been an oasis in the urban sprawl now housed a university campus. Most of the trees were gone, and the top of the hill had been leveled to facilitate the building of dormitories and classrooms. It came to Aki that this development—one he recalled originally being proposed in the late eighties—was the probable cause of Murota's newfound prosperity.

On impulse, Aki stopped a passerby and asked him when they had constructed the university on the site.

"Five years ago," the old man said dispiritedly, peering out from under a broad-brimmed hat and blinking at the bright sunshine. "It's delighted some residents—the ones renting out rooms, that is, or running the cafés, bars, and restaurants in town."

"And the others?" Aki asked, amused, guessing which camp the man belonged to.

"We hate it. This used to be a pleasant, sleepy community. Everyone knew everyone. Now it's full of strangers." He glanced around, looking irritated. "Foreigners. Crooks. Students. Apart from the formal garden, we lost our one nice bit of greenery in town. And the road traffic has doubled!" Then he stalked off.

It might have been the man's suggestion that undesirables had descended on Murota that aroused Aki's suspicions, but he turned around and suddenly noticed a middle-aged man he'd seen earlier at the train station. He wore a hat, suit, and sunglasses.

Yumi warned me! Aki thought, then laughed. It was too absurd. The man was a local or a tourist. He was staring intently at a shop window devoted to a display of men's autumn and winter fashions. It was obvious he had no interest in Aki.

Still, Aki edged towards him, hoping not to attract his attention as he tried to confirm whether he retained full possession of all the digits on his left hand. When Aki had drawn within five feet of him, the man suddenly set off down the avenue, striding briskly toward the town.

As Aki was still loitering, fretting over his ridiculous paranoia and wondering if, after all, he should go to inspect the ferry port, he heard his name called. He looked over to see a bony woman in her early fifties in a shabby black dress, her hair in a bun, staring at him from across the road.

Juno-*sensei!* he thought, overcome by horror. *What bad luck!* Still, being Japanese, he managed to paste on a bright, happy smile as he crossed over to talk to her. She looked older, with gray streaks in her hair, and her mouth had a discontented droop he hadn't noticed before.

"How nice to meet you!" he said in an eager tone he hoped was convincing. "Meeting one of my old friends here makes me feel I've really come home. But I'm surprised you recognized me after all this time."

"Aki Hirakata!" she exclaimed. He wasn't sure if she sounded pleased or dismayed. "It's been ten years, but I'd have known you anywhere. How long are you here?"

"Three nights. I suppose you know Mrs. Muraji is renting out our old house. She contacted Yumi and me and said we needed to take away any things we might still want. While I'm here, I might as well get rid of rubbish like our old clothes, books, things like that."

"It's typical of that woman," said Juno, shaking her head and frowning. "She's completely disorganized. I suppose you know that an American girl working at the university moved in last week, the very day Mrs. Muraji phoned you and Yumi. Ridiculous! Your cousin should have cleared out the place—and cleaned it properly—months ago."

"Well, better late than never," Aki said. As they talked, he had been gazing down the road, but now, when he looked at the missionary, he was surprised to see her face twisted with emotion.

She noticed and turned away, roughly brushing one hand across her eyes. When she faced him again, she had an exasperated expression and said brusquely, "It's just that seeing you brings it all back. What happened to your dear sister, I mean."

Aki felt touched to see her so moved, but also knew she regretted her display of emotion. "It's so awful the case was never solved," Aki said. "That they never found Hiroki Sato and made him face justice."

"I hate him," Juno said flatly. "I hope he's dead. He claimed that someone had left those poisoned chocolates on the door of his mother's house. Liar!" She suddenly raised a hand and looked at her watch. "Well, I must be on my way. I've just been helping with the morning service at the church, and now I have to get to Ishizaki for a mission board meeting this afternoon. It would be wonderful to see you at church next week. Pastor Nakagawa and his wife would be delighted to see you again."

"Sorry, Juno-*sensei*," Aki said. "I can't make it. As I've said, I'm only here a few days." He debated whether he should tell her the truth, then decided it was the best policy. "Anyway, I've lost my faith."

Juno shrugged, looked disappointed, and marched off.

As he watched her heading for the station, Aki wondered whether to laugh or cry. He decided to take a positive view of the encounter. He'd made it through the ordeal of meeting that awful woman and now felt under no obligation to see her again while he was in Murota.

He wanted to efface the memories stirred up by meeting Juno. Aki walked the short distance back to the port and spent a good half hour watching the big boats arriving and departing, remembering how exciting he'd found that spectacle as a child. On Saturday mornings, his father would suggest they walk into town to buy rolls at the bakery for their breakfast. They'd go hand in hand, walking south from their home and taking a detour to spend half an hour watching the ferries. Aki loved the majesty of the huge vessels as they slowly made their approach or set off again to cross the calm waters of the Inland Sea to Honshu.

As Aki stood by the sea, cooling breezes ruffling his hair and caressing his face, he regretted his habit of dwelling only on painful memories of Murota. It wasn't just or fair. That old life had often been a happy one. He watched the sunshine glinting off the rippling waves and gazed at the soft blue of the cloudless sky. It was wrong, too, only to recall the town as being ugly and boring. In some ways, it was lovely, and it was even more so now with the newfound air of prosperity Aki attributed to the new university.

Aki paused, uncertain what to do next. Habit drew him north to his old house, but he wondered if he should get rid of his suitcase first. It wasn't particularly heavy—he'd packed lightly so he could take mementos from his house in it back to Tokyo—but it was awkward and a nuisance. He passed the case from hand to hand, trying to decide. Aki had booked a room for three nights in a small hotel in the center of town. The more luxurious option nearby, the Excelsior, was too expensive.

He set off for the center of town, resolved to check in at his hotel and get rid of his luggage. It would be best, too, to freshen up—to feel and look his best—before he subjected himself to the ordeal of seeing his childhood home again. When he and his family had clambered into the taxi bound for the station ten years earlier, he'd made a point of not looking back, intending never to return. After all, he'd had to.

Then Aki looked at his watch and cursed. Wrapped up in memories of the past, he'd completely forgotten he'd arranged to meet Emi Tada at a café near his hotel. Remorseful he'd not seen her when she visited Yumi, he'd phoned her shortly afterward and made this plan. Emi had mentioned that she would bring the American girl so he could meet her and arrange a convenient time to enter the house and sort out the things he intended to take, discard, or send back to Tokyo.

Aki cursed again. He'd have to run to be on time. Then, spying a taxi, he hailed it and arrived at the café at the appointed time of three. He entered diffidently, still feeling the dread he'd experienced as a shy child at the prospect of meeting strangers. He wondered if Rhoda would be the type of gum-chewing, free and easy American girl Yumi imagined her to be. At least he spoke English, and Emi did, too, so there wouldn't be the awkwardness of communication by gestures or being restricted to simple translations. He set his case by the door, smiling apologetically at the woman at the cash register, then looked for his old friend.

Aki recognized Emi as soon as she stood, even though she had changed since he'd last seen her at Kaori's funeral. She was no longer fresh-faced and young. She had become a plump, heavily made-up middle-aged woman who suffered in comparison with her companion, who was attractive in a Nordic way—tall and blonde. The two women rose slightly and bowed, and Emi made the introductions. "This is my dear friend Aki Hirakata. Aki, this is Rhoda Ellison, only arrived from the States last week."

"I'm thrilled to meet you," Aki said, and he could see the tension he'd observed in the American's face relax. She was relieved he could speak

English. No wonder. He imagined few people in Murota did. "I hope you're enjoying living in my old house."

"Yes, of course, but I hope you won't mind the changes I've made."

"I'm sure I won't. I'm sorry we left it in such a mess."

A waitress hovering nearby approached. "We waited for you, Aki," Emi said. "Now we can order." She and Rhoda wanted tea, and Aki asked for coffee.

"I understand you're working at the university," Aki said to Rhoda.

"Yes, I'm here on a two-year contract. It's all very exciting, but I wish I'd taken Japanese classes before arriving."

She turned to smile at Emi. "You've been a lifesaver. I'm so glad I met you." Then she looked at Aki. "After being offered an advance on my first month's salary, I decided a few days ago to send part of it home to my mother. I was at the international transfers counter of the bank wondering how I could make anyone understand what I wanted to do when this lovely woman came up and said she could speak English and would help me."

Aki glanced at Emi. Her beaming face told him Rhoda's praise pleased her. Poor woman, he thought. Emi probably received far less appreciation than she deserved.

"That was very lucky," Aki said. "What part of the States are you from?"

"Michigan. Have you ever been to America?"

"No, but I'm longing to go," Aki said, lying easily. He couldn't think of a country he wanted to visit less. He imagined it was full of large, blond athletic types who were terrifyingly self-assured.

"How is it you speak English so well? And with an English accent?"

"I don't speak it very well," Aki said. "But the reason I speak it at all is that my older sister—Yumi—used to live in London. After what happened to my other sister, she insisted I come to stay with her. I was only supposed to stay there for a month or two, but I ended up living in England for six years."

"Where were you?"

"Four years in Golders Green, a suburb of London. Then two in Manchester."

"Weren't your parents desperate to have you back?"

"Yes. They'd moved to Tokyo after...what happened to my other sister, Kaori...and said it was like they'd lost all their children at once. Yumi felt it was best for me to be away from Japan for a while. My parents could make a fresh start, away from all the places and people that would remind them of Kaori. And that was true for me, too. Adjusting to a new culture and learning a new language meant I couldn't brood as much on it all as I might have done."

"But wasn't it hard for you when you returned to Japan? You'd have missed out on so much schooling. I know Japanese schoolchildren spend much of their time learning *kanji*."

"That's right. But I attended a Japanese cram school in Camden on the weekends. It was a condition my parents insisted on. Otherwise, they'd have made me come back to Japan."

He gulped, trying to control his emotions. "After all, when I finally *did* come back to Japan, I couldn't spend much time with my parents. My mother died within a year, and my father not long after."

"Awful," Emi said solemnly after a pause. She shook her head. She obviously wanted to change the topic. "Aki, how long are you in town? I just wonder when it might be most convenient for you—and for you, too, Rhoda, of course—to go to the house and decide what you might want."

"How about now?" Rhoda said, putting down her empty cup.

"Fine with me. I just have to check in at my hotel and leave my case, then I'm free."

"And that would be perfect for me, too. Mondays are my busiest days. It would be good if you could come by now and get some idea of the scale of the task."

"And Emi, you must come with us," Aki said. "If you see something you'd like—a keepsake—you must take it. You were like a member of the family—a very valued member of the family." The sight of Emi's face transfigured once more by happiness rewarded him.

After a brief detour to Aki's hotel, where he deposited his case, the three set off. Rhoda had traveled to the café on her bicycle, and Aki wheeled it back to the house for her. On the way, Aki couldn't help glancing about, wondering if he'd see the suited and hatted man with sunglasses he'd suspected of following him from the train station. But it was a bright day, and many businessmen were rushing by wearing light suits as well as hats, although, admittedly, few had dark glasses. Aki decided looking for that man was futile and a waste of time. Instead, as Emi and Rhoda chattered away, Aki found himself immersed in memories as he walked down streets familiar to him from his earliest years.

When they finally arrived, Aki and Emi fell silent as Rhoda opened the rusty gate and they walked down the narrow brick path to the house. "I haven't done any work on the garden yet," she said, but neither made a reply.

As she took the key for the front door from a pocket, Aki said, "Wait. Just wait, please." Using the kickstand, he parked Rhoda's bike on the path, then slumped against the front wall of the house, his legs stretched out in front of him. He felt rather ill. Despite being cheerful at the café, it was traumatic to be back at his old home, and he needed some time to steel himself before entering.

Aki looked up at the big camphor tree beside him. "I used to love this tree when I was a child," he said. "I tried climbing it, but the lower branches were just too high." He nodded at the vine on the other side of the door. "That vine was a different matter. I got up and down it a few times." He took a crumpled packet from a jeans pocket, extracted a cigarette, and then rummaged in the pocket again for his lighter.

He took a deep drag. Exhaling, he closed his eyes. It was obvious he wanted to be alone. Rhoda left him, walking over to the bench by the fountain and sitting on it. Emi joined her. The dirty-faced cherub cut a forlorn figure holding his empty jug above the leaf-strewn floor of the fountain. After finishing his cigarette, Aki approached the women, saying, "I'm ready now."

"Okay," said Rhoda, standing. She fished the key from her pocket and opened the door.

"I haven't been here for ten years," Emi said. "Not since the reception after Kaori's funeral. It feels strange!"

As they entered the hallway, Emi glanced about her curiously. Then she turned to Aki. "I'm glad to be coming back here with you," she said. "I used to think of you as the little brother I always wanted."

"And you were my third big sister," he said, smiling.

Rhoda looked surprised. Emi said, "I should explain. I'm an only child. When I was friends with Kaori, it was like the Hirakatas adopted me, treating me like one of the family. Then they left Murota, and it felt like being abandoned. It's just my mother and me, and she's as good as gone. She's in the early stages of dementia. Sometimes she doesn't know who I am."

It was such a sad story that, on impulse, Rhoda took Emi's hand and gave it a friendly squeeze.

Aki smiled when he saw the phone on top of the hallway cupboard. "A rotary dial phone! It belongs in a museum, not a private house. This is like the place time forgot."

On entering the living room. Emi unexpectedly sank to her knees and held a handkerchief to her eyes. After a pause, as Aki and Rhoda exchanged embarrassed looks, Emi looked up, smiling. "This room brings it all back," she said. "Please forgive me. I didn't know how deeply being here would affect me. I can't help remembering the last time I saw Kaori. We sat on that sofa and argued about her boyfriend."

She rose and went over to the big French windows, looking out at the garden. Aki and Rhoda sat in the two armchairs, Rhoda feeling awkward and at a loss.

Finally, she broke the silence. "Before we go upstairs, I think I need to tell you what I've done," she said nervously. "I've taken most of the things out of the three bedrooms that must have belonged to you and your sisters, Aki, and put them in your parents' room. I wanted to have a bedroom, a study, and a place I can do yoga."

Aki gasped when they climbed the stairs and entered the parents' room. Despite the forewarning, he felt dismayed at seeing so many familiar objects all jumbled together. "Maybe I need to contact Yumi and arrange for her to come help me after all," he groaned. "But I don't suppose she'd have the heart for it. I'm not sure I do, either. Maybe we could just contact one of those services that clear out homes."

"Such services exist?" Rhoda asked, incredulous.

"They're aimed at people who inherit old houses full of *junk!* Masked and gloved men in a large truck simply turn up and take everything away to the nearest rubbish dump. It's all done very efficiently."

"But there must be things you want. Things with sentimental associations."

Aki paused. "You're right. Yumi told me I should leave anything you could use—the things in the kitchen, furniture, and such—but take away mementos like letters and photos."

He paused, considering. "I'll take away a few personal things, but I should also get rid of our old clothes and any items of furniture, carpets, or curtains that are in a poor condition. I've booked my hotel for three nights and plan to go back on Wednesday morning. May I come back tomorrow night and probably sometime on Tuesday, too? I feel too tired—and shaken—to make any rational decisions just now."

"Of course. As I've said, I have a lot of classes on Mondays, but I'll be home tomorrow evening by five. How about then?"

"Perfect."

Rhoda smiled at the two of them. "You're my first guests in this house—even though you know this place far better than I ever can. Will you stay for refreshments?"

They agreed and were soon enjoying tea in the living room. Emi gulped hers down, saying she needed to get back to her mother.

"I'd like to stay a few more minutes if it isn't an imposition," Aki said. "It's been such a shock. I feel I need some company for a little while. I can't bear the thought of being in my little hotel room on my own just now."

He smiled at Emi. "But Emi, again, you must have something to remember Kaori by. Naturally, being Japanese, you're reluctant to choose yourself. Your politeness means you worry you'd want something too expensive or something we don't want to part with. But I have an idea. Wait just a minute."

He ran up the stairs and returned in a few minutes, clutching a dog-eared copy of Jane Austen's *Emma*. Rhoda stared, astonished that Aki could think a battered old book was a suitable present, but Emi clutched it to her chest, tears springing to her eyes.

"Kaori and I spent weeks laboring over that book with dictionaries," Emi said. "We were determined to read our favorite novel in the original. Thanks so much, dear Aki."

After Rhoda had seen Emi off, she returned to the living room, noticing how thin and frail Aki looked as he leaned listlessly back against the sofa cushions.

"Are you okay?" Rhoda asked.

"I'm so glad she's gone," he said unexpectedly.

"Emi?"

"Yes."

"But I thought you two were so close."

"Emi is like a big sister, but she makes me tired. She talks so much, chattering away all the time, and never about anything that matters. Emi never complains, for example, about the rotten cards that life has dealt her. She's so clever, it's a tragedy she couldn't go to a university, that she just couldn't afford it. At the bank, I expect she does all the work, and the men take all the credit and earn lots more than her. And now her mother's got dementia with only Emi to look after her. Bad luck follows bad luck. I sometimes wonder if people like her attract it."

"She sounds very admirable."

"Admirable but tiring. I expect Kaori felt the same. Sometimes I thought Kaori even found Emi a bit frightening, her devotion overpowering. There's also something needy about Emi that's always put me off."

He sighed. "Emi doesn't realize how restful it is to be silent with people you know well or who you love."

Rhoda bowed her head and stared at the floor, feeling embarrassed.

Aki smiled. "I shouldn't be saying such things to you—a total stranger. But it's probably because you are a stranger and because we'll probably never meet again after I return to Tokyo that I can be so honest."

"Oh, yes, of course," said Rhoda brightly. But his words hurt her. She'd found him unexpectedly interesting and attractive and hoped she would see him again.

Then Aki straightened and leaned forward, smiling. "I found this upstairs," he said, taking a small oblong of faded orange embroidered cloth from a jeans pocket.

"What is it?" Rhoda asked, taking it from him. The cloth was soft, as if somebody had fondled it often.

"It's what we call an *omamori*—an amulet wrapped in a brocade bag. It's supposed to protect its owner."

Rhoda handed it back. "Where did you find it?"

"In my parents' bedroom while you were chatting with Emi. I was looking around and saw my sister's jewelry box on my mother's dressing table. This good luck token was inside."

His face darkened. "I'm afraid it holds both painful and pleasant memories. I was eleven when I lost Kaori. She'd given me this charm years earlier as a present, and I always carried it with me, but I got angry with her the day she died and threw it at her. I've always wondered where it ended up."

"Let's go back outside," Rhoda suggested. "It's such a lovely afternoon it seems a shame to spend it indoors." In fact, it was a pretext. Rhoda felt dismayed to see the effect being back in his old house had on the young man she'd just met. She'd noticed how handsome and buoyant he'd looked when Emi had introduced them in the café. But now he was pale and trembling. She felt he needed to get into the fresh air.

Rhoda was relieved to see Aki get his color back after they sat on the bench by the fountain that she and Emi had occupied an hour earlier.

"This place is such a mess!" Aki said. "Not, I hasten to add, that I blame you in the slightest. I think my cousin should have taken better care of the property my parents sold to her."

"Mrs. Muraji didn't strike me as a woman with a great deal of energy or ambition," Rhoda said. "I hope you won't mind my saying that."

"Not at all. I agree completely."

Aki stood and strolled around the garden. When he returned to the bench, cobwebs, blades of grass, and knotweed blossoms covered his black trousers. He looked down, chagrined, and brushed himself off. "I need to look at least presentable," he said. "I've had an idea."

He pointed to a roof visible beyond the wall surrounding the property. "That's old Mrs. Goto's house," he said. "She's your nearest neighbor. You have kindly performed a service for me, and I'd like to reciprocate. It's the custom in towns like Murota for people who've recently moved to a neighborhood to meet the people living nearby. I think I should introduce you to Mrs. Goto, that she should know you. You can look out for each other."

"Now?" said Rhoda, feeling apprehensive.

"As the English saying goes, 'There's no time like the present.'" Aki laughed at Rhoda's anxious expression. "Don't worry. She won't bite. Poor dear. I hear she can hardly even walk these days. She has rheumatism and is losing her sight. Emi told me she can't manage on her own anymore and has had a niece staying with her for the past half year to help her out."

Aki frowned. "The only problem is I don't have a present."

"A present?"

"We always take something with us when we visit somebody."

"I bought a big bunch of grapes yesterday. Would that do?"

"Perfectly. But do you have a pretty *furoshiki* cloth? Or decorated paper? That's another custom. We have to wrap our presents."

When Aki and Rhoda arrived at the Goto house, a sour-faced, middle-aged woman with scanty black hair in a tiny bun appeared at the door. It was an old traditional Japanese dwelling with black outer walls, small windows outlined in white paint, and a heavy tiled roof. The house had a small driveway in front and was set back a short distance from the road.

The woman visibly started at the sight of the unexpected visitors. They bowed while Aki uttered the traditional Japanese phrase, "Please excuse this worthless gift," holding out the grapes wrapped in a blue cloth Rhoda had found in a kitchen drawer. Regaining her composure, the woman soundlessly held out her hands to take the gift, then nodded towards the *genkan*, indicating they should come in.

While they were taking off their shoes, the woman gently placed the offering on a hallway cupboard and hastened to put out slippers, ushering them into a large room decorated with furniture, a carpet, and heavy curtains.

Rhoda started in surprise when the woman said, in fluent English, "I'll get Mrs. Goto. My name is Michiko Ikeuchi. I'm her niece." She sighed. "And housekeeper. And cook. My poor aunt can't do much these days. The only task she insists on doing herself these days is making miso soup. She says I add too much miso, make the taste too strong."

Aki and Rhoda sat on an old beige leather sofa in silence, looking around curiously. Aki appeared interested in the pair of binoculars lying on the windowsill. Rhoda thought the room was musty and like a rarely visited museum, with its shelves and cupboards crowded with decorative Japanese dolls, porcelain vases and dishes, and trinkets—all covered with a gray layer of dust.

"I hadn't expected this," Rhoda said.

"This?"

Rhoda motioned to their surroundings. "This room. It was different at your parents' place. Apart from the tatami mat room housing the Buddhist altar, it looks like a house I could find in Europe. But here, in this traditional old Japanese house? It seems incongruous."

Aki laughed. "You sound disappointed. Did you think you'd find us all sitting on cushions?"

"No, I'm relieved! I've tried sitting that way, with my legs tucked under me, and no matter how thick the cushion beneath me is, I've found it unbearably painful after a few minutes. But this...?" and she shrugged as she looked around.

"This kind of room is called *yoshitsu*—a Western-style room as opposed to *washitsu*—a Japanese-type one. It was the fashion in the seventies for Japanese to have their guest room in the Western style and stuff it with lots of things."

It seemed ages before they heard the creaking of floorboards from somewhere in the house, signaling the approach of their hosts. Finally, an old woman with a shock of thick white hair wearing a faded pink kimono and holding a cane in one hand, supported on the other side by her niece, shuffled slowly through the door. Rhoda and Aki rose and bowed. The old woman bent her head, thanking them for their visit, then seated herself in a large armchair stuffed with cushions obviously reserved for her exclusive use.

Rhoda wondered if the old woman had been lying in bed and Miss Ikeuchi had helped her rise before assisting her in putting on the kimono. That would account for the long time it had taken them to appear.

The niece excused herself, saying she would fetch tea.

Rhoda could only utter a few formal greetings in Japanese. After saying these phrases, intended to introduce herself and explain her circumstances, she was reduced to the status of a listener as Aki and Mrs. Goto chatted. She only understood the occasional word. She heard "Hirakata" mentioned often.

Miss Ikeuchi appeared with a tray holding a delicate teapot and four teacups. Rhoda drank the steaming green tea, thinking she was getting a taste for a beverage that had seemed unpleasantly bitter when she'd first encountered it. There was something bracing yet seductively subtle about the taste. She started when she suddenly heard a few words in broken English.

Looking up, she saw the old woman staring at her and rapping on the floor with her cane to get her attention. Mrs. Goto had moved to the edge of her seat. Her small brown eyes were gleaming brightly in her wrinkled old face.

"Speak English," she announced once she saw Rhoda looking at her. She raised a hand, positioning her thumb close to her index finger to indicate something small. "Little," she said, smiling. "Just little."

"I know young woman in house," Mrs. Goto went on, pointing at the window. The second story of the Hirakata mansion was visible in the distance, looming above the stone walls that surrounded the property. Her lips turned down and her face twisted into an exaggerated expression of sorrow. "Sad. Killed." She smiled at Rhoda. "She pretty. Pretty like you."

Rhoda felt rather than saw Aki shifting uneasily beside her.

Then Mrs. Goto settled heavily back in her chair and launched into a torrent of Japanese. Aki moved to a chair nearer the old woman to converse with her.

Miss Ikeuchi came over to Rhoda, bearing the teapot. "More?" she asked.

"Yes, please."

After pouring out the tea, Miss Ikeuchi put the teapot on the low table in front of the sofa and seated herself beside Rhoda, taking Aki's place.

Rhoda smiled at her. "Your English is good!"

"It was my favorite subject at school," she said. Miss Ikeuchi then moved closer, and Rhoda had to fight an impulse to move away, uncomfortable at the proximity. The small, wizened woman bared sharp yellowed teeth as she went on. "My life is...how can I say? Boring. Studying English, speaking English, it's my hobby, my fun."

Miss Ikeuchi said, "People don't see me. I'm invisible. It's Auntie who's rich and well-known in town. I'm just the person who lives with her. But I know a few things."

Rhoda involuntarily recoiled as she suddenly registered the stink of the woman's breath. Miss Ikeuchi hadn't noticed. She went on, saying, "Auntie told me something once. Then she wished she hadn't. The day before that girl died, a friend visited her. Her best friend! Auntie was at the Hirakatas to deliver something. She was standing in front of the door, ready to knock, when the friend spoke so loudly Auntie heard. Auntie says the friend said she'd kill Kaori if she kept seeing her boyfriend."

Rhoda drew back, this time because the woman's malicious expression repelled her. The niece's eyes glittered as she added, "And I know something else. Auntie told me how she saw somebody buying a box of chocolates at a shop the day before that girl died. She said she recognized the box when she got to the girl's bedroom and saw her dying, said that it was on her bed."

Rhoda sat still and silent, feeling horrified. Then she felt she had to ask. "Have you told this to anybody else?"

"I mentioned it to Emi Tada. I thought she should know." Then the woman paused, drumming her fingers on the table, looking reflectively at her aunt, who was engaged in a lively discussion with Aki. "Auntie was in her room getting dressed when Mrs. Muraji came to explain she was renting out her house. I told her too."

Miss Ikeuchi rose and took away the tray. When she returned, she had a large, white plastic bag that she presented to Rhoda. Peeking inside, Rhoda saw the blue cloth that had wrapped the grapes was now neatly folded over potatoes and onions, a green pumpkin, and some Japanese pears. "Our neighbors are so kind," Miss Ikeuchi said. She gave a vague wave at the window, taking in the neighborhood. "Farmers. They're always leaving things on our doorstep. We're glad to share, but I'll tell them about you. They'll leave some for you, too."

"How nice!" Rhoda exclaimed. "Thanks very much!"

"Everything is so fresh. My aunt especially likes the mushrooms. Whenever we get mushrooms, she wants to make miso soup."

Aki looked over at Rhoda and slightly inclined his head, nodding toward the door. She guessed he meant it was time to leave.

Aki and Rhoda rose. Bowing deeply, they expressed their thanks.

"I explained to Mrs. Goto that you were eager to meet her," Aki told Rhoda on the way back to the Hirakata mansion. "That you're here alone and felt you should know your neighbors, and that's why I came by, to introduce you to each other. She said Mrs. Muraji had told her she'd rented our place to an American girl, and she'd been worried about you living on your own in such a big house."

They walked in silence for a few minutes.

"What did you think of them?" Aki finally asked.

"I had the impression Mrs. Goto has her wits about her, despite her age. But she's frail. I saw her stumble as she entered the living room. She moved slowly, but I guess that's not surprising. She must be in her early nineties."

"And the niece?"

"I didn't like her. She seemed nice, but underneath was something spiteful. She even hinted that Emi—at least that's who I think she meant—could have been involved in Kaori's death because she was so opposed to her relationship with that boyfriend who disappeared."

"Impossible!" Aki said, looking surprised. After a pause, he added, "Although come to think of it, Emi lives in the same neighborhood, in a house only a short distance away from that boyfriend—Hiroki Sato. I suppose you've heard how my poor sister died from eating poisoned chocolates. Emi could easily have left them in a bag on his door without being noticed. I know she hated him and still does. But enough to want to kill him, not guessing he'd take the chocolates to Kaori? Unlikely."

"Miss Ikeuchi told me her aunt had seen a person buying a box of chocolates just like the one in your sister's room the day before she died."

"Who was it?"

"She didn't say, although she mentioned she'd told Emi Tada and Mrs. Muraji about it." Rhoda shrugged, adding, "It was odd how she put it. Miss Ikeuchi said she thought Emi Tada should know."

Aki shook his head. "I'm baffled."

After a brief silence, Rhoda said, "And what do you think of Mrs. Goto and her niece?"

"Mrs. Goto certainly had her wits about her ten years ago when she summoned an ambulance for my poor dying sister, and she still seems very alert and aware. As for Miss Ikeuchi, I agree she's mean-spirited and possibly malicious. And, from what you've just said, she's obviously a gossip."

Aki paused and gave Rhoda a considering look. "By the way," he said, "do you know a woman connected to the Christian church in Murota—a kind of missionary called Juno-*sensei*?"

"Yes, she teaches English part-time at my university and sometimes comes to my office for a chat."

"Do you like her?"

"Not particularly. I pity her while always feeling I'm disappointing her somehow. Why do you ask?"

"Just curious," Aki said. "I know just what you mean about Juno. What you say confirms an impression I had of you, that you're an excellent judge of character."

They parted at the front gate of the Hirakata property. Rhoda held out her hand. "Thanks so much for introducing me to my nearest neighbor. It makes me feel…" and Aki saw her shiver. "Not so alone here."

"You don't strike me as the type to be scared of anything," Aki said.

Rhoda flushed with pleasure at the unexpected compliment.

"I'll turn up tomorrow then, at about five," Aki said, "having spent the day revisiting old haunts. My old primary school. The field I used to hide in for a sneaky cigarette or two. The park where I learned to ride a bike." He smiled, suddenly looking boyishly handsome again. "By the way, I'm very grateful to you for being so kind and keeping me company on my first day back here—a place I've avoided like the plague for the past ten years. It could have been traumatic. Instead, it's turned out to be rather pleasant."

Rhoda hesitated but then said, "Do you hate him very much?"

"Who?"

"That man I heard of—I can't remember his name—accused of killing your sister."

"Hiroki Sato," Aki said, and then groaned. "I'm not sure what to believe. Did he do it? Your telling me what Mrs. Goto said to her niece reminds me. I heard lately that Hiroki Sato claimed somebody had left the bag of poisoned chocolates on his door. That would mean he was the person supposed to die."

Rhoda Ellison

Rhoda met the missionary Aki had mentioned the very next day. She bumped into her in the hall during the thirty-minute break between her first and second classes and, seeing Juno looking somehow sad and lonely, invited her into her office for coffee on impulse.

"I met two of your friends yesterday," Rhoda said, trying to speak in a bright, cheerful manner to hide her mixed feelings about this complex woman sitting opposite her, sipping her mug of coffee.

"Oh, yes? Who?" Juno briefly looked eager.

"Emi Tada and Aki Hirakata."

"Oh, *him*!" she said dismissively. "I've known Aki since the day he was born. I ran into him yesterday, too, outside the train station. He'd just arrived in Murota. I've been expecting him to get in touch to arrange getting together."

Juno smiled, adding, "Such a silly boy, but quite charming. I think I occupy a soft spot in his heart. I'd been thinking of looking him up the next time I'm in Tokyo and then, there he was in Murota, saving me the trouble. He explained he'd come back because his cousin rang, insisting he return and clear the house of anything he and his sister might want because she intends to keep on renting it out after you leave."

Then Juno's mood abruptly changed. She suddenly burst out with a fury that surprised Rhoda. "That Mrs. Muraji!" she said. "What a silly, useless woman! She left the place empty, deteriorating, for ten years. Then she rented it to you. And it wasn't until the very day you moved in that she condescended to contact poor Yumi and Aki Hirakata. I don't suppose she even cleaned the house before you moved in, let alone got anything done in the garden."

She looked at Rhoda curiously. "Is that how you met Aki? Did he come to the house to get some things?"

Rhoda smiled. "Emi introduced us. She'd arranged for us three to meet at a café down the road from the station. Later, we went to the house together. He'll come tonight to get a few mementos. He said he'll leave furniture, kitchen utensils, anything I might find useful."

Looking up, she saw Juno seemed lost in her own world, gazing absently in the distance. "The Hirakatas," she said, thoughtfully.

"Can you tell me anything about them? I'd be grateful. It would help if I had some idea of the family before Aki comes by."

Juno began rattling off information in a monotone as if it were a piece she'd memorized long before. "The Hirakatas were a well-off, well-regarded family in Murota," she said. "Mr. Hirakata married into a wealthy family, the Inoues. I hear the Inoues were dismayed by their daughter's choice of husband. Despite coming from very humble origins, however,

Iwao Hirakata became head of finances at Taniguchi's, the most prestigious real-estate firm in the city. He and his wife gained a reputation as a devoted couple."

Juno sighed, finally looking up at Rhoda. "Then something strange happened. Somebody shot Mr. Hirakata, and rumors swirled he'd been involved in dubious transactions with the *yakuza*. Despite their reduced circumstances, the family could keep their house. I imagine Mrs. Hirakata's parents helped them out."

Juno gave a wintry smile. "It was the hand of God," she said. Her eyes gleamed as she added, "Mrs. Hirakata, who had been raised a Christian, lost her faith upon marrying. I brought her back to the fold as God's unworthy agent. She and her husband began attending our church and got baptized there."

Her face clouded over again. "That's how I met Kaori and Yumi. They were eleven. A year after the parents' conversion, they had Aki. I thought of his birth as a sign of God's love."

"Yumi," Rhoda said. "Aki mentioned her. He said she'd been living in London, and that he went to stay with her after his parents moved to Tokyo."

"That's right. He came back when he was seventeen, and now even Yumi has returned. She works for a newspaper in Tokyo. Never shows her face here." Juno's brow furrowed. "Wait, I think I heard something about her recently. Somebody told me she's involved with some eccentric manga artist. He always wears a black mask in public, and people have compared him to the reclusive English artist Banksy. I suppose he thinks all that air of mystery makes his work more bankable."

"Have you seen any of it?"

"It's second-rate and derivative," Juno said decisively. She held up her mug. "Any more coffee going?"

Rhoda refilled Juno's mug, and she took a sip before going on. "As for the parents, as you've heard, they moved to Tokyo after...what happened to their daughter. I can't think how they afforded it. I suppose it was thanks to the Inoues' generosity. Of course, Mr. Hirakata was no longer working. They sold their house to Mrs. Muraji, Mrs. Hirakata's poor relation, for a song. I understand they lived in a modest apartment near Ueno Park. They never got over what had happened. Soon after Aki returned to Japan, Mrs. Hirakata died of cancer, and her husband followed her not long after."

They were silent for a moment. Rhoda felt moved by this sad tale of the downfall of a once proud and successful family. Then she said, "And that poor murdered girl?"

She was taken aback by the pallor of Juno's face as she stared unseeingly at the office window. "Kaori," Juno said. "She was the most delightful girl. Pretty, but not vain. Kind, caring. Everyone loved her. We are all precious to God, but there was something about her that was special."

Her lips twisted in an ugly grimace. "That's why it was so unbelievable she fell in love with that horrible boy."

"Hiroki Sato? What I can't understand is why the police didn't arrest him for her murder," Rhoda said, pretending ignorance. "From the little I've heard, he was the prime suspect."

"He disappeared!" Juno said angrily. "Vanished right after he'd killed that sweet, sweet child. The monster! It seems his uncle took him to South Korea. I hope he's dead. The uncle is, anyway. That boy brought nothing but bad luck to anyone connected to him."

"But from what I heard, he might have been the intended victim," Rhoda said.

"From what you heard!" Juno repeated scornfully. "What can you know about any of it?"

Rhoda thought it advisable to change the subject. "By the way, I met two other people yesterday you might know. Emi had to hurry back to help her mother. Aki said he'd introduce me to my next-door neighbors. He took me to see Mrs. Goto and her niece, Miss Ikeuchi. They were very kind. They gave me some produce local farmers had given them, and said they'd ask them to leave some at my door, too."

"That's the kind of place Murota is. Friendly. Everyone looking out for each other."

"I was astonished Miss Ikeuchi could speak such good English."

"Can she? I had no idea."

"She said it was her hobby. I got the impression she found it hard being her aunt's housekeeper and caregiver."

"Not surprising."

"But she said something that did surprise me. Both she and Mrs. Goto talked about Kaori Hirakata. They were obviously very distressed about what happened to her. Miss Ikeuchi said her aunt told her she recognized the box of chocolates when she went to help the Hirakatas, that she'd seen somebody buying one just like it the day before."

There was a brief pause. Juno took another sip of coffee. "Ridiculous. It was a popular brand. Still is, for that matter. Anyway, that old woman could hardly walk or see even ten years ago. Everyone knows she's a gossip. She likes to make up tales to make herself important."

There was a pause. Rhoda looked nervously at the clock, hoping she wouldn't be late for her next class.

"God gave me Kaori," Juno added unexpectedly, sitting up straight and speaking solemnly. "The devil helped that awful boy." Then she jumped up and left.

As arranged, Aki turned up at Rhoda's house at five. He held out a large and sturdy carrier bag, saying, "I bought this at a local shop. It should be big enough to hold all the things I want to take back to Tokyo with me."

"If it isn't, I have lots of plastic bags you could use."

"You're very kind."

Rhoda offered him coffee, but he told her he'd prefer to finish first what he expected would be an unpleasant task. She waved him toward the staircase leading to the second floor, and he disappeared.

Rhoda had imagined he'd return downstairs within an hour. Instead, he was gone for three. She prepared a simple dinner for herself, ate it in the kitchen, then retired to the living room, hearing things being moved around in the parents' bedroom above her.

Finally, Rhoda heard a tentative knock, and Aki put his head around the door. "I'm so sorry to have disturbed you, Rhoda," he said. He held aloft his carrier bag again; now, it was bulging and looked heavy.

"Please come in and have coffee with me. But you lived in England for so long. Perhaps you'd prefer tea."

"Yes, please."

As they sat in the living room, Aki said, "I'm very grateful you've been so accommodating, Rhoda. I've got lots of photos and letters in my bag. It would be good to come again. I think you said you'll be at work tomorrow. Perhaps you could lend me a spare key and I can sort out things while you're not here. I'd like to take one more look—see if there's anything else I want to take—but it would also be an opportunity to get rid of some of the useless junk: our old clothes and shoes and books and bedding, things like that."

"Of course. No problem." She rose and walked over to the mantelpiece and upturned the vase, the key she kept inside falling into her outstretched hand. "I got an extra from Mrs. Muraji and put it here. But how will you dispose of those things you plan to throw away?"

"Like I said, there are companies that specialize in this! I'll contact one in Murota and ask them to come by tomorrow afternoon to collect the bags, boxes, and items I'll leave on the curb out front."

Seeing how pale Aki was, how his hand trembled slightly as he held his mug, Rhoda said, "I'm so sorry. This must be very painful for you."

"You can't imagine how much. Now I'm preoccupied with one question."

"A question?"

"Who murdered my sister?"

He grimaced. "Actually, I'm haunted by two questions, not one. The second is, why?"

CHAPTER SIX

Rhoda Ellison
Tuesday-Wednesday, 29-30 September 1998
Murota

Rhoda had three classes on Tuesday and needed to leave her house by 8:30 to be in time for the 9:00 English conversation seminar. It was lucky she lived so near the university, she thought. She could simply jump on her bike and get to work within half an hour. Admittedly, the hill she had to navigate as the last leg of her journey was a nuisance. Even though her bicycle had three gears, she always had to jump off midway up the steep slope and wheel her bike to the top. Still, the exhilaration of zooming down that same hill on her way home was a treat she always anticipated and enjoyed.

Rhoda thought of Aki periodically throughout the busy day. She wondered when he'd arrived at her place and how he was getting on. She imagined he'd welcome a glass of wine with her when she got back. It must be dispiriting, as well as exhausting, having to go through lots of old things that evoked many memories, especially given the tragic circumstances in which the family had vacated the property so abruptly.

When Rhoda cycled down the narrow road leading to her house at half past four, she saw a large quantity of big black plastic rubbish bags piled up on the pavement outside her front gate. A little green plastic bag was hanging from the gate, holding some vegetables. *Hooray!* she thought.

"You *have* been busy!" she said to Aki, who opened the front door to her ring. A black smudge adorned one cheek, and his hair was disheveled. Rhoda looked down and saw he'd left his carrier bag filled with more letters and photos in the *genkan.*

"You didn't have to use the doorbell!" he protested. "After all, this is *your* home now."

"I just wanted to warn you I was back," Rhoda said. Then, pointing toward the road, "When will someone collect all that?" she asked.

Aki looked at his watch. "In about half an hour. I contacted one of those companies I mentioned, which just picks things up and disposes of them—for a considerable sum of money, I might add. Still, it's an essential service in this country where so many people are hoarders."

"Really? I thought the Japanese were very minimalist and Zen."

"Some are, but many aren't. I've been in friends' houses crowded with so many cardboard boxes it looked like they'd just moved in—but they'd been there years." He grinned boyishly. "Rhoda, I hope I haven't thrown away anything you might want. Do you want to check?"

"I'm sure I can trust your judgment," she said, stepping out of her shoes in the *genkan* and into slippers. She held the green bag aloft. "Look! Presents! Lots of fresh vegetables from some friendly farmer."

Aki glanced inside. "Everything looks so fresh. How nice! I saw the bag hanging from the gate earlier, but thought I'd let you inspect the contents first."

"I'll have to think what I can cook with them. But what I'd highly recommend now is that we have a glass of wine." She flushed with pleasure as Aki said, "A woman after my own heart." He followed her to the kitchen.

As Rhoda opened a bottle with a corkscrew, they listened to the satisfying sound of a truck pulling up outside and men shouting as they hurled bags into the back.

"Job done," said Aki happily.

They had each emptied one glass, and Rhoda was pouring more wine when the noise of police sirens and the wail of an ambulance approaching and then stopping in the vicinity startled them.

"My God! What a racket! What's happening?" Rhoda said, rushing instinctively to the French windows in the living room, where she could only see the huge garden bounded by high stone walls.

Aki joined her. "I think they've stopped at Mrs. Goto's place. Let's go and see what's happening."

Rhoda locked the door behind them, and they hurried down the garden path and through the front gate.

"What time is it?" Rhoda asked as they scurried down the road. Apart from the soft halo cast by the sparsely spaced streetlights, it was already nearly dark.

"Just after six thirty," Aki muttered, glancing at the digital watch on his wrist as they ran.

A policeman was standing on the path leading to Mrs. Goto's house. Two patrol cars had drawn up by the side of the road and an ambulance, its lights flashing and back doors wide open, was in the driveway near the front door.

A policeman wearing glasses and a stern expression held up a warning hand as the two approached.

"Stop," he said in Japanese. "You are forbidden to go any nearer."

"My friend lives next door," Aki said to the policeman. "Naturally, she's wondering what's going on. And I'm an acquaintance of Mrs. Goto's and her niece, Ikeuchi-*san*. Can you tell us what's happened?"

Hearing a commotion, they fell silent, staring. From the light streaming out of the open doorway, they could see two men in white coats carrying out a stretcher that had an immobile, stocky figure on it completely covered by a white blanket. The policeman took off his cap and bowed. Instinctively, Rhoda and Aki bowed, too.

The men deposited the body inside the ambulance in complete silence. Then they rushed back to the house with another stretcher, disappearing down the hallway.

Suddenly, a noise became noticeable. It was the sound of loud groaning occasionally punctuated by retching and seemed to come from inside the house.

The policeman beckoned to Rhoda and Aki to follow him to a streetlight. He whipped a notebook out of his pocket and demanded their names, addresses, and phone numbers.

He waved to one of the police cars parked on the street. A thin officer with a pallid face and slightly hunched shoulders got out and approached them. The two officers spoke briefly, the thin officer was given the notebook, and he disappeared into the house.

"The chief inspector is in the house," the officer explained. "I wanted to notify him of your presence. It's possible he'd like to question you."

"Here? Now?" Aki asked. The prospect horrified him. Could it be the same chief inspector who'd led the investigation into Kaori's murder so many years ago?

"In your friend's house," the policeman said, giving Rhoda a small bow. His face took on a faint expression of disgust. "There is some disorder, some...*mess*...in this house. And it's a crime scene."

The thin officer promptly returned and handed back the notebook, confirming what the other had surmised: that the chief inspector wanted to question the two as soon as possible. He advised them to return to Rhoda's house to await his arrival.

They were about to set off when the sight of two men wearing white coats exiting the house again with a figure on a stretcher caught their attention, making them stop and stare. The light streaming from the front door was sufficient for Aki and Rhoda to realize it was Miss Ikeuchi, her body covered by a white blanket, but her head uncovered. They could see her face clearly. Her features were twisted, and she was moving her head vigorously back and forth, as if trying to deny something or shake something off. A trickle of white liquid oozed from her lips, and she was moaning loudly.

The two police officers moved, placing themselves squarely in front of Rhoda and Aki, obviously intending to block their view.

The first policeman told Rhoda, "The chief inspector will be at your house within half an hour."

The Police

Despite her horror at the scene they had just witnessed, Rhoda couldn't suppress a tiny spurt of amusement at what she and Aki did on returning to the house. It was obvious Aki felt as guilty as she did, as though they'd committed a crime in enjoying wine, oblivious to their neighbors' suffering. By tacit agreement, they spoke not a word about what they'd just seen, occupying themselves in tidying away the evidence. Rhoda washed their glasses, drying them and putting them in a cupboard while Aki placed the half empty bottle of wine in the fridge. Then they took turns using the bathroom. After Rhoda had brushed her teeth, Aki washed his face and combed his hair.

Rhoda had just gone back downstairs when she heard the sound she'd been dreading—someone ringing the doorbell. She hurried to the front door, leaving Aki in the front room. In the tension of the moment, Rhoda felt a brief surge of hysteria and had to stifle the impulse to laugh. The pair at the door looked so exaggeratedly different—one man so large and bulky, the other short, pale and so thin he verged on emaciation. They reminded her of the Laurel and Hardy comedy duo.

The officers entered and bowed. Rhoda hurried to place slippers for them and, once they'd stepped up to the hallway, ushered them into the front room. Aki stood and bowed, a surprised look on his face.

Rhoda beckoned the officers to the two matching armchairs facing the sofa, but they had their own ideas. The chief inspector sat heavily in the middle of the sofa while the thin officer with the sallow face and bad posture who'd introduced himself as Lieutenant Miyagi pulled out the piano bench. There they waited, silent and impassive, as Aki and Rhoda seated themselves in the two armchairs.

Chief Inspector Ito bowed, and Rhoda and Aki automatically inclined their heads. Rhoda noticed the thin lieutenant had taken a notebook from a jacket pocket and opened it with a pen poised in readiness. He was so gaunt she idly wondered if he was too busy to eat proper meals.

Then the chief inspector and Aki began speaking in rapid Japanese, and Rhoda's attention wandered. Apart from the occasional word, she could understand nothing of what they said.

"You're a Hirakata?" the chief inspector asked Aki. "Aki, presumably." He glanced about inquisitively. "In that case, I met you in this room over ten years ago when...when the tragedy that befell your family occurred. If I recall correctly, it scarcely seems to have changed."

"It's all the same, but I've changed. I was just eleven then," Aki said. *And you've changed, too,* he thought. Aki had felt shocked, on seeing the senior policeman enter the room, at how old he looked. He felt horrified to discover he was in the presence of the man he would always associate with family misfortune. This was the man who had led the investigation into the attack on his father and then took charge of the case of his sister's murder. In Aki's opinion, both investigations had ended in abject failure. The police had not arrested any culprit. Justice hadn't been done. He knew it was unfair, but he felt such antagonism for the man he found it an effort to be civil.

"But I understood your family moved to Tokyo."

"We did, within a month of my sister's murder. My parents sold the house to my cousin, a woman named Mrs. Muraji who lives nearby." Aki sighed. "I've just returned to collect a few personal belongings at my cousin's request. She'd left the place empty, unused until last month, when she decided to rent it out to Miss Ellison," and he nodded his head at Rhoda. "I came back on Sunday and plan to return to Tokyo tomorrow."

"An odd coincidence," the chief inspector said. "Another tragedy has occurred in this neighborhood. Perhaps it is an unlucky place."

"Or we're unlucky to have useless police," Aki muttered, noting, to his satisfaction, that the thin lieutenant jerked upright and stared at hearing his words.

He noted that Chief Inspector Ito, on the other hand, pretended he hadn't heard. He simply repeated. "As I've said, another tragedy has occurred."

Aki slumped in his seat when he realized the significance of Ito's remark. "Naturally, when I saw that body on the stretcher, I thought that might be a possibility," he said. "I suppose it was Mrs. Goto."

"I regret to confirm that is the case. As for the cause of death, we'll have to wait for the results of the post-mortem," the chief inspector said somberly. "But it looks like a severe case of food poisoning."

He paused as Aki gasped and then exclaimed, "My God! Poisoning again!" After a short while, he went on. "But how awful!" he said. "I liked the old girl. She was a character, carrying on despite age and illness. I admired how strong she was, how she wasn't afraid to speak her mind."

Ito gave him a sympathetic glance and went on. "It was the niece who called us right after she'd summoned an ambulance. She said they'd had their usual early dinner at five of rice, soup, broiled fish, and boiled vegetables. As for the poisoning, we suspect the source was the miso soup because Mrs. Goto had two bowls of it and the niece only a little. Otherwise, they'd eaten the same things. Within half an hour of their finishing their meal, the aunt collapsed, complaining of severe abdominal pain."

He sighed before continuing. "Alas, Mrs. Goto was too far gone by the time the ambulance arrived. The paramedics attempted resuscitation, but with no success. The niece said her aunt had made the soup that afternoon, using mushrooms they'd found in a white plastic bag left on their door this morning."

"A white bag?" Aki said.

"Local farmers are in the habit of leaving produce at the Goto residence."

"They've begun giving some to Miss Ellison, too," Aki said, remembering Rhoda's glee when she showed him the green bag that she'd found hanging from the gate when she'd returned home from work a few hours earlier.

The inspector glanced at Rhoda. He said, "The niece also complained of stomach cramps and had to be rushed to the hospital. Luckily, as I've said, Miss Ikeuchi ate only a little of the soup. The aunt's age and weak health also made her less able to withstand the effects of the poison in the mushrooms."

Aki leaned forward eagerly in his chair, forgetting his earlier hostility. "Sir, would you mind my asking why you've singled out the mushrooms as the culprit?"

"We've found the remnants of those included in the bag left at the Goto home. A few belong to the murderous *tsukiyo take* variety. Mrs.

Goto's failing eyesight meant she simply wouldn't have been able to *see* them properly and recognize they were dangerous."

The chief inspector glanced at Rhoda again before turning back to Aki and saying, "As a matter of some urgency, I need you to ask your friend if she has also received a gift of mushrooms lately."

He noticed a horrified expression suddenly appear on the young man's face as the implication of his request dawned on him. "I saw what was inside the bag. I didn't notice mushrooms," Aki said. "She hasn't yet eaten anything that was in it."

"Could you show me?"

At Aki's request in English, Rhoda brought in the green bag, which turned out to contain a few potatoes, a large onion, and two eggplants. The inspector examined the contents and returned the bag to her, bowing his thanks.

After Rhoda had taken the bag back to the kitchen and resumed her seat in the living room, the inspector indicated he wanted to make an announcement. But as he'd be speaking in Japanese, the chief inspector asked Aki to give Rhoda a brief precis of what he'd said later.

"I've overstepped the bounds I usually observe in coming over to question you," the chief inspector said. "I felt time was of the essence. Normally, I would have summoned you both to appear at the station for questioning tomorrow morning. But I wondered whether you might have seen somebody—the person who deposited that bag on Mrs. Goto's door. And as we spoke, of course, I became worried that Miss Ellison might also have got some of those potentially lethal mushrooms." He looked at Aki. "Did you notice anybody in the vicinity today? Somebody who might have left that bag?"

"No. I was here but busy in the house. My friend's been at work all day."

Ito then said, "Can you please ask your friend the names of the individuals—local farmers, I presume—who have been leaving her these bags: presents of food they've grown?"

When Aki asked, Rhoda shook her head, saying the bag she'd received that day was the first, and that she didn't know who left it.

"I have a question I'd like to ask, sir," Aki said, speaking again in Japanese. "No, two, actually. First, have you made any progress on tracking down the individual implicated in my sister's murder? It's been over ten years, after all."

"You mean Hiroki Sato, of course," Ito said, sighing heavily. "I can understand your anger, Hirakata-*san.* Your disappointment. I regret to inform you we have yet to find him. We traced him to Busan, but then the trail went cold. It's as though he simply disappeared into thin air once he arrived in South Korea. There's a nationwide warrant out for his arrest, and Interpol has his details. However, there have been no reported sightings of him."

The inspector sighed. "And your second question?"

"Given my sister died of poisoning and Mrs. Goto, too, do you think there is any link between the two crimes?"

The inspector hesitated before saying, "I hope you will forgive my asking you a question rather than answering the one you have posed. Mr. Hirakata, you have mentioned you plan to return to Tokyo tomorrow morning. I want to ask you to delay your journey. I'd be glad if you could come to the station at nine. I need to talk to you in private and discuss the answer to your second question." He leaned forward, gazing at Aki earnestly. "I'm sorry to inconvenience you, but I think it's important for us both to have that talk."

Aki sprawled on the sofa while Rhoda saw the two policemen out to the front gate. He felt sad and exhausted. What he wanted more than anything was to get out of the house and be by himself. He needed to process the awful realization that Mrs. Goto and her niece had apparently been poisoned—like his sister.

"I'm sorry to be such a bore," Aki said, rising and bowing. "Please forgive me. This has all been upsetting—more upsetting than I expected. I need to be alone for a while." He hurried to the *genkan,* Rhoda trailing behind, picked up his carrier bag and let himself out.

Aki literally shook the dust off his feet as he slammed the gate shut. He even scraped his shoes on the pavement to dislodge any dirt lingering on the soles. He looked forward to having a bath at the hotel that evening and wished he'd thought to bring more extra clothing. As he'd said to that American girl, being in his old home had proved traumatic, and he wanted to wash himself and discard all he was wearing in an attempt—vain, he knew—to cast off all the unhappy memories it had revived. He hoped never to see, let alone enter, that house again. As for Rhoda, she intrigued him, and he wouldn't mind meeting her again. Perhaps it could be arranged—some other time, some other place. But he hated the thought of burdening that beautiful young girl with his death-haunted thoughts.

The carrier bag thumped against his legs as he rushed down the avenue toward the city center and his hotel. Aki found he had to transfer it from one hand to the other because it was heavy and awkward to hold.

He felt a sense of release and relief once he got to the small, dark room on the third floor of the hotel and closed the door behind him. Dropping the bag on the floor and collapsing on the bed, Aki's lips curled in a bitter smile as he reflected on how he continued to be tormented by painful memories. He'd hoped they were losing their power over him, but being in his old house—seeing it looking nearly as it had when his family had left all those years ago—had brought everything flooding back. And now it seemed the past wasn't content to stay in the past. Somebody had tried to murder his neighbors!

When Aki had been sorting through boxes of letters and photos in his parents' bedroom, he'd felt guilty, like an intruder. He'd kept waiting for somebody to open the door. It might be his dead father and mother, demanding to know what he was doing, rifling through their things. Or his dead sister, giving him a reproachful look. Or it might be his own childhood self—that thin, timid little boy—peering in at him in fearful wonder.

Anticipating he'd be taking a few things back to Tokyo with him, Aki had packed just the bare essentials in his suitcase: his laptop, two shirts— one dressy and one casual—a pair of reasonably good pants, pajamas, and a toothbrush. Now Aki rose, walked over to the case in the corner, opened it, and put the carrier bag in it, feeling no desire to look over those mementos again—or at least, not by himself. He'd visit Yumi once he returned to Tokyo, taking the bag with him. Aki thought of the adage that a problem shared is a problem halved. Sharing the pain with her might rob it of some of its potency.

Aki spied a small fridge in the room and found it held three cans of Asahi Super Dry and a miniature of whisky. He downed the whisky in a few gulps, drank a beer to take away the taste, and then lay on the bed fully clothed, thoughts of the hot bath he'd anticipated forgotten in the hunger for oblivion sleep would bring. As he sank into unconsciousness, he offered up a prayer—*Not tonight! Please! Not that old nightmare!*

Aki Hirakata

Before heading to the police station the following morning, Aki asked the hotel clerk if he could stay an additional night. Noticing the dingy interior and paucity of guests, he'd optimistically left his case in his room before even making the request, thinking it unlikely to be denied.

Arriving at the station at nine, Aki found the uniformed officer at the front desk had obviously been told to expect him. When Aki gave his name, he beckoned to another officer, who promptly escorted him to the chief inspector's office on the second floor of the building.

The officer knocked on the door, opened it, and then stood back, waiting for Aki to enter before closing the door behind him.

Aki was struck again by how old Ito looked. He knew he shouldn't be. Prior to the previous evening, it had been ten years since he'd last seen him—at Kaori's funeral. But the inspector's hair was now completely white when Aki had always remembered it as black, flecked with gray. He imagined the man must be in his early sixties, but his deeply furrowed forehead made him look much older. He seemed prematurely aged. The inspector had also lost what had impressed Aki when he was a boy of eleven as an air of calm competence. Ito had been so obviously an adult, possessing a grownup's confidence and mastery of events. Now he seemed less certain, as if he'd suffered some mighty blow that had shaken and then felled him, and he hadn't quite managed to get up afterwards. There was a tentativeness in his manner that Aki hadn't noticed before.

The chief inspector, seated at his desk, rose, motioned to Aki to take one of the two armchairs, then settled heavily on the sofa opposite.

The two sat for a minute, gazing at each other appraisingly.

Finally, Aki broke the silence. "You look older!" he said accusingly.

The inspector smiled ruefully and, lifting a stubby-fingered hand to his head, combed back his thick shock of pure white hair. "It happens," he said, shrugging. "It's called aging."

Then he leaned forward, smiling. "And you've grown up! You're not that skinny boy anymore, the one who kicked my shin and demanded I stop questioning his mother."

Aki flushed. "Oh, I'd forgotten that. My apologies. I acted childishly."

"I admired you for it. You were brave, trying to protect your parents at a difficult time." He paused. "But you're right. I don't want to sound as if I'm holding any of you at all responsible, but your family has caused me great personal anguish and professional disappointment. Your father and sister figured in the only two cases I was unable to solve."

There was another pause. The inspector stood and looked out the window behind his desk. "I thought of resigning after the superintendent of the Ishizaki police force took over the Kaori Hirakata murder investigation." He sighed and hit the pane of glass lightly with one fist. "It felt such a blow!" Then he turned around to gaze at Aki. "I was demoralized, and so were my men."

"Despite all his superior resources and manpower, the superintendent didn't find Hiroki Sato," Aki protested.

"But he had one breakthrough. He succeeded in tracking down a woman named Risa Inagaki who used to be Hiroki Sato's classmate and friend. She was working as a stripper in Soaplands. He got her to confess that she had harbored Hiroki Sato the day before your sister was murdered. Sato had been staying with his mother but then moved to his friend's house. Miss Inagaki said he needed to hide out at her place, that he was on the run from a member of the *yakuza* wanting to make sure he kept his mouth shut about secrets he knew."

Ito sighed deeply. "But Takenaka didn't follow up on this lead. He didn't identify the gangster sent, it would seem, to silence Hiroki Sato forever. I found that so frustrating. It reminded me of how we never identified the *yakuza* who shot your father. Presumably, he was a local, belonging to a Murota gang."

The inspector drummed his fingers impatiently on his desk. "For that matter, I always had doubts about the whole affair. It seemed hard to believe your father had any dealings with gangsters."

"I know! I *know*!" Aki burst out. He hadn't yet been born when the attack occurred, but he knew his father and couldn't believe the rumors to be true.

"Yet your father seemed deliberately set on obstructing our investigation, and so did his former boss, Mr. Taniguchi. I thought they were concealing something they didn't want us to know. We couldn't proceed without the cooperation of at least one of them."

The inspector pursed his lips and gazed intently at Aki. "One reason I've asked you here today is to tell you I'd like to reopen that investigation. I wonder if you've found any private papers of your father's that might throw light on the matter."

"I know my father kept a safe in our house here in Murota," Aki faltered, looking confused. "But I don't know where it is. I left our home as a child; I've returned to it as a visitor. As you know, Miss Ellison is living there now. I'd need to ask her permission to search the place."

"Isn't there anybody you can ask?" the inspector prodded gently.

Aki frowned. "I seem to recall somebody letting slip that my father had the safe installed when I was seven or eight. Yumi had left for England by then and was gone for years, only returning for Kaori's funeral." He shrugged. "Maybe my father took Kaori into his confidence. But I can't see him having written to Yumi to tell her about the safe." He shrugged. "And now my parents and Kaori are dead."

"Anyone else?"

"I doubt my mother would have confided in Mrs. Muraji. But maybe Kaori told her best friend, Emi Tada. I could ask her."

"Please do."

Aki's former sulky look had gone. "Sir, I want to apologize," he said unexpectedly. "I'd like to work with you. Those two tragedies have cast a dark shadow over my life, too. Kids at school bullied me, calling me the son of a crook. Then, when Kaori died, that old sense of shame was swallowed up in my anguish at losing her. I used to feel furious with you for not having nabbed her killer. I thought you were useless. But now I see your hands were tied, and you did your best. I think we lash out in anger when we are hurt. We want somebody to blame. And it was easy for me to target you."

Aki gulped. He was pale and trembling uncontrollably. "I *wanted* to blame you!" he said. "Otherwise, I'd have had to blame myself! I've always been tortured by the thought that if I'd told my parents what I heard the day Kaori died, I might have been able to prevent her death."

"Just a moment, son," Ito said calmly. He lifted the receiver of his phone and ordered coffee to be brought to his office for the two of them. Aki leaned back in his chair and closed his eyes while the inspector looked out the window. Finally, Lieutenant Miyagi appeared with cups and saucers, cream, sugar, and spoons. He laid the tray on the table and left without a word.

"Do you mind if I have a cigarette?" Aki asked as the inspector put sugar in his own cup.

"Not at all." Ito rose and opened a desk drawer, pulling out a heavy glass ashtray he put on the table and pushed toward Aki. "I used to be a heavy smoker myself, but my wife forced me to give up." He handed Aki a cup of steaming black coffee and said, "Cream? Sugar?"

When Aki shook his head, Ito made a surprising request. "In fact, please give me one," he said, and Aki rose to offer his pack, pulling a lighter from a pocket to light his and the inspector's.

They sat back to drink and smoke in contented silence.

Aki found himself marveling at—and feeling grateful for—the inspector's tact. He must have sensed he was nearing hysteria when he admitted how guilty he felt about his sister's death. Ito had obviously arranged this brief pause to allow Aki to collect himself. Aki gave a wry smile he tried to conceal with a cough. The inspector's sensitivity was at odds with the appearance of the burly man opposite him, with his thatch of white hair and deeply furrowed brow.

The inspector stubbed out his cigarette in the ashtray with a regretful air. "I needed that!" he said. "I miss them more than I let on." He drained his cup and then said, "Go ahead with your story, Mr. Hirakata. If you want to, that is. But I hope you do."

Aki nodded and took a deep breath. "I adored Kaori. I used to follow her around. As you'll remember when you came to the house after her death, I told you I'd been standing outside her bedroom door and then began eavesdropping when I heard somebody in her room. It was someone who came twice, once in the morning and once in the evening."

"Hiroki Sato."

"Hiroki Sato. Anyway, the first time it happened, while I couldn't hear everything, this is what I caught. He said he had a secret to tell my sister that he couldn't keep from her any longer."

The inspector leaned forward, his eyes alight. "A secret? What was it?"

"He said it was something he needed to show her. I heard her gasp and say, 'A tattoo! On your shoulder!' From what they said after that I gathered it was a tattoo of a blue dolphin that was the insignia of the *yakuza* group he'd joined when he was in Tokyo. He also said he was still involved with the *yakuza* even after returning to Murota, only now it was the local gang. My sister was frantic. She kept saying it was impossible and that she could never forgive him. You see, she'd never got over what happened to our father. But he swore he'd made a complete break from them because of his love for her. He finally calmed her down. He said he'd be back and help her get out of the house with her case and then was angry when she told him she wasn't sure she'd go. But I had a feeling she would."

"But why do you feel so guilty about this?"

Aki's face crumpled. "Don't you see? I *knew*. I knew Kaori had a boyfriend and a very questionable one. I knew they planned to elope. But I didn't go down and tell my parents. That's what I should have done. They would have stopped her. But I kept her secret, and then what happened to her...happened!"

"You were an eleven-year-old boy who adored his sister and didn't want to betray her. You couldn't have known what was going to happen. You're being too hard on yourself."

Aki shook his head, refusing to be comforted. "He also told Kaori he was being followed. That he was in danger, and she might be in danger, too."

"Did he say why?"

"He hinted he knew secrets his gang wouldn't want revealed—gambling scams, extortion, racketeering—and they wanted him silenced."

Aki paused. "And there was something else, something I couldn't understand—or I simply couldn't hear his explanation. He mentioned his being ordered somehow to *use* my sister but that he'd refused."

Ito's brow was even more furrowed than usual. "I wonder what that could have been about. Anyway, then you heard him come back later?"

"Yes. I knew he'd be coming that night. I kept wandering upstairs and standing outside Kaori's door, waiting to hear that man's voice again. Finally, I heard it and pressed my ear against the door. They talked. Kaori said she'd go away with him after all. He'd brought her a box of chocolates. I don't know why, but I have the impression he'd found the box hanging on his mother's door. Maybe somebody told me that, or maybe I imagined it."

Aki took his last sip of coffee and put the cup and saucer back on the tray with shaky hands. "After about ten minutes, Kaori began to cough, to choke. I heard him say he was going to get water. He unlocked the door, and I hid in a doorway further down the hall. I saw that man—Hiroki Sato—hurrying to the bathroom. He carried the glass of water back to the room. But it wasn't any good. Kaori told him to go. I heard the creaking of the vine. He must have started climbing back down it. That's when I shouted to my parents, telling them Kaori was sick."

He had his head in his hands and was rocking back and forth. The inspector was silent for a few minutes, then stood and gazed out of the window again until Aki spoke.

"Sorry, sir," Aki said. "I'm all right now."

"I'm very glad you've told me all this," the inspector said, returning to his seat. "For one thing, it must be a weight off your mind. We knew much of this already, but maybe it will give us some leads to follow."

"*Us?*" Aki said, raising his face and looking hopefully at Ito.

"Us. As I've said, I'd be grateful for your help."

Aki heaved a sigh of satisfaction and then thought of a question. "Why didn't you leave, sir? After my sister's murder, when the Ishizaki force took over the case?"

"I have a daughter of my own—a girl about your sister's age. She and my wife had settled down here in Murota and felt happy. We'd lived in several other places before coming here, and I felt I couldn't ask them to move again. That meant I didn't feel free to ask for a transfer to another force. And I couldn't think of another job I could do in Murota—that is, without accepting a huge loss in status and a much smaller salary. The only option that seemed remotely possible was to work for a security firm. But I hated the thought of it. So, I knuckled down and accepted failure." He sighed. "My family knew I was miserable, but I refused to talk about it. My wife guessed it had something to do with Superintendent Takenaka's taking over the case, but I tried to laugh it off, pretend it didn't matter, that I was glad to have it off my hands."

Ito sighed. "We've been talking about some of my failures. But I've had a few successes, too. I think I can trust you. I'll tell you about one—on the understanding you won't breathe a word about it to anyone else. We've discovered the author of those nasty poison pen letters you might have heard about."

"Emi visited Yumi and told her about them, said she'd got a few accusing her of abusing her mother. Disgusting!"

"When we had to visit the Goto household, after she and her niece, Ikeuchi-*san*, ate those poisonous mushrooms, we found a stash of large white envelopes, scissors, and cut-up newspapers and magazines. We plan to question the niece when—if—she comes out of her coma."

"But what possible motive could she have had?"

"I think she was short of money and hoped to supplement the meager income her aunt gave her. But even more, she hated her subservient position. She wanted to exert power. Mrs. Goto's being so nosy and such a notorious gossip meant she had lots of material to work with."

"Congratulations, sir. I wonder what action you'll take."

"I haven't decided yet. We still need to investigate the scope of her unpleasant activities and calculate how much money she's been able to extort from her victims. We'll also have to find out whether it was her trying her hand at blackmail that inspired the attempt on her life—and her aunt's." He smiled at Aki. "So, you see, we police aren't so useless after all."

"Not useless, no!" Then Aki blushed, remembering how he'd used to assert just the opposite.

"Speaking of money and its power to make people do bad things, I want to investigate whether the Taniguchi firm still has dealings with the local *yakuza*," the inspector said. "My theory is they were creaming off a good profit when your father was working there—and when he tried to stop it, they stopped him, and presumably old Mr. Taniguchi hired a more compliant head of finance."

"They occupy the top floor of Murota's most expensive office block," Aki said. "They're obviously a successful business."

"Which might argue for their still associating with the local mob. It's a two-way street. The *yakuza* scare off the competition. The Taniguichis monopolize the market."

"The firm might have been a cash cow the *yakuza* were reluctant to see dry up," Aki said.

When Lieutenant Miyagi returned to take away the coffee cups, he found the inspector and Aki Hirakata sitting in companionable silence, puffing on cigarettes.

Aki felt a lightness of step as he strode away from the police station. A sense of purpose energized him. What could be more gratifying and satisfying than trying to help solve the mystery of the attacks on his father and sister?

After cautioning him to complete secrecy—nobody must be allowed to know what they were up to—Ito had asked Aki to get in touch with Emi Tada to find out whether she knew the location of the safe in the Hirakata house. He also suggested Aki nose around—in a way that wouldn't arouse suspicion—into the affairs of the Taniguchi real estate company. Ito had even hit upon a plausible pretext. Aki could express dissatisfaction with the fact his cousin Mrs. Muraji could buy the family home for peanuts, arguing that he'd come to appreciate the value of the house and garden and wanted to dispute a transaction carried through when his parents were suffering undue stress and had been desperate to sell. Aki could say he hoped his father's old firm would provide the necessary context should litigation be required.

Aki paused and looked at his watch. It was eleven o'clock on a Wednesday morning. Emi Tada would undoubtedly be at work. He wondered if it was worth his while to drop by the bank and see if he could treat her to lunch.

A young female bank employee bowed as the huge plate glass doors slid open at his approach and he entered the building. He took the escalator to the second floor, where he saw Emi Tada sitting at a desk in the international exchange section. She noticed him as he approached and hurried to the counter.

Aki felt a pang of pity. The harsh overhead fluorescent lighting was unkind, picking out the coarse pores of her face that even heavy makeup couldn't conceal, as well as the greasiness of her thick black hair drawn back in a bun.

"Hirakata-*san*!" she exclaimed, her face lit up and eyes gleaming. "I thought you'd be back in Tokyo by now."

"Something has come up," Aki said evasively. "I've decided to stay on a bit longer. Emi, is there any chance you could have lunch with me today? My treat, of course."

Emi flushed with pleasure. "Just give me a minute. I'll check with my supervisor."

She hurried off, and Aki watched as she consulted with a gray-haired man in a suit at the very back of the room. The man nodded, and Emi hurried back to the counter, looking years younger, as if someone had just asked her out on a date.

"Come back in half an hour," she whispered.

Aki was heading for the escalator when Emi called him back. "Wait! The timing of my lunch hour is flexible; I just have to ensure it only lasts sixty minutes. I'll leave soon and meet you at the Café Dolce restaurant. It's around the corner."

The café was a charming white cottage fronted by a flower bed. Framed posters of famous Japanese gardens covered the walls, and each table was adorned with a slender blue vase of red spider lilies and autumn roses. Aki sat at one by the window, admiring its floral tablecloth, and ordered a coffee, explaining a friend would join him shortly. The waitress brought a glass of ice water, a hot towel wrapped in plastic, and a menu to the table.

Aki scanned the menu and let out a noiseless whistle. He'd have chosen the *udon* restaurant opposite the bank, where a delicious meal of tempura and noodles in a savory broth would cost a third of the price of any of the café's offerings.

Aki heard the tinkling sound of the bell on the café door. Emi appeared, smiling excitedly, and hurried over to his table. The waitress brought her water, a towel, and a menu, too, but Emi waved the menu away, saying she'd just have the day's special, with Aki echoing her choice. A breaded pork cutlet with cabbage salad, miso soup, rice, and pickles was placed before them within minutes. The waitress said she'd bring them coffee and a slice of cake after they'd finished their main course.

"I'm ravenous," Emi said eagerly, taking her pair of wooden chopsticks from their paper sheaf and breaking them apart.

Aki observed her with amusement. He was treating her, and for her, it was obviously an unusual indulgence. Aki decided it was his duty to entertain her, and he did his best, regaling her with stories of the high life and the nightlife in Tokyo interspersed with tales of adventures he'd had in London when he'd stayed with Yumi. He took pleasure in hearing her laugh, imagining her daily life afforded her few occasions for mirth.

The waitress began hovering watchfully as they were finishing their meals. Once their plates were clean, she rushed to take them away and bring dessert.

"Thank you so much, dear Aki," Emi said, as she took her last bite of cake. "I haven't enjoyed myself so much in ages." Then she wrinkled her brow, peering down at her watch and finally lifting her wrist closer to her eyes to see it. "I'll have to go in a few minutes. We're expected to be very punctual."

"Emi, before you go, I have a quick question," Aki said, suddenly feeling guilty, as if he was playing a dirty trick on his old friend, offering her hospitality on false pretenses, with the expensive meal serving as the bait. He sipped his coffee, trying not to look too eager. "You were like one of the family when we lived in Murota. I know my father had a safe in our house, but I've never had any idea of the location. Or whether it might still be in the house. With my parents dead...and Kaori...there's only Yumi I can ask, and I don't think she knows—not surprisingly, as she left at the end of her teens." He leaned forward earnestly. "Do you know where it might be, Emi?"

To his great relief, a laugh greeted his question. "I do, Aki, even if it was only by accident. Kaori let it slip when I was visiting one day. I was admiring the reproduction of the Monet waterlilies in your living room when she said there was a safe hidden behind it." Emi grinned. "In fact, I don't think Kaori even recalled having told me. We never mentioned it again."

Aki felt his pulse quicken. He struggled to suppress his excitement. He didn't want to show Emi how much the information meant to him. Even if the safe was still there, it was probably empty. Anyway, he needed to find out the combination to open it. He stood as Emi jumped up, looking anxious at the possibility of being late getting back to work.

"Must go, dear boy," she said and then scurried out of the café.

After paying, Aki loitered in the street outside, wondering what to do next. He could go to the Taniguchi real estate company and act like an aggrieved young man robbed of his rightful inheritance. But what he really wanted to do was go back to his house to check on the safe.

Aki scolded himself. "You're a grownup!" he said. "You can't always do what you want! Go to your father's old firm and get it over and done with. You know you're dreading it. And that's precisely why you should do it."

Twenty minutes later, ignoring his own advice, he was asking the guard stationed at the gates of the new university on the hill for directions to the office of the new American professor.

Aki whistled noiselessly as he made his way to the six-story building he'd been told was the office block. Rhoda's office was on the fifth floor, but the guard had assured him there was an elevator.

Aki was glad to be on a university campus again. They always had their own vibe—a special buzz of excitement—even at a third-rate university like this one in provincial Murota. The students wore the latest trendy fashions, the boys in ripped jeans and T-shirts and the girls in long floral skirts and platform sandals. They sauntered about nonchalantly, but it was obvious they felt privileged, the favored few, as they paused in throngs to chat or strode purposefully down the brick paths to classes or toward the library, carrying books under their arms. Seeing those bright, eager faces, Aki felt an unexpected emotion that he finally recognized as envy.

Aki was surprised when Rhoda opened the door to his knock. He'd imagined she'd be teaching English conversation to a packed classroom of unruly first-years. She blushed when she saw him, which automatically lifted his spirits.

After she said, "I thought you'd be back in Tokyo by now," he began trotting out the explanation he'd come up with—that he'd forgotten a few things in the house and needed to get back in—when he got a guilty feeling again. *Do I use people?* he thought. *Is that something I do? Is that who I am?*

With a sickening jolt, he suddenly remembered Kaori accusing Hiroki Sato of using her. Had he sunk to that level, too?

"Should I go with you?" Rhoda asked. "I've already finished for the day. I only have two morning classes on Wednesdays."

Aki felt he had a chance to reprieve himself. "Yes, come with me," he said. "But I want to tell you I lied. It's not that I forgot to take a few things. I've just found out the location of something important in my house, something I've been wondering about and hoping to find for ages: a hidden wall safe."

Rhoda's laughter was music to his ears. "You had me fooled, but I don't care. You can make up for it by letting me be there when you open it. Maybe it holds some kind of treasure. How exciting! Let's go!"

Aki found Rhoda's insouciant approach charming. It was so different from his own nervy earnestness, which he considered a burden and a bore.

Rhoda had come to the university by bike and planned to go home that way. They arranged to meet at the house in about twenty minutes.

Aki walked as quickly as he could, wasting no time to look at the familiar sights. He was puffing, almost breathless, by the time he reached the front gate. Opening it and hurrying up the narrow path through the overgrown garden, he could knock just once before the door was flung open by Rhoda, who'd obviously been waiting for him.

"It's so thrilling!" she said. "You say you've never seen this safe before?"

"No, I've only heard of it. My father was never inclined to tell me where it was."

Aki quickly stepped out of his shoes and into the slippers Rhoda had put out for him. They made their way to the living room, where Aki pointed at the reproduction of Monet's painting of waterlilies on the wall, saying, "I should have known. I'd always wondered why my father liked this one so much. He was a fan of Impressionist art anyway, but said this was his favorite. Perhaps he was trying to give me a hint."

Aki turned on the overhead light. Then he approached the painting and bowed solemnly, making Rhoda giggle. "Dear painting, please forgive my presumption, but I must take the liberty of *manhandling* you!"

He grasped the frame, lifted the painting from the wall, and, panting from the effort, gently placed it on the floor.

"It's so heavy!" he said. "I somehow feel grateful for it. It's not only brought beauty into this room but also served to conceal my father's safe successfully all these years."

Rhoda approached to take a closer look. The Monet reproduction had completely hidden a steel gray safe with a black dial sunk into the wall.

"Do you have the combination?" Rhoda asked.

"No, but I live in hope. I wonder if this lovely object might not be hiding yet another secret."

After Aki picked up the painting and laid it face down on the sofa, he scrutinized the back. "Ha!" he shouted. Rhoda leaned over to look, too. She saw a five-digit number scribbled in the upper left-hand corner. Aki took a pen and paper from a pocket and copied the number. Then he approached the safe again. Rhoda stood stock still and silent as Aki fumbled with the dial on the gray steel face of the safe. The door suddenly swung open, revealing a large brown wooden box, its lid closed by a clasp.

Rhoda came closer to peer inside. "Wow!" she said. "It's not a treasure chest, but near enough."

Aki reached in and extracted the box, carrying it around the sofa and placing it on the coffee table. He opened the simple gold clasp and lifted the lid.

Rhoda peered over his shoulder at the contents. Packets of neatly folded papers tied with blue ribbon filled the box to the brim. "No jewels or gold coins, but maybe it's something even better," she said.

Aki took out a packet, untied it, read the top paper for a few minutes, and whistled. Returning it and retying the ribbon, he put the packet jubilantly back into the box and closed the lid. Then he sat on the sofa and threw his arms in the air. "Hallelujah!" he said.

Rhoda stared. Aki was grinning, looking boyish and cheerful.

"You're right. It's much better than pirate treasure. I think I've found exactly what I've been looking for," he said. "My father was the most organized person I've ever known. I was astonished when I sorted through his personal papers after his death and didn't come across anything about the scandal that saw him lose his job and his reputation."

He leaned forward and tapped the box. "I think he kept everything here."

"But why didn't he take the box to Tokyo with him?"

Aki's brow furrowed. He was silent for a short while before answering. "One of my sisters used to tell me how my parents were before the scandal that destroyed their lives. My mother loved pretty clothes and dancing, and my father was fond of golf. Maybe *Otoosan* left this behind because he thought of it as belonging to his former life. He used to tell me that becoming a Christian meant forgiving and forgetting. Turning the other cheek. I can imagine him deciding to leave this box in the safe in the knowledge that it might never be discovered, or at least not in his lifetime. He had moved on and didn't want to keep anything that reminded him of the past."

He looked up plaintively. "I wish my sister Yumi was here." He felt small and vulnerable.

"One minute," Aki said. "I've left my mobile at the hotel. Could I use your phone?"

"Of course."

After disappearing into the hallway and placing the call, Aki felt his old self again.

"Who did you call?" Rhoda wondered when he returned a few minutes later. "Your sister?"

"No, just somebody who's ignored me and my family long enough." He grinned. "Well, that bastard doesn't have that option any longer!"

Chapter Seven

Yumi and Aki Hirakata
Wednesday-Friday, 30 September-2 October 1998
Murota

Rhoda insisted Aki stay and have tea with her. Naturally, she pumped him for information on the identity of the "bastard," but he skillfully deflected her curiosity by turning the tables and interrogating her about herself and her family.

On finally leaving what had once been his old home, carrying the big wooden box he'd found in the safe, Aki wrestled with the impulse to call Ito. He supposed he should, but he wanted time and leisure to examine the contents of the box first to digest their significance. Also, he didn't want to discuss that cache of his father's papers with Ito before he'd talked to Yumi. Maybe it was a pathetic habit persisting from childhood—as a boy, he'd often asked his big sister Kaori for advice and assistance. But only Yumi could understand the importance of his discovery, and Aki longed to go over the documents with her first.

Something odd happened on his way to the hotel. Stopping at an intersection just a short distance away, Aki stood patiently, looking at the traffic lights. The street was empty, but like a good Japanese, he was content to wait for the permission conferred by the pedestrian signal.

That's when he heard somebody stop behind him, panting. Finally, the illuminated symbol of a green walking man meant Aki could start across the road. The heavy-breathing individual was right behind him, and Aki suppressed irritation. After all, given his long residence in Tokyo, he'd gotten used to crowded conditions in any public space.

But this individual was really close, so close Aki could hear how heavily he was breathing. Aki was both surprised and not surprised at all when that person—he assumed it was a man—actually trod on his left heel and then shoved him hard from behind. Instinctively, Aki waved his hands in the air, trying to regain his balance, and dropped the box. He collapsed on the ground, on his back, and struggled to breathe. The fall had knocked the wind out of him.

Once he'd recovered from the initial shock, Aki glanced up to see the man who'd tripped him bend over and pick up the box lying on the road. He was squat and short, the front button of his suit straining against his belly, his face obscured by a hat and sunglasses. It all happened so quickly that Aki watched helplessly as the man turned his back on him, ignoring his plight, seemingly intent on running off with the box. "Wait! Stop!" Aki finally managed to shout. And that's when he noticed someone else suddenly appear and, even better, that it was a policeman.

The short squat man saw the policeman, too. He hurried back to Aki and extended a hand to help him get up, holding the box with the other. Aki's sense of horror deepened when he noticed the man was missing his little finger. He tried to see his face, but the hat, its brim pushed down, shielded it. Aki guessed he was in his mid-fifties.

Once Aki was standing, wheezing heavily, with the policeman patting him on the back to help him recover, the short squat man nodded his head and, with exaggerated courtesy, handed the box back to him. Bowing to the policeman, he crossed the road and disappeared down a small street. At first, Aki thought of enlisting the policeman's aid in stopping the man by complaining he'd deliberately made him fall, then tried to steal his box. But Aki had no proof. Anyway, the man was gone, and he didn't imagine the policeman would have any luck finding him. Instead, he thanked the policeman and hurried back to his hotel.

At six Aki succumbed to temptation and called his sister. It took considerable persuasion, but Yumi finally agreed to come, swayed by Aki's explanation of what was at stake. She promised to arrive on the early afternoon train the next day and to bring their father's old briefcase as he requested. It was one of the few mementos Yumi decided to keep when she cleared out their parents' flat in Tokyo after their deaths. After hanging up, Aki went down to the hotel reception and extended his booking for two more nights while also reserving a room for his sister for the same period.

Aki whiled away Thursday morning, impatiently awaiting his sister's arrival. He arrived at the station just as Yumi was nearing the ticket gate. He saw her before she saw him and scrutinized her as he would a stranger, speculating on character and circumstances. As she handed her ticket to the official, he noticed her elegant, arresting appearance. She was the sort of interesting-looking person he occasionally glimpsed and wished he knew.

A feeling of thankfulness suddenly overwhelmed Aki. It was lucky that the distinguished woman was his own beloved sister, his love and gratitude heightened by her agreeing, despite grave reservations, to meet him in Murota. If he discounted Kaori's funeral, which had passed in a blur of emotion, the last time he'd been with Yumi in their hometown was when he was a seven-year-old boy and she was nineteen, on the point of leaving for England. She'd never returned to Murota since the funeral, and he knew she'd had to overcome repugnance and even fear in acceding to his request. How odd that they were all grown up now! And that their parents were dead, and so was Kaori, and that an American girl was living in their old home.

Although they had both lived long in the UK, Japanese ways were so deeply ingrained in their DNA that the brother and sister didn't even consider hugging. They bowed and Aki said, "Was it very hard getting leave to come here?"

"I had to beg my editor. But I promised I might come back with a good story."

"You didn't!"

"I did! That journalist I told you about, Koji Yanagihara, put in a good word for me. But, as I've explained, he's worried I might be in danger here. From what you've told me, the fact I'm a journalist could be perfect leverage to get a satisfactory arrangement with you-know-who."

"The bastard, you mean," Aki said. Then he grinned. "Come to think of it, that would be the perfect revenge—an exposé on how a certain local real estate firm has had dealings with the *yakuza*. I'm glad you thought of it." He picked up Yumi's case, saying, "It's heavy!"

"I've brought *Otoosan's* old briefcase, just as you told me to."

"Good. I think it's very fitting. Even if *Otoosan* can't be with us when we go to Taniguchi's tomorrow, it's poetic justice that his indispensable briefcase will play a role in our encounter. I've got you a room at my hotel. It's pretty awful, but at least it's cheap and near the town center."

"And we'll be together," Yumi said.

"In adjoining rooms. We're booked for two nights. I think we should be able to get everything done by then and can head back to Tokyo together on Saturday morning. The hotel is a twenty-minute walk from here."

Yumi blinked, peering up at the blazing sun. "It all comes back to me—how unbearable Murota is this time of year. So bright! So hot! So humid! Maybe we should take a taxi to the hotel."

"Let's have a drink first."

"It has to be iced."

There was a little café just opposite the train station. Yumi glanced over at the port once they had seated themselves at a table by the window and got their drinks. "I used to love coming to this part of town when I was a girl," she said. "I would watch the ferries heading away, leaving this place behind. Even then, I had dreams of fleeing Murota."

"Because of what happened to *Otoosan*?"

"Partly. Being an adolescent is hard enough without having to cope with family disgrace, too. Some kids at school bullied me, saying that I was my father's daughter and couldn't be trusted. I suppose you had that, too. I also hated how our parents became so religious, insisting we read the Bible and pray before meals. I felt suffocated by it all. And then there was Kaori. I hoped my leaving would toughen her up, that she'd stop putting everyone's needs before her own."

Yumi grimaced and took a sip of her coffee, the ice cubes tinkling in the glass. Aki put out a hand, and she held out hers. They sat in silence, holding hands for a minute. Then Aki let go and rubbed his brow. "It must have been tough. Well, I know it's tough. I experienced some of that, too."

"I also hated having that awful woman, Juno-*sensei,* in our lives. I was escaping from her as well as from everything else."

"I don't like her either," Aki said. "Didn't like her when I was a child and don't like her now. I've met her once since coming back, purely by chance. She made it clear how disappointed she is I've lost my faith. The odd thing is she seems to think we're friends."

"I know that look she must have given you—hurt, as if you'd deliberately let her down. I used to get it all the time. But I didn't care! What I worried about was how she latched onto Kaori. I think she saw her as the daughter she'd never have. Kaori confided to me she didn't really like Juno, but Kaori, being Kaori, she never let on because she felt sorry for her."

"I recall your acting spectacularly bored in church."

"I was! Pastor Nakagawa's sermons went on and on and on. I could feel the will to live draining away as he spoke. Anyway, I'm thrilled you found that box. How lucky Emi knew the location of the safe. I was in England when Kaori sent a letter mentioning *Otoosan* was having one installed, but she didn't think to tell me where."

Suddenly, Yumi shivered and looked around suspiciously. "I enjoy being with you, but I don't enjoy being here. In Murota! I wish we could take the box and go right back to Tokyo. I don't feel safe. Take my being here at all as a testament to my love for you."

Aki smiled. "I know! I'm touched. You've told me often enough you never wanted to come back here. Let's go to the hotel."

The two stayed up until the early hours of the morning, poring over the papers in Aki's hotel room and ordering pizza for their evening meal. Toward dawn, Yumi made a discovery that astonished them both.

"So *Otoosan* wasn't a coward after all," she said, looking pleased.

"But think of the implications of what we've just learned," Aki said, pacing up and down. "Could this mean it was the *yakuza* who poisoned Kaori?"

"As a journalist, I counsel caution. We can't jump to conclusions. Anyway, I hope old Mr. Taniguchi's grandson can clear this up for us," Yumi said.

"Our appointment is at nine," Aki said. "I'm not sure I can wait that long."

Despite getting only a little sleep and needing to spend an hour at a convenience store making copies, the sister and brother presented themselves punctually at the reception desk of the Taniguchi real estate company on Friday morning, Yumi wearing a bulging backpack and Aki holding an old black briefcase. The supercilious young woman behind the desk made a point of insulting them. After looking askance at Aki, dressed as usual in jeans and an open-necked shirt, she claimed she couldn't find the appointment. When Aki insisted and refused to budge, she kept them waiting a good ten minutes before ringing Mr. Taniguchi to tell him they'd arrived.

The reception given to them by her boss was scarcely warmer. "You've got some nerve coming here," he hissed once the door had closed behind his secretary, his thick brows almost touching as he frowned. Makoto Taniguchi might be handsome and sport an expensive haircut, a stylish suit, and glossy shoes, but there was a hint of the pugilist about him, and now anger made him ugly, twisting his regular features. "I can't believe you two even dare show your faces in this place," he added, glaring at them accusingly. "In all its long years, Taniguchi Real Estate has been a respectable and yes, I'll say it, a very successful firm. It was your father who brought shame on us. Naturally, I imagined that his death meant all our connections with your family had been severed."

Aki stood, shifting the heavy black briefcase he was holding from hand to hand. He was only a few years younger than the businessman, but his casual clothing and tremulous expression made him look like a teenager supplicating an implacable adult. In the silence that followed, sun poured through large windows offering a view of the town stretching out below, bounded by the undulating silhouettes of low mountains in the distance.

"May we sit down?" Yumi finally said, pointing to two armchairs in the room.

It was obvious no expense had been spared in furnishing the room. The businessman stood proudly behind his huge glossy desk, positioned on thick green carpeting and lit from above by discreet spotlights beaming down from the ceiling. Plush green velvet armchairs flanked a low coffee table, and expensive-looking watercolor paintings of flowers covered the creamy walls, while heavy green drapes framed the big windows offering views of central Murota.

Makoto Taniguchi heaved an angry sigh, but waved Yumi and Aki to the chairs. After seating himself on the black leather swivel chair behind his desk, he spoke to his secretary on an intercom, ordering coffee for the three of them.

Yumi offered a sharp contrast to her brother. Wearing a tailored white linen suit and heels, her hair swept back in a stylish chignon, she looked perfectly composed and even rather bored. She deposited her backpack next to her chair and began calmly inspecting her nails as her brother spoke in a nervous, tentative voice.

He had just got out the words "I have some documents to show you," leaning down to unclasp the briefcase he'd deposited on the floor, when Mr. Taniguchi unexpectedly leaped to his feet, nearly knocking over his swivel chair as he did so.

"Wait, wait, wait!" he cried, rubbing a hand distractedly through his hair, spoiling its perfect cut. "I don't know why I'm doing this! I should ask you two to leave and summon a guard if you refuse."

His angry words acted like a signal, jumpstarting Aki into action. He sprang out of his chair and, racing to the desk, slammed both hands down on its brightly polished surface, startling Mr. Taniguchi sufficiently that he stumbled backward, collapsing onto his chair that squeaked under his weight.

"No, *you* wait!" Aki said, nearly shouting out the words. "Just listen!" His sister, meanwhile, continued inspecting her nails, but now she was smiling.

Aki strode over to the window and stared out. Complete silence overtook the room until he turned around and walked over to the briefcase. He picked it up, carried it over to the desk, and threw it down on that gleaming surface like a challenge.

Yumi laughed softly, observing Mr. Taniguchi's startled look.

"I'll give you the benefit of the doubt," Aki said. "I'll *assume* you know nothing about what really happened between my father and your grandfather all those years ago."

Yumi suddenly got up and stood beside her brother. "I'm not sure you *should* assume that, Aki. But maybe that's just me. I remember how this man's grandfather used to creep me out, how he always insisted on kissing me and Kaori and hugging us in a way I now realize was completely inappropriate. A pervert."

She coolly appraised Makoto Taniguchi before adding, "As for you, there's the fact your own father was such a loser that he abandoned his family and ended up an alcoholic living on the streets in Tokyo. Where he died. Alone. Abandoned. What does that say about him? About you? Even more, what does that say about your grandfather, who didn't step in to save his own son?"

"Yumi, Yumi, Yumi," Aki muttered, but he was grinning.

Then the grin left Aki's face, and he glared again at the man behind the desk. "Here's another assumption, probably another naïve one. I'll assume you had nothing to do with the low life who tried to rob me as I was on my way to my hotel last night."

Makoto Taniguchi stared, then said in a blustering but (Yumi thought) unconvincing way, "I don't know what you're talking about!"

"I'd rung you an hour earlier to tell you I'd found my father's safe and discovered documents I was taking away with me, intending to show to the police. Documents confirming his innocence and your grandfather's guilt. Could it have been a coincidence some thug suddenly appeared as I walked from my old house to my hotel and tried to take them from me?"

Makoto Taniguchi kept shaking his head wordlessly.

Aki shook his head, too, in disgust. He opened the briefcase and dumped its contents onto the desk. "These are all copies," he said. "We have the originals and intend to give them to the police. I suggest you read all this material very carefully."

Aki looked at Yumi, who nodded in confirmation. "Once you've done that and realize it proves your family committed a crime against ours, this is what we want: a public refutation of the libelous claims made against our father, an admission of your own grandfather's guilt, and financial restitution for the money my family lost out on because my father had to resign his directorship in the firm."

Mr. Taniguchi looked pale. He clutched the edge of his desk so hard that his knuckles turned white.

"I can't. I can't. I can't," he finally said. "My grandfather will disown me. Those thugs will kill me."

"Thugs?" Yumi asked.

"You *know* who!" he said in an exasperated voice. "The men who drive black cars with tinted windscreens. Who have tattoos and, sometimes, no pinky fingers. They were behind it all."

Following a soft knock on the door, the receptionist appeared, bearing a tray holding three coffee cups with sugar and creamer and spoons balanced on the saucers.

She had a smile pasted on her face, but it vanished as Mr. Taniguchi suddenly sat up and assumed a stern expression. "Put the tray there," he demanded, pointing at the coffee table, then barked angrily, "and tidy up this desk."

His fury reduced the scornful receptionist to an anxious girl, looking like she might burst into tears. "Yes, sir," she said, "right away."

Placing the tray on the coffee table, she hastily gathered up the papers scattered over her boss's desk and aligned them in a neat heap in one corner. Bowing, she exited the room.

But the coffee was destined to turn cold and remain undrunk. Yumi nudged her brother. "Remember? We still have the most important question of all to ask."

"You're right, of course," he said. Aki approached Makoto Taniguchi's desk once more, again slamming his hands down so hard the young man jumped.

"We found one more document in the safe we'd like you to explain to us. It's a copy of a letter my father sent to your grandfather dated the fifteenth of September, 1988."

"Is that date significant?" Makoto Taniguchi whispered, his lips white.

Yumi joined her brother at the desk and also slapped its surface with both hands. "Pay attention!" she demanded. "Our sister was murdered with poisoned chocolates three days later."

"But I don't see the connection," the man said, almost whimpering.

"The letter makes it plain our father intended to clear his name after keeping silent for so many years. He explicitly blames your grandfather— for the firm's questionable links with the *yakuza* and for having him shot."

Yumi's eyes blazed as she hissed, "*That's* the connection! Now we just need to know if our sister was another victim of your family's despicable greed and corruption and links to thugs. If she was killed to silence our father."

After a long pause, the young businessman spoke in a subdued voice that was almost a whisper. "No, I categorically deny we had anything to do with your sister's death. But I'll admit to some of the other accusations you've made. I know a bit of the story. My grandfather told me snippets of it when he began training me to take charge of the firm. He swore me to silence. I'll look over your papers and see what I can do."

He looked up piteously and added, "In return, can you promise not to give the originals to the police until I've spoken to you?"

Aki and Yumi looked at each other and then, by common consent, at Mr. Taniguchi, shaking their heads.

The man shivered as he added, "In that case, I'll have to mention that when I...consult...certain individuals concerned."

Hearing these words, Yumi and Aki rose. Aki picked up the empty briefcase and Yumi put on her backpack. After they bowed deeply and turned to leave, Aki looked back as they were exiting the office and saw the young businessman sitting at his desk, head in hands, muttering, "No, no, no..."

As the brother and sister left the building, Aki put down the briefcase and turned to Yumi. It was instinctive. They lifted their hands and clapped them against each other's in a gesture of celebration. "*Yatta!*" said Yumi. "We did it! What an unpleasant man. I disliked the receptionist at first, but now I feel sorry for her. Where to next?"

"The police station. It's just a little way down this road. But first I'll call and see if Chief Inspector can meet us." He insisted on taking Yumi's heavy backpack, giving it a conspiratorial pat. "It's just lucky that creep didn't realize we have the originals of the documents with us. I wouldn't put it past him to have attacked us to get at them."

The Police

Miyagi was happily chatting with Miss Hino at the station nibbling almond cookies she'd baked herself when the phone rang. He grimaced at the interruption. They'd moved on from anecdotes about the Bear to gossip about certain officers well known to them both.

"Is the Bear in his office?" Miss Hino asked, holding a hand over the receiver.

"I suppose so. I was with him half an hour ago," he said.

She took her hand away from the receiver and spoke into it, saying, "Please wait a moment." She put Aki on hold and rang the chief inspector, who confirmed he was free to see Mr. Hirakata and his sister.

"At last!" Ito thought as he put down the phone. He'd been waiting for good news so long he'd nearly lost hope. He knew Aki would only come to the station if he had made a breakthrough in any of the lines of inquiry proposed to him.

But the chief inspector wasn't experiencing unmixed joy, and he knew why. For all his years of experience, he'd come up blank in the two cases related to the ill-omened Hirakatas. So how had young Aki contrived to find answers so quickly? Ito knew he had to be honest with himself—chagrin and envy marred his happiness.

He instructed Miyagi to bring in coffee. Celebrations were in order despite his mixed feelings. He stood as Yumi and Aki walked in. They all bowed, then the siblings sat in the two armchairs, with Aki depositing a heavy-looking backpack by his chair and Yumi a battered old briefcase by hers, apparently empty. The inspector took his usual place on the sofa opposite.

Ito looked closely at Yumi. "I last saw you at your sister's funeral," he said.

"A decade ago."

"I can't believe it's been so long. And I imagine you feel the same way."

"I think of her every day," Yumi said. "I miss her every day."

And I feel guilty about her every day, the inspector thought.

At that point, Miyagi walked in, bearing the coffee tray. Once everybody had a cup, Ito turned his attention to Aki.

"Right, son," he said, hoping he didn't sound patronizing. "Out with it."

He watched as Yumi and Aki smiled at each other. Then Aki moved the tray to one side, lifted the backpack, and emptied its contents onto the tabletop.

"I've got it! That is, I've got the proof," Aki triumphantly said. "Proof that my father was unfairly accused and unfairly punished."

"How did you come across these documents?" Ito said, untying a packet and flipping curiously through the pages.

"Emi Tada knew the location of the safe. My father had hidden it in plain sight behind a painting in the living room, and these papers were in it, stored in a big wooden box." He smiled ruefully and lifted a hand to tousle his hair. "Granted, it was a pretty obvious place to hide a safe. I'd probably have found it if I'd looked for it."

Yumi looked exasperated. "Whatever," she said. "The point is, we've got them now. My father was a very organized man. What you see here is typical: all the papers kept in meticulous chronological order, every packet dated. They tell the story of how the rot set in—that is, the illicit transactions between the Taniguchi real estate firm and the local *yakuza* in the seventies—when old Mr. Taniguchi began paying them protection money. His father, who'd founded the firm decades earlier, refused. But the son didn't have the nerve; he gave in to their demands."

Aki took over. "What we've discovered more or less confirms that theory you proposed to me, Inspector. It started as protection money, but then the *yakuza* decided to sweeten the deal—and force the firm into a closer relationship with them—by advancing loans at low rates of interest.

Which old Mr. Taniguchi used to expand his business. My father felt devastated when he discovered the firm's mutual benefits system with Murota's thugs. They had set it up long before he joined, when he first worked as a lowly accountant. After he advanced up the ladder and became the director of finances, it didn't take him long to see what was happening. Some papers are pages torn from a diary my father kept. They describe how he agonized over the situation and tried to find solutions. By then, the *yakuza*'s demands had grown so exorbitant Mr. Taniguchi couldn't cook the books sufficiently to hide what was going on."

Ito was frowning, trying to take it in, as Aki continued, "When my father said the whole affair had to be made public, old Mr. Taniguchi freaked out. First, he attempted to bribe my father, offering a generous sum of money in exchange for his silence. Then he appealed to his sense of loyalty, implying that if my father made any disclosures, the firm would probably go bankrupt. Finally, he made threats. I don't know whether it was him or the gangsters who decided to frighten my father by having some hoodlum shoot him in the leg. I hope you can find out."

Yumi raised a hand to halt her brother's account. Her face pale, she said, "The worst is how they played upon our father's love for us to agree to take the blame, acceding to his own public humiliation. He was told something along the lines of, 'This time you got shot. Next time it'll be your wife or one of your daughters.'" She looked tearful.

Aki leaned over to give his sister a consoling pat on the arm. "It's all there, Inspector, in one form or another. It seems my father kept everything. Maybe he cherished a vague hope that someday all this would come out and exonerate him."

"Is the name of the man who fired the shot given?"

"Not exactly," Aki said. "Mr. Taniguchi admitted to my father that he had paid a local *yakuza* handsomely to do the deed, but he didn't divulge the identity. The old man must have engineered the whole scam and eventually told his grandson about it. Young Taniguchi looked guilty enough when Yumi and I confronted him."

"We've just come from meeting him," Yumi explained. "He's such a shameless hypocrite! He does his old grandfather proud. At first, he implied we were besmirching his precious company just by turning up there. He sang a different tune after we gave him copies of these documents and told him we were taking the originals to the police."

"I loved the look on his face when we made our demands," said Aki.

"Which were?" the inspector said.

"That they rehabilitate our father's reputation, confess to their own guilt, and compensate us for the financial losses incurred. Makoto Taniguchi was angry at first but finally indicated he knew the *yakuza* had been involved and said he'd be contacting them himself to let them know the game was up."

"That's when he didn't look angry anymore—when he began to look scared instead," Yumi said. She smiled, shaking her head ruefully. "It's so odd. It's what I've wanted for ages. But now I find it makes me feel worse, not better. When we left that horrible man's office, I was thrilled, as if I was walking on air." She looked at her brother. "But now the whole thing just makes me feel soiled. Dirty and sad. My heart aches for my poor parents, who paid such a heavy price for old Mr. Taniguchi's wickedness. I wonder if you feel the same way, Aki."

"Totally." Then he looked at Yumi. "Shall I tell him?"

"Of course."

"We've left the best till the last. The icing on the cake. We discovered a copy of a letter from our father dated three days before Kaori was poisoned. It's addressed to old Mr. Taniguchi and threatens to make everything public. My father said he was going to the police with incriminating documents. Could that be a coincidence?"

The chief inspector's eyes were gleaming. "I'd been wondering if this had anything to do with your sister's murder."

Aki shrugged. "The grandson strenuously denied it, but I don't trust him an inch. We think it needs to be investigated."

A beeping sound broke the silence that followed. "That's mine," said Yumi, taking her mobile from her pocket and leaving the room.

She carried her phone out into the hallway. On her return, Ito felt startled and noticed surprise on Aki's face, too. Yumi had gone out looking wan and miserable. The woman who reappeared had lost five years in as many minutes. She was glowing and girlishly excited.

And she clearly knew it. "Sorry to be so ridiculous," she said, shaking her head in self-deprecation. "You wouldn't think I'm in my early thirties. I hope I'll grow up someday. That was my boyfriend. Well, a Japanese man who used to be my boyfriend when we were both living in England. We got reacquainted when we both moved back to Tokyo and have been spending lots of time together. He's coming to Murota this evening, says he's worried I'm going through a hard time and wants to be here to offer support."

She grinned. "He's so amazing. He's not only a good manga artist. He can cook. He can speak Korean and English and a little Spanish."

"A marvel," said the inspector.

"Tetsuya Kataoka? How sweet! I'll finally get to meet that mysterious suitor you met in England and got hooked up again with when he moved to Tokyo. But does that mean I need to book another hotel room?" Aki said.

Yumi shook her head, laughing. "We're grownups. We'll manage."

When the Hirakatas left his office taking the briefcase and the backpack, Inspector Ito bundled up all the documents they'd brought and carried them out to the staff room, dumping them unceremoniously on Lieutenant Miyagi's desk.

"Deputize two officers to note down the salient points," Ito said. "They'll also need to visit Mitsuo Bank—where the Taniguchi firm has an account. I need to have the firm's statements examined from the seventies onward and those of Mr. Iwao Hirakata. As far as possible, the officers must try to find verification for any points raised in the documents. Depending on what they discover, I may want to issue a search warrant for the Taniguchi real estate firm."

"Yes, sir. Right away, sir," Miyagi said. He paused, considering, then said, "I have two officers in mind, sir, both very good with numbers."

"How quickly can you have them start?"

"Within half an hour. I'll take them off any other duties."

"Good. Once you're done, I want you to accompany me to a house in the Soaplands district. It's about time we addressed a loophole in Superintendent Takenaka's investigation of Kaori Hirakata's murder. He'd found a woman named Risa Inagaki who harbored Hiroki Sato for a night before he fled to Busan. That was his only breakthrough in the case, but unaccountably the superintendent only interviewed her once, got little out of her, and never bothered seeing her again. She's someone I want to question."

Ito added, "She works nights. We need to catch her before she goes off to her job."

"Yes, sir." Miyagi rose and picked up the documents. After he had left the office, Ito heard his voice in the corridor, summoning two officers by name to attend a short briefing on an urgent matter.

A short time later, Ito sat in the back seat of the patrol car chauffeured by Miyagi, watching as they passed down the broad avenue bisecting the heart of Murota's bustling and prosperous commercial district where trim men and women in suits carrying briefcases hurried down the sidewalks or waited impatiently at the traffic signals. As the car proceeded south and passed the entrance to the town's famous old traditional garden, Ito noticed how the tall commercial buildings gave way to less imposing structures. Fast-food joints and convenience stores proliferated, with the occasional old Japanese dwelling featuring a tiled roof and garden of bonsai trees in pots was wedged between the oil-stained concrete forecourt of a large gas station and the crowded parking lot of a garishly lit pachinko parlour.

The urban landscape deteriorated even further once they'd entered Soaplands, a dismal district of factories made of ugly corrugated iron, houses little better than shacks, and brothels advertising themselves as bathhouses that offered massage services. At night, Ito knew these bathhouses would be illuminated with a warm pink glow to attract customers. Black-suited burly men in sunglasses would prowl outside, supervising the clientele and refusing admittance to any potential troublemakers.

After taking a labyrinthine route through the most densely populated section of Soaplands, Miyagi was told to take the next left. "We're nearly there," Ito said, reassuringly, knowing his lieutenant didn't care for this part of town. They soon found themselves on a dusty road lined by five shabby houses in a row, each with its own breeze-block wall. "Park at the end of this street," the inspector said. "The woman I wish to interview lives in the last house."

Miyagi trailed behind the inspector as he walked up a dirt path, opened the gate, and knocked on the cracked, plywood door, visibly starting when a waif-like woman with huge breasts, her face nearly hidden by a mop of brassy blonde hair, opened the door.

"I wondered when you'd turn up to question me again," she said, beckoning them to follow her. "I only had to wait ten years."

Miyagi wrinkled his nose as they took off their shoes in the *genkan* and stepped up into the slippers she'd left in the hallway for them. Obviously, these houses had not yet been connected to Murota's sewage system.

She led them to a room dominated by a huge leather sofa. "Sit there," she ordered. "I'll get tea."

She returned within minutes, carrying three steaming cups of green tea on a tray that she placed on a low table in front of the sofa. She then seated herself on a cushion opposite them.

"So, what do you want to know?" she asked, looking at her watch. "My show begins in an hour. I can only spare you a few minutes."

"Thanks for seeing us, Miss Inagaki," said the inspector. "I'm very grateful. I have a few questions I'd like to ask. First, we're still unclear how Hiroki Sato came by the box of chocolates he took to Kaori Hirakata's home. Do you have any information about that?"

Risa Inagaki peered at the two officers through her thick fringe of yellow hair and said, "He came here the day before he was going to elope and stayed the night, saying he said he thought his house was being watched by *yakuza* creeps. The next morning, Hiro-*chan* told me he was going to look at his old home for the last time. He had his hoodie on, his face covered, trying not to be seen. When he came back to my place a little later, he had a white plastic bag with a box of chocolates in it. I remember his saying he was happy because his mother must have left it for him. He said it showed she cared, that she'd been thinking about him and would miss him."

"I've heard that story before," the inspector said thoughtfully. "Do you think it plausible?"

She scowled. "Yes. That poor fool Hiro-*chan* showed me the box, and I noticed some chocolates were missing. I remember thinking that was just like his mother. She was greedy and selfish."

"She was also very lucky," said the chief inspector. "That is, if she did find the box and took some chocolates for herself. About half of them were poisoned."

"Lucky!" Risa laughed. "I doubt she'd agree with you. She was always complaining about how hard her life was."

The young woman frowned. "She was an awful mother, but I can't see her trying to kill her son, however bad he'd turned out. Anyway, she couldn't help herself. If she ever bought her boy anything good to eat, she'd want some of it for herself. Most, probably. But Hiro-*chan* never minded. He was always pathetically eager for her to show him some sign of affection, always ignoring the signs she couldn't care less. The only person who ever paid him proper attention was his uncle, Itsuki Beppu. Naturally, it was his uncle he turned to when he decided to escape to South Korea— eloping while also escaping from those thugs who were after him."

"About Kaori Hirakata, are you convinced he had nothing to do with her death?"

"Hiroki could be rough sometimes, but it's not surprising. He grew up in the school of hard knocks. He slapped me once or twice when we'd had a blazing argument. Gave me a good shaking, too, a few times. From all I hear, he adored her. If he knew she was going to dump him, he might have done something drastic. I just don't know. He's a complex character. Even as a little boy, he longed to see the world, and he was always more mature and self-aware than anybody I knew. And talented, to boot."

She smiled wryly. "I might as well tell you. I was in love with the guy. I *am* in love with him. Always have been and always will. Faults and all. But he's only ever seen me as a friend. If anyone wanted to give that girl poisoned chocolates, it would have been me. I felt so jealous when he used to talk about her, I wished she was dead."

She noticed Miyagi's shocked expression and let out a loud, raucous laugh. "But I didn't kill her. Maybe we're all capable of murder, given the right circumstances. Still, I like to think I'd never kill anybody, and especially not in that devious, horrible way." She shuddered. "Poisoning! That's so cruel, so sneaky."

Then Risa Inagaki rose from her cushion in a neat, feline movement and said, "Sorry, I must get ready." Cradling her large breasts provocatively, she added, grinning, "I have to make myself presentable." Then she collected the cups and took them to the kitchen.

The inspector and Miyagi were waiting by the front door, having left the slippers in the hall and put on their shoes, when she reappeared. Stepping down into the *genkan*, she stood by the lieutenant and lifted a hand to stroke his hair. "You're cute," she said. "Please come see me perform. I'm at a place called 'Girls, Girls, Girls'. I'll see you get a big discount."

Seeing the look of puzzlement on his face, she said, "I'm a stripper!"

Ito had to suppress a laugh. Miyagi, with his disheveled hair and astonished expression, suddenly looked like a callow junior high student.

"Miss Inagaki," Ito said. "I have one last question. Well, actually, it's three, but they're all related."

She smiled at him. "Yes?" She glanced at her watch. "But really, you'll have to hurry."

"Have you been in touch with Hiroki Sato since he disappeared ten years ago?"

"No."

"Do you think he's dead?"

"No."

"Would you let us know if he contacts you?"

"Again, no," she said, laughing, and slammed the door behind them.

Tetsuya Kataoka

On their way back to the hotel, Yumi told Aki she wanted him to meet Tetsuya Kataoka that evening. He would arrive at Murota's train station at five on an express from Tokyo and spend the weekend.

"I'd like us to go out to dinner together," she said.

"That sounds great," Aki said. "Do you mind if I bring somebody?"

"A double date! That sounds perfect. But who?"

"I've met somebody nice," he said. "It's that American girl who's living in our old house, in fact. Her name is Rhoda Ellison."

"I'm not sure I *can* like her," Yumi said, "however nice she is." She shuddered. "It's creepy to think of her being in our home, using our things."

"That reminds me. You should look at the stuff I've taken. It's all in my room. I think I'll mail everything back to Tokyo because it's a nuisance to carry it. Yumi, now that you're here in Murota, you should go to the house, too. Check whether there's anything you want. Rhoda won't mind, and it'll probably be your last chance. And if you're serious about this Tetsuya person, maybe it would be nice if he could see where you used to live."

"I don't think I can face it."

"With him beside you, holding your hand, you can do anything," Aki said, making such a ridiculously adoring face, Yumi began laughing.

"Maybe," she said. "If Rhoda can come, we could all go over to her place after dinner. You should call her, see if she's free."

She looked at her watch. "I need to meet Tetsuya's train. Where should we meet?"

"There's an excellent place near the station called "Yakiniku Nakamura." It's got wonderful *wagyu* beef."

"Yummy! I just hope your American isn't a vegetarian," Yumi said.

"I'll book a private room for the four of us for six thirty."

Yumi grimaced. "It's a bit early."

"This place gets fully booked for any later on a Friday night. It's very popular."

"Are you so sure Rhoda won't be busy?"

"I live in hope."

Aki hurried to his room and rang Rhoda at the university. She was gratifyingly excited by his proposal. "Yes! That would be wonderful," she said. Then, after a short pause, she added, "Should I ask my friend Aggie Snow to join us? I think she's lonely sometimes."

"I'm sorry for that, but no, I forbid you to ask her. This is a date."

"A date! I'm so glad. I can meet you at the station at about six."

"Perfect. Let's go for a drink at a bar I know nearby, then meet my sister and her boyfriend at the restaurant." He was about to say his farewell when he remembered Yumi's words. "You're not a vegetarian, are you?" he said. "It's a famous *yakiniku* place."

"*Yakiniku?*"

"Fried meat, with wonderful dipping sauces."

"I can't wait. My favorite meal is steak with a baked potato."

Aki was pleased to see that Rhoda had dressed for the occasion. She wore a long red velvet dress, had her blonde hair up in a chignon, and her pretty face was framed by dangling earrings that glittered whenever she moved. He was proud to be seen with her and glad he'd thought to pack his best black shirt.

After they'd had beers at a noisy snack bar near the station, they made their way to the restaurant. It was the kind of place that insisted customers store their shoes in a large cupboard by the door and don the slippers provided. Everything was elegant and tasteful. They followed a beautiful young woman in a kimono who shuffled down a polished hall in her white tabi stockings. Kneeling gracefully, she bowed deeply as she opened the sliding doors to the private room Aki had booked.

"We got here before them!" Aki said jubilantly. "I always like to get places first."

"Right, I've got that fact about you stored away then. 'Aki likes to be first.' I suppose that must mean you're secretly very competitive."

"Not so secretly," he protested.

Then the door slid open again. Aki looked over and saw Rhoda had a nervous grin on her face as she watched the other two enter the room. He tried to imagine her feelings. Perhaps she thought the tall woman with long black glossy hair possessed the sort of remote elegance she could never achieve and found the man equally daunting. He was also tall, wearing a beret and sunglasses that lent him a certain exotic air. He bent down to rub an ankle.

"Sorry we're late," Yumi said, speaking in English. "There was a creep waiting outside, wanting to have a word or two with my friend, Tetsuya, here." She turned, smiling at her boyfriend, saying, "But you didn't want to play ball." She turned back to Aki. "My friend gave the man a swift kick. He was a loser wearing a wrinkled suit, a hat, and sunglasses. Such a cliché! He got the message, took to his heels, and scampered down the road."

Rhoda and Aki rose and bowed. Aki made the introductions while Yumi's boyfriend stood apart, observing them impassively. He had a small mustache and a thin face. A thick lock of hair escaping from the beret seemed to be dyed blue. Aki hoped he wasn't some poser. He sensed rather than saw Rhoda trembling slightly as she stood beside him. It endeared her to him. When they'd first met, he thought she was one of those terrifyingly confident Americans. But she was human, after all. Maybe she was just worried, wondering if the man spoke any English.

Once they all sat down, Tetsuya said, "I'm glad you could join us, Miss Ellison."

Aki was taken aback. He knew Tetsuya spoke English, but it was surprising he did so with a faint American accent.

"You sound like you're from my part of the States!" Rhoda cried. "Michigan?"

"Chicago," he said, his sunglasses glinting in the light cast by the overhead lamp. "I spent a few years there. Took classes at the Art Institute."

"You never told me that!" Yumi exclaimed.

"You never asked."

"I have asked about your past often, but you've only told me a few things."

"You need to ask specific questions," he said. "You can't expect me to compress my entire life into a brief biography for your benefit." Yumi looked a little hurt, but Rhoda grinned, and then began laughing when he winked at her. Tetsuya then took Yumi's hand and kissed it, as if to apologize for his rudeness.

"I see you're all in black," Rhoda said. "Are you in mourning?"

"Yes, I'm mourning my lost innocence," he said.

Changing the focus, Yumi said, "Rhoda, you're beautiful. I'm impressed, Aki. I didn't think you could attract such a good-looking girl."

"My sister," he said, his eyes rolling. "As you can see, my greatest fan."

Everything went smoothly during the dinner. The kimono-clad woman soon returned, bearing a huge platter holding an artistically arranged variety of thin slices of beef and offal as well as sliced eggplant, green pepper, onion, mushrooms, and cabbage. The table had a built-in grill and was soon covered with glasses, chopsticks, plates, bowls, and four types of dipping sauce. Yumi took over the cooking. Tetsuya insisted on keeping everyone's glasses filled to the brim, pouring from the pitcher of beer on the table that was replenished at least twice.

They concentrated on the food, carelessly chattering in English as a courtesy to Rhoda. Once they had satisfied their initial hunger pangs, they lounged on their cushions, leaning against the wall, laughing and joking, and refilling each other's glasses. Finally, the platters of sliced meat and vegetables were empty and, flushed with drink, they decided they should go.

Aki insisted on paying. Standing outside the front of the restaurant, they hesitated, wondering what to do next. Tetusya held up a hand and examined his wristwatch by the beam cast by a streetlight. "It's only eight o'clock," he said.

"Shall we go to a bar?" Yumi wondered. Then she pursed her lips, looking uncertain. "Or I have another idea. Aki, you suggested earlier we might go back to our old house so I can see if you've left anything I want." She looked at Rhoda. "That is, of course, if you wouldn't mind."

They were startled by the sound of somebody shouting from across the street, "Rhoda! Rhoda Ellison!" They looked over to see a thin woman in a black dress, her hair pulled back tightly in a bun. She held a big black purse in one hand and was waving at them with the other.

"Oh, God," Aki muttered. "It's Juno-*sensei*. Again!"

"You're right. I haven't seen her in ages, but I'd recognize her anywhere," Yumi said, looking disgruntled. "Still, for our parents' sake, we have to be friendly."

Rhoda looked at her companions curiously. Aki noticed, thinking he and his sister had made it too obvious they didn't much care for the woman. Still, he and Yumi put polite, friendly smiles on their faces and waited patiently as Juno made her way to the nearest intersection and crossed over to join them.

Aki found it amusing that Rhoda seemed to feel obligated to perform the introductions. "You know Aki Hirakata, of course," she said. "You mentioned you'd met him two mornings ago when he'd just arrived in town. And I think you know his sister Yumi, too."

They all bowed, with Yumi politely saying, "I hope you are well, Juno-*sensei*. It's been a long time!" She hid it well, but Aki knew his sister must be disappointed to see a woman she'd told him she hoped never to meet again. Aki felt the same, but being Japanese, their greetings were effusive and appeared genuine.

"And this is Miss Hirakata's friend, Tetsuya Kataoka, who's come to Murota by train this afternoon."

Tetsuya, his beret pushed low over his face, nodded and bowed his head, saying nothing.

"What luck!" Juno said, her cheeks splotched an ugly red with excitement. "I'd usually be home by this time." She looked confidentially at Aki and Yumi. "I'm still living in the church, so I can be on the spot to help Pastor Nakagawa and his wife."

They nodded.

"I've been out all day!" Juno gushed, oblivious that her sudden appearance hadn't been to everyone's liking. "I had to go to Ishizaki to chair another mission board meeting. I was hoping you'd get in touch, Aki. I told the pastor and his wife about seeing you, and they said they imagined you'd turn up at the church to see us. But it's all worked out, and much better than I could have hoped for. It's such an unexpected bonus that I can see you, too, Yumi!"

There was an awkward pause.

Finally, Rhoda seemed to feel she had to step in to rescue the situation. "I have an idea!" she said brightly. "Why don't we all go to my place? In fact, I bought a selection of nice cakes this afternoon, just in case. Juno, you can catch up with Aki while Yumi sees if there's anything left in her old home that she'd like to take away."

Yumi hesitated. "It holds unhappy memories but many happy ones, too. After all, I would like a chance to see it again," she said. She looked at Tetsuya. "Would you mind? Just for half an hour?"

He nodded his assent.

Within a few minutes, they'd managed to hail two taxis and were on their way.

The Police

It was a hot, muggy Friday night and Chief Inspector Ito, sitting on the sofa at his family home following dinner, was feeling at a loss. His wife was in the kitchen, washing the dishes. He felt a sudden longing to see his daughter. It was so sharply painful that he had to suppress a groan. She'd moved to an apartment in Ishizaki some years earlier, having got a job as a paralegal at an attorney's office. They were proud of her. She'd become independent. But he missed her. And his wife fretted their daughter was already in her thirties and not yet married. She wanted grandchildren!

Ito was alone—alone with his thoughts—which was just what he didn't want. He thought of turning on the television. Or the radio. Or flipping through the day's paper again. Anything to distract him. But no, that was the coward's way out. He'd just have to grit his teeth and be content with his own company.

Ito nursed the can of beer his wife had given him. He mused over the five cases that were finally coming together. He had a gut feeling that there had to be a connection between them, but he couldn't find that link.

Kicking it all off was the attack on the prominent businessman Iwao Hirakata in August 1976, shot outside his home. Then his daughter Kaori

Hirata died twelve years later after eating chocolates laced with thallium. One week following the murder, Tokyo journalist Koji Yanagihara was assaulted during his visit to Murota to report on the local tragedy. Shortly after, Itsuki Beppu, the uncle of Hiroki Sato, the primary suspect in the case, was fatally stabbed. Fifth, Mrs. Goto and her niece received a bag of produce that included poisonous mushrooms. Mrs. Goto had died, and Miss Ikeuchi was seriously ill. On being rushed to the hospital three nights earlier, she had been placed in an induced coma, and her doctor hinted that she might never regain full possession of her mental or physical faculties. Ito felt he was close, closer than he'd ever been. He was just hoping he could close them once and for all.

One, two, three, four, five. Ito looked at the raised fingers on his right hand. Then he curled them into a fist and hit the coffee table. It was too frustrating! He had the tantalizing sensation he was on the verge of a breakthrough, but it still felt just out of his grasp. One problem was, there were too many improbable coincidences. For example, the first, third and fourth cases had established *yakuza* involvement. Certain individuals figured in more than one case in various capacities. It was like trying to unravel a tangled skein of yarn.

Ito emptied his can and put it on the coffee table, wondering if he should shout out that he wanted another beer. He and his wife had been together so long that she often sensed his wants and needs. He hoped she'd miraculously appear in a few minutes with another can of Asahi Super Dry straight from the fridge and maybe even a dish of rice crackers or dried octopus.

As he waited for that miracle, Ito returned to feeling sorry for himself. He wanted somebody to blame. Superintendent Takenaka was the obvious candidate, having abruptly and, Ito felt, unjustifiably, taken over the Kaori Hirakata murder investigation. Of course, Ito had derived a guilty pleasure from the fact that, after all, that little terrier-like man had failed.

But now he felt ashamed of himself, knowing it was selfish egoism that drove his ambition to be the one to solve the mystery of who killed that poor young woman and why. On reflection, he realized it would have been preferable if the superintendent had cracked the case. That would have brought the Hirakata family *closure,* much though Ito hated that word.

Why? He thought the concept was essentially meaningless. The parents were gone, their end prematurely hastened by what had happened to their daughter, but Yumi and Aki continued to serve a lifelong sentence with no chance of parole. Kaori's murder had been of many blows leveled at that unfortunate family. Ito always thought people were mistaken when they demanded that life should be "fair." It wasn't, and neither good intentions nor social engineering could make it so.

Ito heard the phone in the kitchen ring. His wife carried it into him, along with a can of beer so cold it nearly froze his fingers. On putting the receiver to his ear and listening for a minute or two, Ito said *Wakarimashita*—understood—before jumping up and hurrying to the kitchen to return the can to the fridge. "I must go out," he told his wife before retreating to his bedroom to put on his uniform. He paused midway, having put on his trousers but not his tunic, remembering he'd just drunk alcohol. That meant he couldn't drive. He rang Miyagi and asked him to swing by and pick him up as quickly as possible.

CHAPTER EIGHT

Friday 1 October 1998
Murota

After they had passed through the front gate, Rhoda was struck by Yumi's clear dismay at the state of the place she had once called home. In fact, Yumi was too loud and frank for anyone to be in any doubt as to her feelings.

"How awful!" she exclaimed as they wandered down the narrow brick path through the overgrown garden, their way dimly lit by a streetlight. "It used to be immaculately maintained. A gardener came once a week." Then, catching sight of the house itself, she said, "Oh, no! It needs a coat of paint. But first, those cracks have to be plastered." She paused, apparently realizing her comments might cause offense, and added, "Please forgive me, Rhoda. It's nothing to do with you. Our cousin Mrs. Muraji has been very negligent, very remiss in her duty to keep this place in a good condition."

On entering, Yumi said, "Now I'm here, I must see my dear old home. I used to be happy here!" She hurried off toward the living room, followed by Aki and Juno, while Tetsuya Kataoka loitered in the *genkan*, taking a long time to take off his shoes. Rhoda felt she couldn't leave him. It was her house now and she should act the part of the attentive hostess.

"It's hardly changed at all," he muttered softly as he stepped up to the hallway and put on the slippers that she'd laid out for him.

"Have you been here before?" Rhoda asked, staring.

"Oh, no," he said, quickly. "I mean, this kind of home always looks the same. The same architecture. The same furniture. The same paintings. All typical of the regrettable sense of style entertained by middle-class Japanese in the late twentieth century."

"I rather like it."

"Too influenced by Western fashion, if you ask me. But never mind." Tetsuya scrunched his face up in a comic expression denoting intense concentration. "Don't tell me," he said, eyes closed. "Let me guess. The paintings in the living room. Impressionist reproductions, right?"

Rhoda laughed. "Yes!"

"A gray sofa and matching armchairs, plush texture. French windows. A piano that nobody plays. A disused fireplace with a vase of dried flowers on the hearth."

"Again, yes!"

When they joined the others in the living room, Yumi was looking around and commenting on various objects.

"I used to lie on this sofa on weekends and spend hours reading novels," she said. "And I loved *Otoosan's* art preferences. Of course, I've been to Paris and seen the originals of Monet's *Waterlilies*." She turned to Aki, laughing. "How perfect that he hid the safe behind it. After he became religious, he went in for the austere, but he used to have wonderful taste. And a great sense of humor. Pity you never knew him when he was fond of making jokes. He was very good at it."

She grabbed Tetsuya by the hand. "At last! I suppose you were loitering in the hall to avoid hearing me reminisce about my childhood. Still, I insist you see the piano where I first learned to play! Not that I'm much good." She dragged him over to it, seated herself on the bench and launched into a perfunctory rendition of Beethoven's "Für Elise." Then, jumping up and laughing, she said, "Okay, the piano is out of tune, and I'm mediocre, but it's fun to bang out a few tunes."

Aki was tapping a foot impatiently. "Yumi, I know you're enjoying your little stroll down memory lane, but I think we should go up now and see if there's anything more you want. This is your last chance. But you'll have to be quick. It must be nearly nine now." He looked at Rhoda. "And then, if you don't mind, we can sample those cakes you've mentioned and maybe have some coffee or tea before we head back to the hotel."

"Yes, of course," Yumi said. "Rhoda, do you mind if we make our way upstairs by ourselves?"

"Not at all!" Rhoda said. "Just wait one minute." She rushed off to the kitchen and returned with a large plastic bag. "Please use this if you find anything you want to take away. Of course, I have lots more if you need them."

The brother and sister went up the stairs, chattering excitedly in Japanese, while Rhoda, Tetsuya, and Juno stood awkwardly in the living room.

"Please sit down," Rhoda said. "Anywhere you like." She smiled at her guests. "If you'll forgive me, I'll go to the kitchen to heat water for our drinks and get out cups and saucers. And plates and forks for the cakes."

Juno sat in the center of the sofa, placing her purse beside her, while Tetsuya chose an armchair opposite. She finally broke the silence by asking conversationally, "Have you ever been to Murota before, Mr. Kataoka?"

"Many years ago."

"And what do you think of our fair town?"

"I'm a big city type."

Rhoda appeared at this moment, proudly bearing aloft a white cardboard box with the name of Murota's premier patisserie emblazoned in gilt letters on the side. "Only the best for my honored guests," she said, placing it on the coffee table with a flourish. "I just need to sort out the dishes. Back soon."

There was another slight pause before Juno said, "You remind me of someone. Someone I knew a long time ago."

"I have one of those faces."

"But it's not your face. I can scarcely see it with your beret pushed so low on your forehead and your mustache. It's your figure, the way you move, that seems familiar."

"People are always telling me that. I seem to resemble lots of men of my age. I'm not sure if I'm offended or pleased."

Juno suddenly stood and, leaning over the coffee table, knocked his beret to the floor with a swoop of her hand. "*Shitsurei!*" she said. "Please excuse my rudeness!"

Staring hard at his face, she suddenly began to tremble. "You've dyed your hair blue. You've lost your earring, grown a mustache, and lost weight, but I know who you are," she exclaimed. Seeing Tetsuya sit impassively, making no reply, Juno shrieked so loudly that Rhoda ran in from the kitchen and Yumi and Aki could be heard thundering down the stairs.

"It's him!" she shouted. "Hiroki Sato!"

Rhoda, Yumi, and Aki stood near the sofa, too dumbfounded to move or speak.

"It's him! It's him! It's him!" Juno kept saying. And then she said, "Rhoda, call the police."

Yumi had gone pale. She walked over to pick up her boyfriend's beret, placing it back on his head, and said, "Juno-*sensei*, you're mistaken. This is the well-known manga artist Tetsuya Kataoka."

"He's Hiroki Sato," Juno said adamantly. "You never met him when he used to hang around your poor sister. I did. I *know* what he looks like!"

She turned to Rhoda. "If you won't call the police, I will. I know where the phone is."

She began marching off to the hallway when Aki rushed forward and put a restraining hand on one arm. "Let me. I'll call for you. I'm friendly with the chief inspector. I can't imagine he's at the station, but I've got his home number. Still, I'm sure it's all a terrible mistake."

An embarrassing scenario ensued. Juno refused to sit in the same room as Tetsuya Kataoka. After exacting a promise from him he wouldn't run away, she insisted on going into the kitchen with Rhoda, saying she'd wait there for the police to arrive. Yumi pulled the matching armchair next to Tetsuya's, and they held hands.

Yumi shook her head. "How strange! I remember Juno-*sensei* being odd and irritating, but I didn't know she was mad. Maybe it's early onset dementia."

Tetsuya said, "Never mind, Yumi. I think you should go back up and look for anything you want to take away. The police won't be here for another half hour. There's no point in you just sitting here waiting."

"Then you must come upstairs with me. And don't worry. I don't believe a word that awful woman says." She dragged him to his feet and planted a big, sloppy kiss on one of his cheeks. He was silent as he followed her up the stairs.

When the doorbell rang, Rhoda was in the kitchen with Juno, feeling uncomfortable at the unexpected turn of events. She'd been happy and excited when Aki had rung to ask her out, envisaging a lighthearted dinner with him, his sister, and her boyfriend, followed by coffee and cakes at her home.

The first half of the scenario had played out as planned, but now she felt abruptly plunged into something like a nightmare. Juno sat perched on a stool, her purse propped against the toaster on the counter, making unpleasant accusations about Yumi's boyfriend. The missionary Rhoda had only known as a pitiful but also remote and intimidating figure was obviously in the grip of powerful emotions. It was as if she had a fever. She moved her hands in excited, jerky gestures, her cheeks had a hectic flush, and her eyes were glittering. As Rhoda cowered behind the counter, pretending to busy herself with teacups and matching saucers, spoons, a jug of cream, a sugar dish, and tiny forks and small floral plates for the cakes— arranging and rearranging them on a tray—Juno went on and on, barely pausing for breath.

Meanwhile, Rhoda could hear strange noises overhead—the scrape of furniture being moved and objects flung on the floor. She could just make out the distant murmur of male and female voices conversing.

Finally, Rhoda heard the sound she'd been waiting for—the doorbell. Juno cast a sour look at the clock on the wall. "Well, they've certainly taken their own sweet time getting here," she said. "It's been nearly an hour since we called." Juno sighed. "I regret to say, dear Rhoda, that in the last few years, I've noticed a marked deterioration in public services in this country. It's a global trend, of course, but somehow, I thought Japan would be immune."

"Oh, dear," Rhoda said, shrugging. "Anyway, I'd better get the door."

It felt like *déjà vu*. On opening the door, Rhoda saw the burly chief inspector and his lanky, stooped lieutenant behind him. She bowed and shuffled backward, turning around to step up to the hallway to line up slippers for the two officers. That's when she noticed Juno had followed her.

As the officers slid out of their shoes and into the slippers, they all looked up, hearing a noise at the top of the stairway. Aki, Yumi, and Tetsuya were standing there, looking down. They seemed to share a similar expression, but Rhoda found it impossible to read what it was. Aghast? Amused? Japanese inscrutability was a cliché, but Rhoda thought it perfectly true.

Gazing down the stairs at Rhoda and Juno standing next to the inspector and his lieutenant, Aki felt a surge of anger at the missionary who'd made his childhood miserable. Why had she come to spoil their last night in their old home?

He hurried down the stairs, shaking his head ruefully and saying, "My apologies for bringing you out so late, Chief Inspector Ito. It's all a terrible mistake—a case of mistaken identity, I mean. But our guest, Juno-*sensei*, insisted we call you. I imagine you know her, or at least know of her."

"Of course," Ito said, bowing. "She's a local celebrity." Looking at Juno, he added, "Even if our visit is in vain, it's a privilege to have the chance to meet you again, Juno-*sensei*," and he bowed again.

Juno temporarily looked flattered, even flustered, but then her typical stern and determined look returned.

"Never mind all that," she snapped. She pointed to Tetsuya, still standing at the top of the stairs with Yumi. "It's *him!* It's Hiroki Sato. How he can have the effrontery, I can't think. He's standing only feet away from the scene of his crime—Kaori's bedroom! The place where he gave her a box of poisoned chocolates. The place he fled from when he saw she'd eaten enough of them to die. To add insult to injury, it seems he's attached himself to the poor dead girl's sister."

There was a cry, then Yumi thundered down the stairs, stopping just in front of Juno, glaring. She looked so angry, Aki wondered if his sister might even slap her.

"No!" Yumi cried. "Stop telling these horrible lies! I can't think why you're doing it! That man is my boyfriend, Tetsuya Kataoka. As I've told you, he's a highly regarded manga artist."

Yumi turned to the inspector and his lieutenant. "I have no idea why Juno-*sensei* has identified my friend as my sister's murderer or why she's insisted you come here. It's hard enough being back in my old house for the first time since Kaori's funeral. Tetsuya, busy as he is, kindly offered to come here from Tokyo simply to offer me support. It's intolerable he's now subjected to such insults, and especially by somebody I used to consider a friend of the family."

The inspector listened, looking unflappable and unfathomable. He beckoned to Tetsuya. "Please come downstairs, Kataoka-*san*." While he was descending, the inspector added, "I propose we all adjourn to the living room, have some tea, and talk about this calmly."

He asked Aki to explain in English what had just happened. Rhoda shuddered at what she was told, walked back to the living room, picked up the box of cakes she'd left on the table, and took it back to the kitchen.

Everyone followed her to the living room. Within a few minutes, Yumi was sitting on the sofa with Rhoda between her and Aki, while the chief inspector and Juno occupied the matching armchairs. Tetsuya had dragged a hardbacked chair from an adjoining room and positioned it by Yumi. The lieutenant occupied his usual perch on the piano bench. Aki wondered what would happen.

As he settled in his seat, the inspector ordered his officer to the kitchen to make them a hot drink. "English milk tea," he instructed. "Make it very strong and very sweet."

They sat listening to the rattle of dishes, the sound of the kettle boiling, the clink of spoons against saucers and cups. The chief inspector commanded their immobility and silence through sheer force of will. He gazed toward the French windows, as still as a statue, as if enraptured by the view even though it was dark and nothing of the garden was visible.

The lieutenant returned with a large tray loaded with cups, saucers, the sugar bowl, a jug of milk, and the teapot. "You had it all ready, miss," he said to Rhoda, apparently not realizing she didn't understand Japanese. "I've just left the cake and the plates in the kitchen."

It was only after everyone had been served and Miyagi had positioned himself on the bench again, notepad and pen in hand, that Ito spoke.

"I've been summoned here at a fortunate moment," Ito said. "I'd intended to contact you, Aki, to ask you and Yumi to come to the station tomorrow morning. I have some good news."

The brother and sister leaned forward expectantly, Rhoda all the while wondering what was going on.

"We've had Mr. Taniguchi in for questioning. Taniguchi the younger—Makoto Taniguchi—I should say. He's been surprisingly forthcoming. You could say we have him between a rock and a hard place. We'd already contacted the local *yakuza* boss, who turned out to be very keen to incriminate Makoto's grandfather."

Ito smiled at Aki and Yumi. "I think your family is in line for a substantial payout—a reimbursement for damages incurred—as well as a public apology that will rehabilitate your father's reputation."

"But did the *yakuza* have anything to do with my sister's death?" Yumi demanded.

"No, they categorically deny that, although they confessed to targeting your father and shooting him. Of course, that's more their style. Guns or knives, not poison."

"Have they identified the individual who actually pulled the trigger?"

"Yes, he's a local."

Seeing Aki looking indignant, the chief inspector hastened to add, "The *yakuza* have apologized and helped to facilitate the man's arrest. He's in custody now."

Ito looked around. "As you all know, I imagine, our criminal gangs in Japan like to insist they obey a certain code of honor. According to the *yakuza* boss I spoke to, old Mr. Taniguchi completely misrepresented the situation. The boss indicated his indignation at having been lied to. Old Mr. Taniguchi wanted to have his cake and eat it, too, and he's done just that all these years, keeping up his lucrative association with gangsters by scapegoating Mr. Hirakata. We intend to arrest him, too."

The inspector bowed to Aki. "I'm grateful for your help in clearing up this mystery, one I've long considered a stain on my career. The shooting was my first case when I joined the Murota force. I desperately wanted to prove myself, but at every turn, my inquiries were thwarted, and I was finally forced to abandon the investigation."

He sighed heavily. "It was so frustrating. And that's how I felt twelve years later when Superintendent Takenaka took over the investigation of Kaori Hirakata's murder. Hiroki Sato had gone to South Korea and vanished. Soon afterward, someone killed his uncle, who might have offered further information. His mother refused to help me and then died herself. Risa Inagaki, a friend of the suspect, was too loyal to be tempted into revealing any secrets she might be hiding."

Juno had been listening to all this with increasing impatience, tapping her fingers loudly on the arm of her chair. Then she began fidgeting, shifting about impatiently. Finally, she'd had enough.

"Chief Inspector Ito," she said, rising and picking up her purse, "this has all been fascinating. But I think it's time you arrested the culprit sitting here, only a foot away from your own chair. He's given me his promise he won't run away, but what worth is a promise made by a criminal? By a murderer?"

Ito turned his attention to her. "Juno-*sensei*, please sit down. I need to detain you all a few minutes longer."

Ito turned to Tetsuya Kataoka. "Unlike our respected missionary here, I think I can trust you. I believe you will tell me the truth. Now I'd like to ask—are you Hiroki Sato?"

There was complete silence. Then Tetsuya rose and put a hand on Yumi's shoulder. "Yes," he said.

An audible collective intake of breath echoed around the room.

After a brief pause, Yumi cried out, horror etched on her face as she looked up at him, "No! It's impossible. I can't believe it!"

"Please forgive me, Yumi. I've wanted to tell you for so long—ever since we met in London."

Yumi shook off his hand and jumped up. Standing by the windows, she stared at her own reflection, frowning.

Tetsuya gave a hopeless shrug and slumped back in his chair. "I imagine you know Hiroki Sato had a blue dolphin tattoo on his left shoulder. I can take off my jacket and shirt if you'd like to see it. I admit I've been living under a false identity for many years. I was forced to abandon my true identity and pretend I was somebody else. I had nothing to do with Kaori's death—apart from giving her the box of chocolates I thought my mother had left for me. I ran and kept running because...because I had to. I didn't think I'd get a fair trial. I wanted to escape from Japan—from the *yakuza,* but most of all, from memories of Kaori."

He looked over at Yumi, then focused his gaze on Ito, addressing him. "Chief Inspector, I *did* cause Kaori's death, but not intentionally. You may have heard how we chanced to meet at a bus stop. Of course, her beauty initially dazzled me. But then I found myself even more attracted by her kindness. She was the sweetest person I've ever met, the most genuinely good."

He gulped and went on. "I was working at the Nissan car factory but still had links with the local *yakuza.* Stupidly, I boasted to one of them I'd fallen for a woman with movie-star looks who, astonishingly, seemed to love me back. When he asked her name, I told him." Tetsuya smacked his forehead dramatically, looking chagrined. "I can't forgive myself for that. I never should have said. That creep was surprised. And then delighted. He said it was lucky because it meant I could help the gang out of a tight spot."

Tetsuya gave a bitter laugh and said, "Inspector, it's you who's been told lies. Of course, the local *yakuza* boss knew that Mr. Taniguchi had framed Kaori's father for his own crime. The myth of the honor of the *yakuza* is just that—a myth. It was expedient for them to have Kaori's father shot and his reputation ruined. It meant they could still demand an enormous chunk of so-called protection money from the Taniguchi firm while retaining an even firmer hold over its boss."

Tetsuya rose and paced up and down for a minute, giving the space in front of the windows where Yumi was still standing a wide berth. Whenever he passed within a few feet of her, she trembled. It seemed she wanted nothing more to do with anyone in the room or with what they were discussing. But the taut rigidity of her body told another story—she was listening intently to every word.

Tetsuya gave a deep sigh and resumed his seat, shaking his head. "About Kaori..." His voice broke. After a pause, clearing his throat, he went on. "Falling in love with her meant I wanted nothing more to do with the *yakuza*. I wanted us to run away and start a new life together. The problem was her father had decided he couldn't keep silent anymore about all the lies. He told Mr. Taniguchi he planned to go to the police and had documents proving his innocence. On hearing that, Mr. Taniguchi immediately contacted my Murota *yakuza* boss, who'd heard about me and Kaori. He pressured me to stop her father from blowing the whistle on their scam. I refused. He threatened me and warned that Kaori would be targeted, too."

Tetsuya briefly held his head in his hands. Looking up, he said, "That's why I was in danger, why I hid, why there was an urgency about our plans to elope."

He stood again, restlessly shifting from foot to foot, looking up at the ceiling as he added, "I feel as guilty about Kaori's death as if I'd poisoned those chocolates myself. But I didn't. As I said, I thought they were a gift from my mother, who'd heard from her brother I planned to leave the country. Once Kaori got poisoned, it was terrible having to accept it was the *yakuza* who'd left the bag on my door, knowing I planned to run away with Kaori that night. I realized it was a win-win situation for those bastards. I'd be out of the way if I ate the chocolates myself. If I took them to Kaori and she died, her father would feel so guilty he'd give up trying to exonerate himself."

Tetsuya walked over to stand a short distance from Yumi.

"When Kaori died, I wanted to die," he said. "I wanted death even more when my uncle got killed because of me. But the will to live is strong. As I've said, I ran. And ran and ran. Still, I could never run away from myself. Yumi, I'm ashamed! Ashamed of joining the *yakuza,* ashamed I didn't tell your sister from the start, ashamed I didn't stay with her as she was dying, ashamed it was because of me that a very good man—my uncle—had to die."

Yumi heaved a great sigh but didn't turn around. He went on in a quiet voice, staring at her back. "I like to think it was fate we met in London, that it's something Kaori would have wanted. But we broke up after a few months, and I know why. You couldn't bear how secretive I was. I loved you then. I love you now. You saved me. But I didn't know how to tell you the truth. Then, when we met again in Tokyo, I think we both realized how much we cared."

He sighed. "I am Hiroki Sato. I didn't deserve Kaori. I didn't deserve my uncle. I don't deserve you. I won't blame you if you can't forgive me."

Juno jumped up again. "You see? You *see*? I was right." She looked at Miyagi. "I think you should put him in handcuffs so he can't escape."

The chief inspector intervened. "Thank you for your advice, Juno-*sensei*. I'd be grateful if you'd sit down now, please. And you, too, Kataoka-*san*. Or, if you prefer, Sato-*san*."

Ito looked at his watch, saying, "It's getting late. I hope I can release you soon. First, however, we need to look at a troubling recent incident—another poisoning—which took place in this neighborhood. We have to ask why somebody decided Mrs. Goto and her niece Miss Ikeuchi had to die."

He looked around. "Some of you here might not know that we've identified Miss Ikeuchi as the person who wrote the poison pen letters some of you have received. When we were summoned to the Goto household after the old woman had suddenly collapsed, we found evidence of her activities. I doubt any of you made the connection, but the poison pen letters began appearing in Murota not long after old Mrs. Goto invited her niece to stay with her."

Aki said, "I thought she was unpleasant, but when you told me about this the other day, it shocked me. I hadn't realized she was capable of that!"

"I'll grant you Miss Ikeuchi can be unpleasant. And sour! Sufficiently unpleasant and sour to make anonymous threats to supplement the meager income allotted to her by her aunt. Miss Ikeuchi is a rich woman now. She's inherited all her aunt's money and property. But her aunt gave her only a pittance when she was working as the housekeeper and caregiver. In my opinion, Ikeuchi-*san enjoyed* writing those letters. Blackmailing people gave her power over them. Made her feel superior, stronger than them. At her aunt's beck and call day in and day out, I imagine it was that sense of power that gave her the greatest satisfaction, pleasing her far better than any money she extorted with her accusations."

"Is that why she got poisoned, sir?" Aki asked. "Was it somebody she was blackmailing?"

"That was my original idea," the inspector said. Now he directed his gaze at the occupant of the armchair next to his. "Juno-*sensei*, I need to tell you that in the course of our investigations into Mrs. Goto's death, we have had cause to examine Miss Ikeuchi's bank statements. We've noticed she recently received a very large payment, and we have traced it back to you."

Juno stared straight ahead and said nothing.

"Juno-*sensei*?" the chief inspector persisted. "What hold did she have over you?"

Still, she said nothing.

Finding she didn't intend to answer, the inspector went on. "With or without your cooperation, we think we've established the reason. Shortly before you rang the station, asking for officers to be dispatched to this address to arrest the suspect in a murder inquiry, I had an earlier call. It was from Murota Hospital, informing me that Miss Ikeuchi had come out of her coma."

He ignored Juno's gasp, adding, "We had the foresight to take a tape recorder to the hospital. She proved surprisingly alert and articulate. It all just poured forth without us even having to ask. She wanted us to know that her aunt had told her she'd seen you, Juno-*sensei*, at a shop buying a box of chocolates identical to the one she saw in Kaori Hirakata's bedroom. She saw it as the girl lay dying on the floor."

Juno laughed humorlessly. "Absurd! Someone mentioned the brand in an article about the case. It's very popular in Murota and all over Japan. I buy a box now and then, but so do countless other people."

"According to Miss Ikeuchi, Mrs. Goto was adamant that it was you she saw buying it, and that it was the day before Kaori Hirakata died."

He paused. "Few people in the late '80s would have known of the existence of the poison thallium, let alone of its properties. Odorless and tasteless and soluble in water, thallium is easy to administer and difficult to detect. Juno-*sensei*, you're a local legend—as a missionary fluent in English but also as a fount of wisdom and local lore. Even I have heard you described as a bookworm who knows lots of curious facts."

Ito sighed and looked over at the gaunt woman sitting stiffly beside him. "I think that one day, you chanced upon an article about poisons and found it fascinating. And perhaps you learned how thallium could be inserted into a food item–say, chocolates–with a syringe, leaving a hole scarcely perceptible to the naked eye. As for how you got that information, perhaps in the course of your prison visits as a missionary, you met somebody who was forthcoming about such matters."

He looked at Miyagi. "In fact, I think we should investigate the records of the Ishizaki prison and find out which inmates you met and when."

"Ridiculous. I'm tired of being insulted. I think I'll go home," Juno muttered, rising and looking dissatisfied and angry.

"For the third time, I must ask you to sit down. As I've said, for a woman who had just woken from a coma, Miss Ikeuchi was surprisingly forthcoming when we interviewed her. She also told us she thought it was you who'd deposited the bag of vegetables, including poisoned mushrooms, on their door. She said she'd heard somebody leave something on the door and, peering out, saw a figure retreating. It was a woman, not a farmer, as she'd have expected. She said that should have aroused her suspicions, but it didn't."

Ito looked at Juno. "Of course, I found the coincidence striking. Two bags containing poisoned items left on doorknobs—first chocolates laced with thallium and, a decade later, mushrooms of a poisonous variety." He pursed his lips and closed his eyes. "And then I recalled something my wife mentioned once. She'd met you in the local supermarket. Apparently, you'd looked into her basket containing lots of fresh vegetables, saying disdainfully—that's why it lodged in her memory—that you preferred looking for edible plants in the countryside around Murota to buying plastic-wrapped food in shops."

There was a sudden flurry of movement. One moment, Juno was sitting in her chair, fumbling in her purse, presumably for a tissue. The next, her bag fell to the floor with a loud thump, and she was crouching beside Hiroki Sato, whose beret had fallen to the floor again. One of her hands was pulling back his head, gripping a thick sheaf of blue hair. The other held something at his throat that glittered in the light cast by a lamp near his chair. It was a knife.

"It's *you* who should have died!" Juno shrieked, her face splotched with patches of red. Holding the knife in her powerful hands, she drew a line around Hiroki Sato's neck marked by tiny beads of blood bubbling up and dripping as red droplets down his throat, disappearing as they reached the neckline of his black jersey.

"I hate you! I hate you!" she cried. "I loved Kaori. You were going to take her away from me! I've had to live all these years with the agony of knowing she'd taken the poison I meant for you." She shook her head violently. "I've felt guilty every minute of every hour of every day ever since. I knew she loved chocolates. But I never guessed you might take them to her. I even took out some chocolates, so you'd think they were a present from your hopeless mother."

She shrieked and drew another line around Sato's throat even deeper, and he gasped.

The police lieutenant leaped from his piano bench and stood a short distance from Juno.

"Come any closer, and I'll kill him," she hissed.

Everyone was on their feet, staring at the spectacle with horror.

"No, Juno! No! No! What are you doing?" Rhoda moaned, twining her hands together helplessly. "That knife, that knife is from my kitchen!"

Hiroki Sato struggled to free himself from Juno's grip, but she simply held the blade closer to his throat, pressing it into the flesh, causing him to choke.

"*You* should have died!" Juno repeated, her face livid as she screamed, "*Die!*"

It happened in a flash. The lieutenant was suddenly beside her, grabbing the hand holding the knife. The two figures wrestled briefly, as if performing an intricate dance. Then it was all over. With a clatter, the knife fell to the floor. The officer kicked it away, grabbed Juno's hands and, while she whimpered and moaned, pinned them behind her back.

The lieutenant glanced at the chief inspector, who rose and approached, interposing his big solid body between Juno and Hiroki, slumped in his chair and gasping for breath. His authoritative presence intimidated Juno, who stood motionless, allowing Miyagi briefly to release her and, taking the pair of cuffs hanging from his belt, snap them on her wrists.

It was as if Juno had suddenly lost all her strength; she collapsed like a broken doll. "I would never have hurt my darling," she panted between sobs. "I decided I would do *anything* to protect her from that monster. But now, the anguish! The guilt of her death! When she died, a part of me died, too. I'm dead. I'm *dead*!"

Ito glanced down at Juno-*sensei* as she lay huddled on the floor, moaning and weeping, dismayed to see how this proud woman had relinquished her dignity so completely. He whipped out his mobile phone, first ringing for an ambulance, then calling for backup from the station. Yumi hurried to her boyfriend, taking a handkerchief out of a pocket that she held to his neck, trying to wipe up the drops of blood. "Tetsuya! I love you—whoever you are, whatever you've done."

Rhoda ran to the kitchen to fetch a cloth. Giving it to the lieutenant, he tied it expertly around Hiroki's throat. Yumi knelt by the chair, the red-spotted handkerchief discarded on the floor, nestled against her boyfriend while he clutched his neck, making choking sounds.

Within minutes, the ambulance and a patrol car arrived, and they carried Tetsuya out on a stretcher. The inspector briefly consulted with a paramedic and got permission for Yumi to join her boyfriend in the ambulance. With another policeman suddenly appearing, Lieutenant Miyagi accompanied Juno out to a patrol car to be driven to the station.

The inspector stood by Aki and Rhoda in an otherwise deserted room. He saw Aki take one of Rhoda's hands and hold it tightly.

"What happens next?" Aki asked the inspector. "How about Yumi's boyfriend? I'm not sure what to call him now!"

"The paramedic assured me it's a superficial wound just requiring stitches," Ito said. "And muscle relaxants. His throat has seized up. Once they have done all that and given him painkillers, he will spend the night resting at the hospital. I hope we'll be able to question him tomorrow morning. We need to find out what he's been doing all these years. I'd like to hear the details, for example, of how he got a false passport and established a new identity. It would seem he's spent considerable time in South Korea, England, and in the States."

"The authorities in those countries might decide to bring charges against him," the chief inspector sighed, looking grim. But then again," and a smile flitted across his face, making him look almost cheerful, "they might not!"

"No?" asked Aki.

"No. There is no doubt, in any case, that he will be acquitted of your sister's murder. Juno-*sensei* acknowledged her guilt before too many witnesses for her to get off, however she tries. And he might be able to provide us with some interesting information about the *yakuza*." He shook his head, looking mournful again. "But it was such a waste, your poor sister dying with all her life before her."

"I can never forgive Juno," said Aki.

"Whether you do or not, they will charge her with the murder, and all those tattered old wanted posters of Hiroki Sato in the post offices and police stations around the country can finally be taken down. But I think we haven't seen the last of him. It's only a matter of time before we see his photo again, but I predict it will be in a feature in a national paper on the current crop of Japan's most talented artists. I've asked around, and people who know about such things tell me he's very good."

Taking his mobile from a pocket, the chief inspector rang the station and asked for a patrol car to be sent to collect him.

After slipping on his shoes in the *genkan* and turning around to take his leave, Ito made his farewells. He noticed Aki had one arm around Rhoda's waist, and they both had flushed faces and bright eyes.

"I hope you can make this a lucky place," he said. "However long you two might stay. There's been too much tragedy here."

Ito hoped the two would see his smile as a benediction. "Love each other," he said. "But not too much."

About the Author

Lea O'Harra has published four crime fiction novels: *Imperfect Strangers*, originally published in 2015 by Endeavour Press, republished in 2022 by Sharpe books; *Progeny*, originally published in 2016 by Endeavour Press, republished in 2022 by Sharpe books; *Lady First,* originally published in 2017 by Endeavour Press, republished in 2022 by Sharpe Books, and *Dead Reckoning*, published in 2022 by Sharpe Books. The first three books comprise the so-called 'Inspector Inoue murder mystery series' set in Japan. The fourth book is a standalone in small-town America. Her website is: http://leaoharra.com

Note from Lea O'Harra

Word-of-mouth is crucial for any author to succeed. If you enjoyed *Sayonara, My Sweet*, please leave a review online—anywhere you are able. Even if it's just a sentence or two. It would make all the difference and would be very much appreciated.

Thanks!
Lea O'Harra

We hope you enjoyed reading this title from:

BLACK ROSE
writing™

www.blackrosewriting.com

Subscribe to our mailing list – *The Rosevine* – and receive **FREE** books, daily deals, and stay current with news about upcoming releases and our hottest authors.
Scan the QR code below to sign up.

Already a subscriber? Please accept a sincere thank you for being a fan of Black Rose Writing authors.

View other Black Rose Writing titles at www.blackrosewriting.com/books and use promo code **PRINT** to receive a **20% discount** when purchasing.